ASSASSINS' WALL

GARE DE LYON

By Amanda Dubin

DEDICATION

First and foremost, to Jack Kramer, for persuading me to take my script and turn it into a book. Thank you for believing in this story and me. Secondly, to all my friends and family, who through blood, sweat, and tears helped make this possible.

Assassins' Wall: Gare de Lyon

TABLE OF CONTENTS

PROLOGUE

No one moved toward the restrained man. All four stood in complete silence for a minute, staring at one another to see who would act first. No one made a sound or moved.

"It seems no one is up for torture," said Marise with a little glee in her voice.

"Some fearless group we are," said John, half joking and half annoyed with the situation, and with Saif for putting them in it. "Ready to fight for our lives if need be."

Why did Saif go through all this trouble to bring this man here if he didn't have the stomach to interrogate him? The irony hit John at once. Of course, Saif didn't have the stomach for it. He probably expected one of them to get information out of the man. John guessed the only person, besides the man about to be interrogated, who had seen anything resembling torture that wasn't in a movie, was Saif. And he backed out, not that John could blame him. He couldn't do it either.

"Well, at least we all have risen above," said Lexi, who was quietly grateful that her companions could not stoop to such measures. Why lower their dignity to the level of the assassins? It would make them no better. Granted, she had no idea how they were going to get any information out of the man, but at least they all keep their humanity and their integrity. And that was worth something — no, *everything!*

Lexi turned and smiled at the group, even at Saif. It said a lot about his character that he couldn't do it. And she knew immediately, she could trust him.

The restrained man stared at the group, disgusted. "You weak humans," he said in English, his tone almost accusatory.

The four turned in unison toward the man tied up across the room. They all had, in their discussion and debate about torturing him, had almost forgotten about the soon-to-be-tortured.

"You mean '*WE,*' don't you?" demanded Saif. The man's statement shook him to the bone. Something was not right.

"No. I mean *YOU!*" replied the man, looking at the group as though he was the one in control, not the one duct-taped to a chair about to be tortured, well, almost tortured.

PART 1

The most amazing mechanism in the known universe is the human brain; it takes in information all the time then uses it, all of which is happening, of course, without human cognizant knowledge.

Typical ...

CHAPTER 1

The Glass Wall

GARE DE LYON, PARIS. LATE AFTERNOON.

Wednesday

A passenger train slowly rolled into Paris's Gare de Lyon train station. Inch by inch it crept toward the end of the line, letting out a long high-pitched squeal from the brakes. With a giant whoosh, it suddenly stopped. The passenger doors opened, and a flood of people poured out: one after another, after another, no stopping or slowing.

In the middle of the train, Alexandra Peters struggled with her heavy suitcase. Lexi, as her friends called her, stepped off the train, but the wheel of her large bag got caught in the door. It wasn't ready to go to Paris, or perhaps it didn't want her to go — as if she was not listening to the universe. She pulled the handle, a little too hard, causing the bag to fall sideways hard onto platform C. She paused for a moment to straighten her suitcase. Unfortunately, this also stopped the flow of people behind her on the train and on the narrow platform, causing a mini traffic jam.

"Excuse me, I am so sorry," said Lexi with an American accent, discomfited by the major backup she was causing. She dragged her bag, still sideways streaking against the ground, to the opposite side of the platform to get out of the way of passengers heading into the main terminal. She paused for a moment to straighten her suitcase and remove the carry-on bag from over her shoulder, which she laid strategically on top of her luggage. She pulled out a hairband and put her shoulder-length brown hair into a ponytail. Now, she felt ready to tackle Paris.

Ahead of her was a very lengthy walk into the main terminal. Two trains were parked on the same platform, making the trek into the station appear excruciatingly long. She had never traveled through Gare de Lyon train station before, and was embarrassed to admit, being in her late thirties, that this was her first time in Paris as well. She'd been all over the world: to Asia, Europe — including Germany, and Italy, even other cities of France — but never here, the home of great art and artistic movements.

The other passengers from the train were still efficiently filing past her, zipping down the platform toward the covered station. The sun shined low in the afternoon sky, making it impossible to see inside; the interior looked black against the sunlight.

Lexi glanced up to the sky, squinting her eyes a little. She wondered if she should get her sunglasses. It was bright outside, but not too bright to bother her eyes. Instead, she covered her eyes, creating a little bit of a shadow over her face, and she started briskly walking down the platform.

As she approached the overhang of Gare de Lyon, she briefly scanned the exterior, noticing the light green color of the building. It was almost a mint color. She always felt every city had a color, and the color tended to match the city's personality. Perhaps Paris was green? Green was one of her favorite colors. It immediately elevated her mood, making Paris feel warm and friendly.

It was an interesting game to play, one which she had tried in many other cities: New York felt silver, a little cold, sleek, and sharp. Washington, D.C. felt cream, elegant with a sense of history, classic. Boston felt reddish brown. Los Angeles light blue, Miami white ...

Her first color impression of Paris: Green. She made a mental note to herself.

NOTE TO SELF: Look up the color symbolism for green in Goethe.

It took her a few more minutes to reach underneath the overhang. Lexi was temporarily blinded by the light change when she stepped inside the interior of the station. She blinked her eyes a few times, allowing them to adjust to the darker light, and then all was visible inside Gare de Lyon.

Once she was past the trains, it allowed for a wide view of the station and the flurry of activity, colors, and excitement of the main floor. It was very bright and open. The high ceiling was made up of crisscrossed beams along the entire ceiling; it looked like beams, beams, and more beams. And the light green color continued from outside, into the interior walls. The color made Gare de Lyon welcoming to new visitors, like Lexi.

And there was something else on the main floor.

At first, she couldn't perceive all of it, but as she quickly hustled forward, it became clear why she didn't. *It* was clear. Or transparent.

Standing in middle of Gare de Lyon was — a giant glass wall.

"Oh," she said a little surprised.

The wall wasn't a single piece of glass: The main body was made up of large square pieces piled high, like a tic-tac-toe board, but the center and bottom-middle pieces were missing creating an opening. Shiny silver metal support beams held all the glass pieces firmly together. It created a glass arch curvature, like the Arc de Triomphe. It was at least 30 - 40 feet tall, just missing one of the metal crisscrossing beams of the station.

Lexi couldn't believe what she's seeing. A glass wall was in the middle of a train station.

"What an odd place to put a wall?" she said out loud to no one in particular.

But she couldn't take her eyes off it. It was stunning.

As she walked through the main terminal, she tried to observe it from every angle since she felt she couldn't stop now, pull out her phone, and take pictures. It was probably at the bottom of her carry-on bag, anyway. And she didn't want to cause another backup. Lexi quickly turned around, glancing at the large line of people still behind her walking briskly.

She mused to herself that no one in America would put a large glass wall in the middle of a train station, for absolutely no reason. She quietly laughed to herself, and then thought better of it. Who was she to snicker at other cultures? Who knows why the wall was there? The French must have their reasons.

She wanted to stop and see if there was any information about the wall, but the main terminal floor was densely packed. Hundreds of people were standing around waiting for trains, and even more, like herself, were moving forward toward the doors and escalators leading down to the metro or outside. The station hummed from all the activity. She barely had anywhere to go but with the flow of passengers from her train to the escalators or nearest exit. Truthfully, she couldn't get near the wall even if she wanted to, not with her bulky suitcase. She would literally have to shove people out of the way.

When she was within 20 or feet of the wall, she glanced up at it again, and noticed something she hadn't seen before.

Maybe she was too far away, or the angle wasn't right? Or maybe, she just wasn't truly focusing.

On the left side, in the second pane of glass from the bottom, was a picture of a man's face. But this wasn't an ordinary photographic picture. It was a hologram. It had depth, appearing three-dimensional in the two-dimensional glass. The man in the hologram was handsome. He appeared to be in his late forties or early fifties, with a nice head of dark hair that was slightly graying; high cheekbones; and blue eyes. But it was hard to tell exactly because the colors in the hologram were all pastels: light blues, pinks, greens, yellows, red, and oranges.

"Oh, wow!" said Lexi, realizing for the first time the wall must be an art sculpture. She gazed at the holographic image. She had only seen holograms on really cheap postcards or stickers. This was so much more advanced than anything she had ever seen before. It was truly remarkable. She didn't realize holographic technology had taken such a giant leap forward. But, she thought to herself, 'artists are always on the cusp of new technology.'

She remembered an art installation at the American Art Museum in Washington, D.C., that used light diodes running from the ceiling to the floor to spell out words. It was incredible, but nowhere near the technological sophistication of this installation.

The man's face was three-dimensional, and it had depth inside the glass. She didn't need glasses. It made all the movies she had seen requiring polarized 3-D glasses look flat and lifeless.

The artist who created this wall needed to call up James Cameron or Peter Jackson and give them both a serious lesson in dimensions. This wasn't 3-D as seen through a 2-D movie frame, like looking through a window. The man looked like a living human being, not a flat photograph.

Lexi finally made it to the back of the main terminal floor. She veered to the right, passing the downward escalators, as she slowly walked around, she never took her eyes off the glass wall.

The wall was probably best viewed from far away anyway, hence why the holographic image was high up on the second pane of glass, not in the first. That way the whole station could view it and admire its beauty and innovation.

As she walked up to the hallway leading out, she glanced back one last time to have a final look at the wall, admiring its splendor. If this was a taste of all the art, she was going to see in Paris then she was in for a cultural extravaganza. The glass wall was truly one of the most extraordinary installations she had ever seen — the imagination. Who would think to do that to a wall? No, was not just the glass wall itself; it was the three-dimensional hologram that made this sculpture touch the cutting edge of technology and innovation. And wasn't that what art in the twenty-first century was all about?

She wondered who the man was. Why was his face chosen to be up on the wall? Her best guess: he was the artist himself showing off his accomplishment. As she turned away from the glass wall and Gare de Lyon, she made a mental note to herself.

NOTE TO SELF: Always appreciate innovation, it's the future.

Lexi walked down the short hallway, reached the outside door, and walked through the large plaza in front of the train station, over to the line of taxis.

●

A

A = (a point)

A *point* is a member of a set.

Assassins' Wall: Gare de Lyon

CHAPTER 2

The Face

STREET, PARIS. EARLY MORNING.

Thursday

Early the next morning Lexi left her hotel wearing a brand-new suit with a light scarf wrapped around her neck. She was off to do battle, of sorts, and this was her armor. The battle was business, and her suit was the jousting attire of a modern fighter — no horses or lances needed. A briefcase and a laptop computer were all the tools a modern man or woman needed for fighting today.

Walking down the sidewalk, she glanced down at the map on her phone, trying to find the nearest metro entrance, Lexi saw a small newsstand on the street corner. She walked up to it, picking up one of the few English newspapers.

It perhaps seemed redundant to buy a newspaper in this day and age of twenty-four-hour internet news cycles, but she loved the feel and smell of the paper. She knew it was old fashioned and as everyone said, "soon to be a wasteful thing from the past," but a paper gave her, and the news, a sense of hard reality. On the internet, information changed from minute to minute, always being updated, revised, censored, or deleted. A newspaper was definitive. It was solid, a remnant of the past in an all-consuming digital world. And psychologically, it made her feel as though she had accomplished something. No one cared if you read the latest newsfeed from any number of websites and social media, but to say you read a complete newspaper was truly concrete. Not that this was her rationale.

It was a routine her dad started with her as a young child. "Always start your day with the newspaper, Alexandra," he used to say. Granted, she was only "reading" the comics section in her youth. But as she grew up, she moved on to the metro section, then sports, and finally the opinion pages. Her father would always graciously take the time to discuss what she had read, ask her thoughts about a given topic, and then gave his advice and perspective along the way.

A newspaper every day was a nod to him, and the love he had for all the happenings in the world, and the love he had passed on to her. "Be involved with the world Alexandra, because *IT* is involved with you," he used to say. She was probably the last person on her block, and even in the building, that still had the daily paper delivered to the door. Most newspapers were going out of the paper business. The question was how much longer were they even going to be doing physical papers? The thought depressed her.

As Lexi was handed today's English newspaper, she noticed another paper. The headline was in French, and the front-page cover featured a large picture of a man. She took a moment to try and register where she had seen him before. She knew the face, but he wasn't a celebrity or any political figure that she could think of, not that her knowledge of French political figures and celebrities was impressive.

She grabbed one of the newspapers from a pile in front of her, staring at the face. Glancing up to the man behind the newsstand, "Good morning. Can you please tell me what this says in English?" She pointed to the newspaper headline.

The man appeared annoyed and didn't acknowledge her request.

Of course! The French hate it when you assume they speak English, which they probably did. She held up the paper, pointing at the headline above the face. "*Pardonnez-moi. Qu'est-ce que cela signifie ... en anglais?*" she said stumbling over the words.

The man scanned the paper, then away, even more annoyed. "Man found dead in home."

"Really?" The words came as a shock to Lexi. "Dead? Who is he?"

"*Je ne peux pas dire,*" he said, shrugging his shoulders.

She wondered what all that meant in English. She thought better of getting out her translator app on her phone. The man probably wouldn't repeat what he said into it, but that didn't matter. There was something about the dead man's face. She looked down at the paper again, perplexed, handing only the English paper to the newsstand man. As she was about to put the French paper back in the pile, her heart twinged; it jumped and felt heavy, all at the same time. She hesitated for a moment. There was something there. It had to do with the dead man on the paper.

"And I'll take this one as well," said Lexi, handing over the French paper.

The man stared at her for a moment, not moving.

French! She forgot to say it in French. But how did she say that in French? "*Merci,*" she said kindly to him, hoping that would be enough to get him moving. Sometimes a quick, sincere thank you can go very far. People often took for granted what a little kindness and appreciation could accomplish.

"Ten Euros," he said flatly, staring at the next customer behind her.

She handed him the money and walked away; eyes transfixed by the face on the French paper. There was something about this man. She couldn't put her finger on it. But she knew him.

While staring at the paper, Lexi almost ran into someone on the sidewalk. "Excuse me," she said, then folded the newspaper into her bag. She glanced at her phone for the time and quickly rushed down the street toward the nearest metro entrance.

Assassins' Wall: Gare de Lyon

CHAPTER 3

Vision

LA GRANDE ARCHE, LA DÉFENSE, PARIS. MORNING.

Walking up stairs to exit the metro, Lexi was at her
destination: La Défense. At the top of the steps, she paused to
look around: in front, around, and behind her was a grand
pedestrian plaza lined by tall glass skyscrapers. The size of the
plaza was difficult to fathom. She guessed it was what the vast
size of Tiananmen Square would look like, at least from pictures,
though she'd never be allowed in China because of her security
clearances. And beckoning at the very end of the plaza was her
final stop for the morning, La Grande Arche de la Défense.

Lexi wasn't exactly sure why they call the building an
arch. The steps at the bottom made the building look more like a
cube than an arch. It probably should have been called La Grande
Cube instead. But the Parisians, again, must have had their
reasons.

La Grande Arche stood like a beacon at the end of La
Défense pedestrian plaza: tall, white, and ... square. What made
the structure so unusual was the hollow center that was open to
the air. It impressed Lexi. Who would have thought to construct a
building in the shape of a cube without a center? And to have it as

an actual workspace! Parisians appeared to blend art with everyday functionality seamlessly. Why not have a building that was also art? She wished that Americans would place more emphasis on such architectural importance.

As she started walking down the plaza toward La Grande Arche in the bright morning sunlight, she quickly glanced up at the sky. The sun was very intense, and it was bothering her eyes. She stopped for a second, opened her bag, and started rummaging through it, looking for her sunglasses. It had been cloudy earlier this morning, so she didn't need them, but now they were nowhere to be found.

She observed two people walking by. Bright sunlight pierced her eyes, and she started to see a white wavy highlight all around each individual, an aura. She knew what this aura was called, metamorphopsia — when objects appear wavy and distorted in space. She had seen it before.

Without a moment's hesitation, she immediately stopped searching through her bag and hustled toward La Grande Arche.

Yes, the sun was definitely too bright for her eyes this morning. She picked up the pace of her walk to a brisk stride while taking another look inside her bag for the sunglasses that weren't there. She remembered putting them in her carry-on bag last night. "Why can I never find anything in my bag when I really need it?" she whined out of frustration to no one in particular, perhaps to the universe itself.

She gave up on her sunglasses and looked toward La Grande Arche to see how far she had to go. It was still a hell-far walk in direct sunlight, so she rushed even faster, holding her hand above her eyes to shield them from piercing sunlight.

She quickly glanced at a few more people walking by, trying to assess how her eyes were doing. Now besides the white highlight, she was also seeing a human shadow shape following behind each person.

She knew what this issue was; many an eye doctor had tested her for it. Her eyes, or more precisely, her retinas were having a reaction to the sunlight. It was called solar retinopathy. Her eyes were very sensitive to light, especially harsh sunlight, which could damage her retinas, causing lesions.

Her ophthalmologist had once joked that with the symptoms she was reporting, her retinas should look like those of a middle-aged man who had just stared at a solar eclipse. He then asked her if she was, by chance, part of a religion that worshipped the sun. She didn't even realize they existed anymore; wasn't that only in ancient Egypt?

The doctors, and she had seen many, weren't sure why her retinas were reacting this way to sunlight. Her retinal vascular system was perfectly functional and normal, she didn't have diabetes, and she hadn't been exposed to high levels of radiation. They knew only that she had this condition, so they were more concerned with prevention at this point than the initial cause, which was probably genetics.

The first time it happened, Lexi was a twelve-year old playing soccer on a bright summer day. The goalie suddenly had a white fuzzy aura all around her. And the longer she played in the sunlight, the worse her condition got. By the end of the game every single player had a white aura.

The episode prompted the first visit to the eye doctor, and by high school she restricted herself to outdoor sports like cross-country running, softball, and tennis. Soccer was no longer an option because she couldn't wear sunglasses.

And her eyes only got worse with age. When she was in her twenties, it really started to worry her because if her retinas were this sensitive, this young, she couldn't even imagine how bad her eyes would be in her eighties. She guessed she would eventually have to wear sunglasses on cloudy days or pray science fact finally caught up with science fiction, and her imagination, and they could clone her new retinas. She was still holding out hope for that one.

Walking even faster down La Défense pedestrian plaza, Lexi couldn't believe she forgot her sunglasses. It is so unlike her. She knew how important they were for her eyes. She usually had two extra spares on her, at all times. Lexi searched through her bag one last time and huffed. Just her luck, they weren't there. She didn't think Paris sunlight could be so bright. She would expect this in Florida or some other tropical location, but not Paris! She needed to buy a cheap pair of sunglasses. Immediately!

Looking down the plaza, she realized the effect on her eyes was getting worse. Now the overwhelmed retinas were seeing an afterimage — where the image persists after the original image was created in bright light. She saw, in the middle of the plaza, even in empty spaces, more human shapes, besides the shadows walking behind the people. The plaza looked three times as busy as it actually was.

The sight before her eyes then changed again. The walking shadow shapes then started turning every color of the rainbow from a brand-new symptom, chromatopsia — where objects appear to be colored. The rainbow-colored shadow shapes — and now some seemed not quite human — walked this way and that, following the people.

All three symptoms of the solar retinopathy — the metamorphopsia, afterimages, and achromatopsia — culminated together, creating a view of the plaza with thousands of shapes, sizes, and colors around the few hundred actual people walking around.

The sight was too much for her brain and eyes to process, so she glanced high up in the sky to the top of La Grande Arche, trying to give her eyes a break. But the bright white color of the building just exacerbated the symptoms in her retinas, and she started seeing little white shooting stars in the bright blue sky.

21

This brand-new symptom had never occurred before. She didn't have a name for it yet. She knew this is bad ... very, very bad. Covering her eyes completely with her hand, she looked down only at the ground immediately in front of her and broke into a run.

She sprinted up to the large steps, made all the more difficult by the nice suit, heels, and bag. It was better to get inside quickly. The longer she stayed outside in sunlight, the worse it was on her eyes. With this level of retinal symptoms, it could take hours or even days for her eyes to recover, hopefully without lesions.

The last time this happened, and it was many years ago, her eyes took four hours to stop seeing afterimages. She was lucky there weren't any lesions on her retinas. But somehow, she always managed to escape that fate: attributing it to her hyperawareness of the eye condition, catching it when she was young, and always having a pair of sunglasses ready ... Well, except for now. Hopefully, her eyes wouldn't interfere with the meeting, even if the conference room appeared to be a little more crowded than it really was.

She made it up the stairs of La Grande Arche and quickly jolted inside the building.

CHAPTER 4

Satellites

CONFERENCE ROOM, LA GRANDE ARCHE, PARIS.
AFTERNOON.

After more than 10 hours, Lexi was finally feeling and seeing like herself. Once inside, and out of the bright sunlight, her eyes settled down and allowed her to get to work.

Sitting at a conference table, Lexi momentarily stared at some white empty wall space, trying to assess how her eyes were recovering. Only faint glimmers of the shadows from the solar retinopathy were left. As soon as she got back home, it would be time to call up her eye doctor again. It had been over a year since she last saw Dr. Strun, but obviously things were getting worse. This time she'd be lucky if there weren't any lesions from whatever new symptom caused those shooting stars. She bet it had to do with blood flow or a detached retina. The thought put a pit in her stomach. Hopefully she didn't need eye surgery.

Lexi turned back to the conference table and the man sitting at the head of it. He was an older French gentleman in a military uniform speaking formally to the group of people. He spoke in English; she guessed for her benefit. She was the only non-French-speaking person in the room.

"Before we finish, I would like to thank you all for joining us today for our first joint status meeting. As we mentioned earlier, there are a few obstacles the Ministère des Armées found with perfecting the metal matrix composite of the lightweight aluminum beryllium alloy for our communications satellite. There are problems with its long-term durability against solar wind, solar flares, solar radiation, micrometeorites, ultraviolet light, and any number of environmental degradation factors in high atmospheric orbit, not including ISS fecal dumping."

The conference room let out a small laugh.

Lexi knew, as did the rest of the room, there was a little-known secret that the International Space Station stores the crew's fecal matter and then dumped it, via unmanned spacecraft, into the atmosphere so it can burn up on re-entry. The atmosphere did make the perfect waste incinerator, and the practice soon gave a whole other meaning to the saying "the world is full of shit," prompting never-ending jokes inside the aerospace community.

"Also," he continued, "this particular aluminum beryllium alloy is highly susceptible to atomic oxygen. So, we will have to take into consideration how the material is anodized. The satellite and this new alloy will have to be at least twice as durable as previous satellites because of the increased amount of space junk the Americans have left behind in orbit."

All the twenty people at the conference table turned to Lexi, who was surprised at the pointed blame toward the word "American."

"Don't blame us," she said, trying to lighten the mood. "The Russians were up there first." Lexi smiled slightly.

"Indeed, Mademoiselle Peters, and still going up," said another man from the French Ministry of Defense who was sitting across the conference table. "They've never stopped sending people up themselves."

Lexi quietly sighed, "True. Very true."

His words sting her heart. Americans now faced competition from China as well as Russia in the ever changing and evolving space race. And space was the future. Not in a science fiction moon colony kind of way, no, not yet. That was still a decade, or two into the future, but presently space was the communications and materials engineering frontier. The only way forward was up and out: more satellites for GPS, military weapons, Starlink, and spying. Eventually space might not only be militarized; the internet, telephone, and television, all media would be transmitted through space for a global audience.

She guessed that within the decade, they all would be watching a single global news network, broadcasting to every inch of the planet for every human being to see. All of them would be watching the same program, at the same time: no more time delays or national channels, but a true global merging of television/internet, which would be broadcast, of course, through these satellites. A GNN, as it were. And the world would be global because a phone would be in the hands of every human being. Well, almost ... She was sure there was a Maasai warrior or two somewhere in the middle of Africa who would never want or need such a device. And could she blame them? They didn't need an app to avoid a lion. Well, not yet ...

Lexi watched as the Ministry of Defense official finished his speech to the officials assembled around the conference table. She knew France had secure communications satellites to connect with their armed forces around the world. But governments were too far behind nowadays, including America's. It seemed only a matter of time before private industry fully surpassed government space programs. The government super-subcontractors of the Mercury, Gemini, Apollo, and space shuttle days were almost over. Soon private businesses, run by billionaires, would be the leaders and innovators, trailblazing through space. Governments were cutting budgets, which meant cutting out space.

When the meeting ended, Lexi stood to pack her bag. She pulled out the two newspapers from a side pocket, making room for all the additional paperwork from the meeting. She saw a person waiting patiently next to her and turned to shake the hand of the woman who had been sitting next to her. "Thank you for everything ... *Merci*." This process repeated ten more times as the other individuals in the room quickly departed.

After her bag was packed with paperwork, Lexi glanced down at the French newspaper. Stuck in the corner of the paper were her folded sunglasses. "Ah! There they are," she said excitedly, grabbing the glasses and securing them to her shirt. She picked up the newspaper before putting it back in her bag, staring at the man on the front page. Her heart twinged again.

"See you later this evening, Mademoiselle Peters," said the older gentleman who chaired the meeting.

Focusing on the newspaper and only half listening, she quickly looked up. "Yes. Will do. Thank you ... *Merci.* This evening." She turned and firmly shook his hand, putting the newspaper in her bag, and headed out of the conference room.

The Ministry of Defense official was left alone, shaking his head slightly as she left the room. Sometimes it was very hard to understand "American."

Assassins' Wall: Gare de Lyon

CHAPTER 5

Sculptures

LA GRANDE ARCHE, LA DÉFENSE, PARIS. LATE AFTERNOON.

Lexi was perched high above the plaza on the La Grande Arche main outdoor entrance, with her sunglasses on. She walked over to the top of the stairs to take in the beautiful view of the spacious plaza.

It was spectacular. It reminded her of standing at the top of the stairs of the Lincoln Memorial in Washington, D.C. That view started at the reflecting pond and ended at the Washington Memorial. But here at the top of La Grande Arche steps, the view flowed past the plaza, down a large boulevard, stretching all the way to the Arc de Triomphe de l'Étoile.

Lexi couldn't believe her luck. This was the first time she had seen the Arc de Triomphe in person. It must be huge for her to have seen it from so far away. It was an amazing feat of architecture. She could see the top curvature of the arch and the middle portion, but she was too far away to see the bottom. Lexi knew the massive structure must have been at least two or three miles away.

Digging through her bag to find her phone, Lexi pulled out the French newspaper and then her phone. She quickly glanced at the Arc de Triomphe, then looked at the picture of the man on the front page of the newspaper. For the briefest of seconds, she saw an arched glass wall around the man, like double vision. His face was perfectly placed on the second pane of glass.

That was it! She'd figured it out. He was the man from the glass wall in Gare de Lyon. The face looked a little different in a 2-D photograph instead of a 3-D hologram. But it was him. She blinked her eyes a few times, looking at the photograph. The double vision was gone, and the paper had only the portrait of the man, no glass wall. Maybe her eyes were still getting residual afterimages from earlier, carrying the arch shape from the Arc de Triomphe over to the picture of the man.

She squeezed the paper back in her bag and with her phone took a picture of the plaza and the Arc de Triomphe. Hundreds of other people were taking pictures of the view, lounging on the stairs, and enjoying the vista. She decided on a panoramic picture, starting on the left, and she noticed another unusual sight, not for the first time — or the last time — in Paris. To the left of the main plaza was a giant sculpture of a thumb.

Now she had seen everything: a glass wall in the middle of a train station and a giant thumb right in the middle of La Défense. She had to hand it to the Parisians. They had a penchant for putting sculptures of the strangest things in the oddest places … But hey, why not? They're French.

She jaunted down the stairs of La Grande Arche and veered left over to the large thumb to get a better look. As she got closer, she realized the thumb was bronze and enormous, at least thirty feet tall. It had a fingernail, wrinkles, and a fingerprint, everything. And she wasn't the only person interested in this peculiar sculpture. People were constantly stopping and staring at the giant thumb.

Maybe it meant "yes," as in "thumbs up." But she did not know if the cultural connotation was the same for the French. She always thought the thumbs-up gesture originated in the Roman Coliseum to save a gladiator's life. Maybe it originated in Roman Gaul? Whatever this thumb meant doesn't matter because art always comes down to the interpreter. Did it really matter what the artist had intended? Or was it up to what the viewer saw and interpreted? She didn't know.

Lexi stood at the bottom of the thumb looking up at it. She thought the thumb meant "yes." So, "yes" it was. Maybe it was an encouragement from the universe. Yes! She's headed in the right direction. Keep moving forward. Or perhaps she was sticking out like a sore thumb?

As she walked back to the metro entrance, down the long plaza, she noticed another two sculptures that towered high above the ground. She didn't notice them this morning, probably because she was walking in the opposite direction toward La Grande Arche.

She strolled past a beautiful carrousel, up to the sculpture on the left side of the plaza. She knew it was definitely an Alexander Calder. There was another one that looked similar to this in Washington, D.C., on the National Mall. It had bright red steel beams arched to the ground ... a play on balance or gravity.

The other sculpture on the opposite side of the plaza was another mystery, even more so since it had no obvious meaning or symbolism. The sculpture looked like giant clay blobs, almost like Play-Doh, in bright blue, red, and yellow. The sculpture could be child's play, as if a kid left some colored clay after playtime and a grownup took it as inspiration.

And she didn't want to be harsh, but it was ugly. Very, very ugly, but that is just her personal opinion. Art is allowed to be ugly. The ugliness often held a meaning.

Lexi pulled out her phone, using it to jump onto social media. She typed in: Sculptures. La Défense. Paris. *That should be enough*.

Under images, the sculptures, and the name Joan Miró immediately popped up. "*Deux Personnages Fantastiques*."

Standing on the plaza between the two sculptures, Lexi turned back to the Arc de Triomphe in the distance. She slowly walked over to a balcony overlooking another lower section of the plaza, all the while staring at the French icon. The arch reminded her of the glass wall in Gare de Lyon.

She typed into her phone web browser: Gare de Lyon. Paris. Sculpture.

Nothing.

She typed: Paris. Gare de Lyon. Interior. Sculpture. Glass Wall.

Nothing.

She typed: Gare de Lyon. Glass Wall. Sculpture. Hologram. *That should work.*

Nothing.

Lexi pulled out the French paper and stared at the man's face again. His image pulled at her heart. This couldn't be the man she saw yesterday on the glass wall. She re-read the French headline. Why would he be found dead? There was only one way to find out.

She quickly put the paper in her bag and turned around, heading toward the metro entrance. She had to go back to Gare de Lyon and check.

Assassins' Wall: Gare de Lyon

CHAPTER 6

Name

GARE DE LYON, PARIS. LATE AFTERNOON.

Still wearing the same business suit from the morning, Lexi briskly walked up the escalator from the metro below and into the main terminal of Gare de Lyon train station. It was very busy. Not as congested as the day before with all the trains dumping off their passengers, but it was still very crowded.

Directly in front of her were the trains and to her right was the glass wall, but at this angle she couldn't see the front glass, only the side. To get a better look she had to stand back from the wall, and unfortunately like yesterday, the main terminal was at capacity. There were hundreds of people standing around, milling about, and sitting on the benches. She would be hard pressed to make it through the people without getting crushed.

She turned to the left, away from the wall, and casually walked around, just as she has done yesterday, in a semi-circle around the escalators. She passed the hallway she used yesterday, and finally stopped at the row of benches in the very back of the station. The benches were occupied, so she stood right behind the seats, looking up at the wall, which was now directly in front of her. And again, just like yesterday, on the second pane of glass was the hologram of a man's face, but from this side of the station it was on the right-hand side of the wall.

She continued to stare, analyzing every aspect of the hologram. He looked very similar to the face she saw the previous day. Was he the same man? Maybe? It was hard to be sure.

The man sitting in the seat directly in front of her got up. She quickly grabbed the empty seat on the bench. She needed a moment. There was only one way to prove her theory.

Lexi pulled out the French newspaper and stared at the photograph intently, then up at the wall, back and forth a few times. It reminded her of the visual game in the Sunday newspaper where she had to compare two exact pictures to see which one had something missing or changed. She hardly ever got all the answers correct, so why would she get these two correct? Also, it was hard to accurately tell if it was the same person because the pastel coloring of the hologram wasn't like a normal picture. The shades of skin, eyes, and hair made the analysis difficult.

She scrutinized the picture in the newspaper again, then looked up at the wall, then back to the newspaper, and back up at the wall. There were subtle differences between the two men: the face in the paper was a little narrower, his eyebrows were a little farther apart, and the hairline was slightly farther back. The man currently up on the wall didn't exactly match.

She began to feel annoyed, not at what she was seeing, but at what she started feeling in her heart. It reminded her again that something was not quite right with this whole situation by giving another slight twinge, but she ignored it.

Just to be sure, positively sure, Lexi held up the paper, so the two images were right next to each other, side by side. It was a close call. The two men could have been brothers, they appeared so similar. Older gentlemen, brownish-graying hair, light eyes, distinguished facial lines, and wrinkles, but the man currently on the wall was *not* the man from the newspaper. He had a slightly deeper brow, rounder eyes, and a larger nose. It was the little distinctions that made the difference.

She spoke quietly to herself, in a reassuring tone. "I knew it. It's not the same guy." Here she had gotten herself all into a flurry about the French newspaper, and it wasn't even the same man. She felt a little foolish for thinking the man from the newspaper was the man on the wall. "Of course, it wasn't him!" she said firmly to herself. Why would a man from a giant glass wall in Gare de Lyon be found dead? How ridiculous!

She let out a long sigh, in relief. "There. Done!" she said, putting the newspaper back in her bag. She stopped for a moment to appreciate the atmosphere of the beautiful train station. She had some time to kill before the dinner party that evening.

She scanned the train station, watching the people walking around, sitting in the seats waiting, and talking to each

37

other. Yesterday when she went through the station, she was in such a hurry that she never took the time to really study the travelers around her. One of her favorite pastimes was to sit and people watch, trying to guess who they were, where they were going, and perhaps take a shot at why they were going there. She tried to conjecture about their lives using the clothing, hair, posture, accessories, and even the expressions on their faces as guidelines. And she was pretty damn good at it. She could tell if people were friends, lovers, relatives, or business associates. And Gare de Lyon offered the perfect opportunity for her to perfect these skills. The station was a hive of people. It gave off the energy, excitement, and momentum of somewhere to go, in the same way airports, amusement parks, and sporting events do.

She turned and saw a young couple, three seats over, who looked like newlyweds. They were all over each other. Maybe they were about to go on their honeymoon? They were wearing wedding rings, had their legs crossed toward each other, and spoke intimately. Yes, they must be newlyweds, and they were obviously very happy and in love. Every word they shared brought a smile or a small kiss as opposed to the two men sitting across from her. They were sitting as far apart as humanly possible while still talking to each other. They must be relatives or friends, but their body language revealed they only tolerated each other's company. The obvious giveaway was their bags. One of the men kept pushing his bag slightly away from the other so they wouldn't touch, as if even their bags took offense at being too close to the other person.

Slowly, Lexi gazed around the station observing the couples, friends, and business people waiting for trains. Her eyes eventually made it back to the glass wall. What an odd thing it was. Who would put a giant glass sculpture with people's faces on it in the middle of a train station? But then again, why put a bronze thumb in the middle of a plaza? She wondered if the glass wall was a statement on their fast-moving twenty-first century lives and the picture was supposed to remind the world that people, not technology, made up these lives. But that wouldn't explain the glass. Why not make it stone like the Arc de Triomphe? Why make the wall transparent? What aren't they seeing? Ha! The irony.

Looking down from the holographic picture, she noticed something she hadn't seen before. Wait. That would make three "notices" in the last two days ... or was it four "notices"? The hologram, the thumb, the Calder, and now this. That would be four. Her observational skills were slacking. She needed to open her eyes and start paying attention! Or as she once heard a cop discussing, be *In The Yellow*. He explained that red was a high state of awareness, remembering minute details like a license number or a type of car, while he was working as a policeman. Yellow was just a general awareness of his surroundings, seeing if someone was out of place or acting oddly, while he was off duty but still being a cop; he was aware if anything went wrong in case he needed to help. And finally, green was not paying attention to the surroundings, while he was at home, safe and sound. Since she arrived in Paris, she had been acting like she was in the green. Maybe it was the station wall color rubbing off on her? But with all she had missed, she needed to step it up a notch.

NOTE TO SELF: BE IN THE YELLOW.

She observed three men standing at the bottom of the wall. They were the only people, literally, directly below the wall, waiting. They seemed to keep to themselves, but that's not what caught her eye. They had no luggage, no roller suitcase, no messenger bag, duffle, carry-on, nothing. They had no visible sign of why they were in Gare de Lyon. Maybe they were waiting for a friend to arrive, and they stood so close to the trains to be the first to greet the friend as they disembarked. It was a plausible explanation.

Lexi stood and took a few steps closer, angling for a better view of the wall and the men. As she approached, she realized the men at the bottom of the wall were Middle Eastern. They had dark hair and were in Western attire: dark basic pants or jeans and a shirt. She read a while ago that France had a very large Arab immigrant population, and they were the country's largest minority. All of the men's pieces fit: clothing, hair, but something about them didn't *feel* right. Maybe it was their lack of accessories.

40

Her eyes peered up from the men to the hologram on the wall. "Oh," she said to herself, intensely staring, stopping in place about halfway to the wall.

She squinted her eyes. "Didn't see that before," she said to herself. Next to the 3-D picture of the man was a name in large letters, also holographic, which made it a bit difficult to read. "Louis Calendrier," she read aloud slowly, trying to make out all the letters. No one heard her in the cacophony of sound: from the loudspeaker blaring a woman's voice in French to the never-ending ambient noise of people conversing.

Her heart twinged again; this time she couldn't ignore it. She reached into her bag and pulled out a notepad and pen. Looking back at the picture on the wall, she squinted her eyes a little, writing down the name. "OK Lex, C.Y.A.," she said to herself.

She knew deep down inside why she did this. Her heart was still nagging her, it had this feeling ... it was so crazy she didn't even want to think it, but her heart kept insisting that the man she saw yesterday up on the wall was the dead man from the newspaper, and this man, Louis Calendrier, was a totally new person. There was something not quite right with this whole situation. But she had to be sure. Yesterday she took it for granted. Today she would not.

NOTE TO SELF: Stop taking things for granted.

Lexi was about to take a step closer to the wall when she stopped. She stared at the three Arab men at the bottom of the wall, realizing what it was about them. Their posture was wrong. They looked like they were glued to the wall. Everyone else was just walking by, or if they stopped, they weren't so close. It appeared these men were almost drawn to it — there was a possessiveness toward the wall.

"Something's not right with those guys," she said, oh so quietly to herself. Their posture was the same as the couple sitting three seats over from her. There was a gravity to their position, a magnetic pull, but these men were standing that way, not with a person, but with a glass wall. It was theirs.

Lexi watched one of the Arab men abruptly leave the wall and head toward the nearest exit of the station. The other two men stayed behind with the wall, as though guarding it.

She took one last look at the hologram, talking to it. "OK, Louis Calendrier. You better hope I'm crazy." She quickly turned and left the station, feeling assured that with his name in her proverbial and literal pocket, all of the world would soon be back to normal. Or at least she hoped so.

CHAPTER 7

Reminders

ARC DE TRIOMPHE DE L'ÉTOILE, PARIS. DUSK.

That evening, as was the custom in business, there was a celebratory dinner at a restaurant near the Arc de Triomphe. Lexi, wearing a vintage pencil thin black dress and a blazer, had purposely planned her route to take in the arch so it would be silhouetted against the evening sky.

Leaving the metro station and walking up the street toward the Arc de Triomphe, she saw it beautifully lit by the reflecting sunset in the clouds. She stopped at the roundabout enshrining the arch. Cars zoomed by, creating a moat of motion, protecting the Arc de Triomphe from the rest of Paris. It was even more massive than she had imagined. It must have been over a hundred feet tall, maybe more. The people standing at the bottom looked like tiny ants in comparison.

As the Paris evening slowly crept in, surrounding the Arc de Triomphe in the pinks, blues, and purples of a perfect sunset. The colors reminded her of the holographic picture on the glass wall and Louis Calendrier.

She never realized how similar the two structures actually were. The glass wall and the stone arch evoked an overall majesty. Both were a reminder for French ingenuity and victory. Perhaps the creator of the glass wall took inspiration from the Arc de Triomphe? It made logical sense.

As the colors in the sky began to fade away, Lexi opened her small evening bag and took a picture of the arch before all the pinks and blues faded into the black of night.

She reviewed the pictures on her phone. "Beautiful," she said, smiling. She glanced back as the night floodlights totally encompassed the Arc de Triomphe and the car headlights merged into one, creating a wall of light. To her, the Arc de Triomphe was the beating heartbeat of Paris, not the Eiffel Tower.

CHAPTER 8

Questions

RESTAURANT, PARIS. NIGHT.

At the predinner cocktail hour — or had it been hours (she lost track of time) — Lexi had only two things on her mind ... Louis Calendrier and the glass wall in Gare de Lyon.

Everyone from the business meeting mingled, except for Lexi. She had eyes for only one person: the Ministry of Defense official. With a glass of wine in hand, probably one of the best she'd ever had in her life, she waited patiently for the opportune moment to catch him in between conversations.

She saw her moment just as he finished speaking with the man who earlier berated the American space program. She quickly approached him. "*Pardonnez-moi*. Monsieur Calbe, may I ask you a question?" She smiled, took a little sip of wine, trying not to seem too awkward.

"*Oui*, Mademoiselle Peters," said Monsieur Calbe, turning toward her, figuring she wanted only to discuss work in their time off, as all Americans are apt to do.

"On my way into Paris through Gare de Lyon train station, I saw what I think was a sculpture. It's a large glass wall. Have you seen it?" asked Lexi, trying to act nonchalant about the whole thing, while inside her heart was racing. *Why was it racing?* She also started sweating a little.

A look of total surprise was visible on the man's face; a sense of relief washed over him. She wanted to talk about something other than work. "No. I haven't. I never travel through Gare de Lyon. I use Gare du Nord on the weekends," he responded.

"Oh," said Lexi, taking another quick sip of her drink. "Well, it's really an interesting installation. The sculpture is made up of glass, and a steel skeleton supports the whole thing. It also has an arch, like the Arc de Triomphe. But the most intriguing part of the wall is on the second piece of glass, on the right side. There's a holographic picture of someone's face. The hologram has so much depth ... I've never seen anything like it before. I was just curious about the artist, and if he or she used pictures of Parisian citizens for the wall, or perhaps it's a self-portrait?"

"*Qui sait?*" said Monsieur Calbe, slightly shrugging. "Paris always has new art installations all over the city, all year long. I'm hardly able to keep track of all the new pieces. A while ago there was a huge statue of a chicken, made from garbage. It appeared out of nowhere in one of the gardens, I don't remember which one, and then it was promptly gone after a month. Did you see, next to La Grande Arche, there is a statue of a giant thumb, Le Pouce, almost twelve meters high?"

"Yes, I saw that statue today," Lexi said with excitement in her voice. At least he knew about one of the sculptures she saw today. "After our meeting I saw some others along La Défense plaza ... a Calder, I think, and a Joan Miró. May I ask why the giant blobs of yellow, blue, and red? Do you know what it symbolizes?"

"No. But as you know, Mademoiselle Peters, art is not my field of expertise." He politely touched his shining military uniform and turned around to another guest.

"Yes, well, *merci*." Lexi smiled, after he turned away. She slightly huffed to herself ... *Well, that's a dead end.*

Assassins' Wall: Gare de Lyon

CHAPTER 9

Chance

LEXI'S HOTEL ROOM, PARIS. LATE NIGHT.

Lexi walked into her hotel room, turning on the lights, and the television for some background noise. She dropped her purse and her jacket on the bed, then headed around the corner into the bathroom.

The sound of the sink running from the bathroom was barely audible under the blaring French late-night news. The voice of a reporter echoed throughout the room. "*Mais d'abord, ce soir, nous avons des nouvelles tragiques: Louis Calendrier a été retrouvé mort à son domicile. Louis Calendrier ...*"

Lexi popped her head around the corner from the bathroom. "What? Louis Calendrier?" she said, confused. She quickly ran towards the screen half undressed, her hair pulled back in a headband, and her face wet from washing. She quickly ran over to the television across the room.

"What? WHAT? WHAT!" she yelled to the television.

She perched right in front of the television like a little child would watching a favorite show.

On the screen the news reporter stood in front of a small house. In the background behind him were an ambulance and a police car. Speaking into a microphone; his tone was grave. "*La police enquête et traite cette affaire comme un homicide, mais il n'ya pas de signes d'une force dans l'entrée.*"

"No! What are you saying!" she pleaded with the television.

A picture of Louis Calendrier appeared up on screen with his name in bold print along the bottom. Lexi gasped, almost falling back, but she caught herself. She knew this face.

"No. No. No. No ..." She kept repeating the word out loud, hoping this wasn't true. She had to be wrong. This couldn't the same man from the wall. *It is just a coincidence*, she repeated in her mind, but her heart started sinking heavily.

She ran over to her bag on a chair, pulled out the notepad, and quickly ran back to the TV, pad in hand. She opened it up, looking down at what she wrote. In giant letters it read, "LOUIS CALENDRIER. You're crazy, Lex!" She paused and turned back at the TV, dumbfounded.

The face of Louis was on half the screen while the reporter took up the other half. "*Un voisin a vu la porte ouverte plus tôt dans la journée; pensant que c'etait inhabituel il se dirigea à l'intérieur pour trouver le cadavre.*" The picture showed a body bag being pulled out of the home and being put into an ambulance.

Lexi glanced at the piece of paper again and then back to the television, a few times. She walked over and slumped on the bed. "Oh, my God." She quickly got up and retrieved the French newspaper from her bag, staring at the picture. She unfolded the whole newspaper for the first time and skimmed the caption under the picture to find the man's name.

"Georges Martin," she said aloud to bring the reality of this man's death home. She put down the paper and stared at the television. "And Louis Calendrier are dead."

This was the second time. This was the second person. It couldn't be chance.

"What do I do?" Lexi uttered hopelessly to herself, and then her heart twinged a bit. It knew what to do. It told her to go back to Gare de Lyon and the glass wall. There was something very unpleasant going on.

Assassins' Wall: Gare de Lyon

●

A

$A = \{. \ . \ . .\}$

Every *set* has a group of points and is said to contain its members.

Assassins' Wall: Gare de Lyon

CHAPTER 10

Decision

HOTEL LOBBY. PARIS. MORNING.

Friday

The next morning on her way out of the hotel, Lexi
stopped at the front desk. The waiting clerk asked politely, "Will
you be checking out today, Mademoiselle Peters?"

She paused for a moment.

Thank goodness, at least the hotel staff was willing to
speak English without her attempting to butcher French. "Umm.
... no," she replied. "Is my room available for another day or so?"

The clerk typed into the computer. It took an eternity.
She had always noticed this: What should take a few quick
keystrokes to find out basic information in fact took twice as long
as it should. What was it with hotel desks, airport counters, and
rental car check-ins?

"Yes, Ms. Peters, it is. We don't have it booked until
Monday."

"Great. I'm going to stay ... for some sightseeing." She
smiled. It was an American custom. One could even say, a
southern American custom, to always put 'it' forth with a smile. It

was like saying thank you; you always got more with honey than vinegar.

"Very good. Mademoiselle Peters." The clerk began typing endlessly into the computer ... again.

"*Merci*," she said and quickly began heading out of the hotel, not waiting for the latest typing marathon to end.

CHAPTER 11

Address

GARE DE LYON, PARIS. LATE MORNING.

Lexi slowly moseyed into the Gare de Lyon through the same entrance that she always used. Unlike the dense crowds on her previous visits, today only a few passengers milled about here and there, waiting for a train. She noticed the hollowness of the sound without hundreds of people talking.

She paused just past the entrance and investigated the station. No one in particular took notice or even cared that she had entered the building. Slowly she walked over to the last row of benches, farthest from the wall, and sat down.

The entire time she had kept her eyes away from the glass wall, only daring to look at the right side of the station at the Express café, the destination board, and below at pastry-sandwich shop. She didn't have the courage yet to face the wall and what was truly going on with it.

Once seated, she inhaled a huge breath, like the extra lungful of oxygen would help calm her nerves. She slowly shifted left toward the wall, gazing up at the second pane of glass. The wall was empty. There were no pictures on it. Nothing. It was the first time she had ever seen it empty — Just glass and steel. No pretty hologram. Nothing.

A huge smile appeared on Lexi's face. She teared up a little and let out the air in a huge sigh of relief. "YES! It's gone," she whispered softly to herself. She kept her voice extra low since there were so few people in the station. She didn't know how far the sound carried.

All of this worrying was for nothing. The wall was empty. Louis Calendrier's name was not on the wall anymore. Maybe she wrote down the wrong name? Or spelled it wrong? Maybe it was Louis Calendr*eir*, not Calendr*ier*. It could be a common name in France, like Smith or Jones in America. But why worry? There weren't any faces on the wall anymore, and no one might be killed. The wall was empty now. It was all over. It was done. There was nothing to worry about.

Happily, she scanned the station, almost laughing at herself and the world. There was nothing to worry about. All of her fretting last night was for naught. She even changed her travel plans. Now she could really enjoy the sightseeing around Paris: the Eiffel Tower, Notre Dame, the Louvre, but no Arc de Triomphe.

Lexi took a minute to watch the people in the station going about their own business, enjoying the day. Soon she would be doing exactly the same.

As she was about to get up from her seat, she checked out the wall one last time. It was still empty. She smiled brightly. All of this was for nothing. She felt foolish and started to get up while looking at the empty wall. A new picture popped up in the glass.

Lexi froze in place, staring at the picture. She'd never seen a face pop up on the wall before — the other two times, the face was already up there. She didn't know they could just pop up like that. Unfortunately, she took the empty wall as a sign that the wall was no longer working, but it was worse than that. Someone completely new was up on the wall.

She dropped back heavily into her seat. There was no mistaking it this time. The picture on the wall was very different from before. He was an older gentleman, probably in his late fifties or sixties, who was very heavy set and almost totally bald. The previous two faces were the complete opposite of this man.

She was crushed by the new picture. "No. You're not Louis," whispered Lexi to herself. She peered around the station in a panic at the other people roaming about, seeking the comfort of another human being with whom to share this devastating news, but no one was paying attention to her or the new face on the wall. She returned to the holographic picture again.

For the first time today, she noticed the bottom of the wall. She couldn't believe she forgot to check.

Standing in the exact spot under the wall where they stood yesterday were the same three Arab men. One of the men was looking up, staring directly at the man's picture on the wall. He turned back and began speaking with the other two men at the bottom.

Lexi was surprised. He had never done that before, not that she had noticed. Were they involved with the wall as well? "Oh, my God!" she cried quietly to herself, not believing what she was seeing: First the new picture popping up, and now the three men might somehow be involved. She quickly surveyed the station, praying someone else besides her was paying attention to what was going on with the wall. No one was.

Quickly she dug in her bag and pulled out the notepad. Looking up at the wall, she squinted her eyes. She was too far back and couldn't read the name next to the picture. She frantically began rummaging through her bag, "Come on. Where the hell are they?" Giving up the search, she stared back at the wall.

The one man who was also gazing at the picture suddenly left the bottom of the wall and was walking straight toward her. Lexi caught herself staring obviously at the man as he approached. She quickly diverted her attention, busying herself by sorting through her bag again. She waited a few seconds with her head down to see if he was coming *for* her. Did they see her staring up at the face on the wall? Or notice her writing down the name yesterday? The thought gave her goosebumps.

The man passed by without even glancing in her direction. She turned around, pretending to adjust her jacket, and watched as he made his way toward the exit behind where she was sitting.

"Where the hell is he going?" she said to herself, just above a whisper.

Looking back at the wall, Lexi squinted her eyes again. She casually got up, grabbed her bag and jacket, and slowly walked toward the wall, taking the occasional pretend glance up to the destination board.

The two Arab men left behind were now standing on the opposite side of the wall, looking out toward the incoming train tracks. They must have walked to the other side of the wall while she was watching the third guy leave.

Trying to appear nonchalant and lackadaisical by looking at everyone and everything but the wall itself, Lexi approached the wall. She was a little nervous. She had to get close to read the name without her eyeglasses. When she got within twenty feet of the wall she quickly peeked up at the holographic picture. This was the closest she had ever been to the wall before. She read the man's name next to his picture just like before, but underneath the name was something faint. She took another step closer, and the hologram became clear. It was an address.

An ADDRESS!

Lexi was shocked. She never saw an address the previous times. When she originally walked past the wall, she caught just a glimpse of the picture at odd angles. Maybe this was there the whole time, but it could only be seen from a certain angle? Holograms and lenticulars work that way; different angles offer a new perspective of the entire picture. Maybe the closer she was to the wall the easier it was to see the information?

Lexi glanced at the two men standing by the wall. That would explain why these guys were literally at the base of the wall. And unfortunately, until now, she never took the time to pay attention to the little things, like why they were positioned next to the wall. She got angry with herself for not getting closer to the wall and seeing the address before.

NOTE TO SELF: Pay attention to the little things in life.

She peeked up to the glass again, and then made a sudden right turn, walking away from the wall and quietly mumbling to herself to try and remember the full address. When she was about fifteen feet away from the wall, heading toward the exit, she quickly wrote down what she could remember of the address in the notepad, her hands shaking.

CHAPTER 12

Recon

STREET, PARIS. NOON.

As Lexi walked down a beautiful street crowded with tall four-to five-story buildings, she navigated the map directions on her phone. Like Boston's twisting streets, the labyrinth of Paris alleyways was not to be taken lightly. Boston roads were most likely drawn under the influence of some hard liquor in early-seventeenth-century America. Paris streets must have been drawn under the same influence, only wine was probably the drink of choice back then, not hard liquor, or perhaps both? Her history of wine was fuzzy.

As she continued through the residential neighborhood in the heart of Paris, she stopped at a street corner. She looked around at the street, then down at her phone map. "What are you doing, Lexi?" she asked herself while moving the map, searching for a blue dot pointing to her current location. "What if I can help this man?" she said to herself while glancing up again at the buildings, scanning for a street sign. "But what the hell can I do?" She stared down at her phone again. Taking in a long breath, she watched down the street. "See if you're crazy and he's still alive, that's what."

She stepped forward into the road, glancing to her right. "OK. Was it Rue du ..." She froze. Coming out of an alley across the street was the Arab man from the wall. Lexi took a few quick steps back, hiding behind the building.

The man hesitated on the sidewalk in front of a building for a moment. He turned in the opposite direction, away from Lexi, and began walking.

Peering around the corner, she watched him leave. She took in another long, slow breath, waiting until he walked away. "What are you doing in there, buddy?" She glanced down at her phone. The map showed a big red dot, on the opposite side of the square at the end of an alley, the same alley were the man just left.

She crossed the street and sauntered down the block toward the alleyway between two buildings, trying to act as if she was having a nice leisurely afternoon mosey down the street. She strolled up to the opening, doing everything she could not to draw attention to herself on the street. Running up to the alley, like her heart wanted to do, would make her an easy target for the guy if he returned.

If that man did come back, Lexi figured she could continue walking on down the sidewalk as if it was no big deal. Who was she? He didn't know. For all he knew, she could be on her way out for a nice lunch date. So, walking with a smile on her face, head up, and a confident stride was in order.

As she was about to pass the alley, she took another quick glance down the sidewalk in the direction of the man and then turned down the tiny street. She ran down a dark tunnel, for at least fifty feet, her heart racing. It suddenly opened to the sky, with greenery along the walls and a small stone path barely wide enough for a small car. She continued running through what felt like a small garden walk, when abruptly it opened to a large courtyard surrounded on all sides by buildings. The only way in and out was through the passage she just took.

Lexi stopped and eyed the pathway for any sign of the man returning to this location. All was quiet. She took a breath and a moment to straighten her hair and clothes, then continued walking a little farther into the courtyard, which was covered in trees and greenery, almost transporting her into a mini park. Across the courtyard were stairs leading up to two open doors. She checked the map on her phone again, a bright red dot flashed directly in front of her blue dot. She found the building.

Slowly, she walked up the stairs and through the front door. Once inside she waited a few seconds, listening and watching. No one was following her. She was alone in the small foyer of the building. She gazed up the spiral staircase of the semi-dilapidated apartment building, checking out the premises. It wasn't poor or unkempt. It was just old, very old — a few hundred years old at least. But so was almost every building in Paris. Parisians take great pride in antiquity and in having something so old still in use. The building looked like it hadn't been touched for the last hundred years or so, or most probably since World War II.

She began the meticulous walk up the stairs, passing the first landing, not seeing the apartment number, and continued up, very cautiously. She made it to the next landing and stopped in front of an apartment. She pulled out the notepad with the address. She checked. This was it.

The door was slightly ajar.

Confused by the open door, Lexi squeezed through the opening. *Why would he leave the door open? Is that a common French sign of hospitality?*

"Hello? *Bonjour?*" she called out, stopping just inside the threshold of the apartment. "Hello? Monsieur Lapeyre?"

The apartment was very elegant on the inside, not shabby like the building itself, and well furnished. It was the opposite of the dilapidated apartment building entrance and staircase. It looked like a mini version of Versailles. Everything was lined with gold: doorways, molding, mirrors, and even the wallpaper had little gold filigrees. The furniture was antique wood and the fabrics on the chairs and the couches were fine silks.

"I'm sorry to ..." Lexi froze. Sitting on the beautiful settee with his back to her was Monsieur Lapeyre. From behind it was apparent that he was a very large, heavy-set man with only a few gray hairs left on his bald head.

66

"*Bonjour*," Lexi said light-heartedly from across the room, relief in her voice. She casually walked around the settee and side table, over silk rugs to Monsieur Lapeyre. As she made it around the table, she realized there was something wrong. He hadn't moved an inch since she arrived. Who had a visitor without saying hello? Or turning his head?

A pit settled in Lexi's stomach and her hands started to shake a little. Her heart recognized the answer before she saw it.

Monsieur Lapeyre was sitting perfectly still, looking as though he'd been frozen in time, eyes wide open staring ahead at something, drool drizzling slowly out of his lifeless mouth.

She reached out, hands shaking, and she touched his shoulder. "Hello?"

His head fell over. Lexi jumped back with the sudden movement and took a moment to survey the room, paying attention to the little things to see if anything seemed out of place.

The apartment looked immaculate. There was no evidence of ransacking or rummaging for valuable goods. The only thing out of place in this picturesque portrait was Monsieur Lapeyre, dead on the couch. A large amount of saliva was now running out of his mouth, down his neat vest and perfectly tailored shirt.

Then the true implications hit her. This man was dead. She was at the crime scene and obviously now the main suspect. What should she do? Call the police and tell them what happened?

But how could she explain coming up to this apartment? Knowing this man's name and address? She had no connection to him at all, and the French justice system was legendary. It could take months to work this out, or even years.

What if, God forbid, she was accused of causing his death? She had no idea how he died. She knew that this killer ... No. He wasn't just a normal killer, who picked his victims at random, according to his own emotional whimsy. This man was told where to go and whom to kill. That made him an assassin. The assassin from the wall did this. But how? How did he kill this man? And would an autopsy show that? Exonerating her and implicating him? There were too many unpredictable variables.

Another thought kept echoing in her mind over and over again — What about the others? What about all the other people on the wall? How many more would be killed in the months it would take to clear this whole situation up: one hundred, maybe two? The wall seemed to average at least one person per day. She could no longer help Monsieur Lapeyre, but maybe she could help the others.

Lexi was staring at the dead body of Monsieur Lapeyre for what in her mind felt like an eternity, but in actuality it was just a few moments. Slowly she started backtracking, heading out the door. She knew, in many ways, this was the cowardly way out. This poor man deserved better than to be left dead on his beautiful settee. Her eyes teared up a little as she stared at the back of the dead man's head.

"I'm sorry, I promise," she pronounced, not just to herself, but also as if Monsieur Lapeyre could hear, "to make it up for leaving you here dead. I won't let this happen again." Tears started welling up in her eyes. "To *ANYONE*!"

Lexi squeezed out the front door of the apartment, making sure not to touch anything, and turned down the stairs at a run.

Assassins' Wall: Gare de Lyon

CHAPTER 13

Trigger

LEXI'S HOTEL ROOM, PARIS. NIGHT.

That evening, just like the night before, the late news with the same reporter was on, but instead of Louis Calendrier, now it was Monsieur Lapeyre whose death was the lead story. The news reporter was standing on the same landing where Lexi was just a few hours ago. He was speaking in French, of course, but she didn't need a translator this time. She guessed exactly what he was saying and wondered if it was the exact same copy as last night, only the names were different.

This broadcast solidified the feeling in her heart from last night. Three *different* men from the wall were killed. She couldn't deny it anymore. The first man was Georges Martin from the newspaper, the second Louis Calendrier, and now Monsieur Lapeyre. Three people killed in three days. People died in greater numbers all the time, all over the world, but not because of her lack of observation. Maybe if she had acted faster, somehow Monsieur Lapeyre would still be alive?

Tears began to build up in her eyes for a myriad of reasons, so many in fact it was hard to keep track: tears for this man's death, tears for her inability to walk away now, and tears for the blame she laid upon herself for this man's fate. A few more tears were also shed for the three men's lives: Did they have families that loved them? Wives, mothers, and daughters? What about every person who knew and loved them? How were they feeling right now? Did someone else find him dead, like she did?

In her mind, it was one thing to die from natural causes or even an accident, but to be purposefully and maliciously killed for some unknown reason was unacceptable! And it was right under the eyes of every person in Gare de Lyon.

Could she somehow stop this? No. She had no idea who these men were or how the wall worked in order to shut it down. And there were three of them and only one of her. She couldn't overpower them, not like she'd have any clue how to do that, anyway. In her everyday ordinary life, she did everything possible *not* to fight with people. In fact, she had never been in an adult physical altercation with another human being in her entire life, not having any siblings. And the United States of America was geared toward creating a safe, violence-free environment, and most of the time, exceptions being acknowledged, of course, that was what they had. Out of more than 350,000,000 people, fewer than 22,000 were murdered each year. Lexi had a better chance of getting killed in a car accident than getting murdered, and her chance of being murdered by an assassin was even less.

Lexi's Face Time chimed. She picked it up, looking at the caller ID before taking a moment to compose herself, wiping away some tears. She cleared her throat before she answered the call, "Hi, Mom."

"Hi, sweetie, how did the meeting go?" An elegant older woman was staring straight at her.

"It went OK. There are a few issues we have to work out, but this is only our first meeting on the project. It's going to take some time." Lexi turned back to the television; the reporter was showing the inside of Monsieur Lapeyre's beautiful Versailles-clone apartment.

"Well, Rome wasn't built in a day, sweetie, nor was Paris. You having fun?"

Lexi quickly turned away from the news broadcast and back to her mom. "Oh, I like it here," she said, taking in a deep breath to sound slightly more composed. "I'm going to stay a few extra days to go sightseeing and maybe visit the Louvre. And the architecture here is amazing, and so are the sculptures I've seen. Did you know they have a twenty-foot bronze sculpture of a thumb?"

"You feeling OK, sweetheart?" Her mother had a concerned look on her face.

Lexi was just barely keeping it together. She wiped another tear from her eye. "Yeah. Yeah. I'm fine. Long, long day. It's frustrating. How are you doing?"

"Fine." Her mother paused for a moment, "I went to Arlington Cemetery to visit your dad today. I put new flowers on his grave and was telling him all about your meeting and your trip to Europe."

That was it, the knife to her heart. Lexi became even more upset, failing to conceal it well. "Good. Good. I bet he liked that," she said, pretending to be cheerful. It was an old habit, talking about her dad as though he was alive in the present, hearing every word they said. It made her mother feel better, like he was still around, just not physically. For Lexi, it was heartbreaking.

More tears trickled down her face. She turned away from the phone and Monsieur Lapeyre's apartment. It was just too much.

"Look, sweetie, you seem so tired," said her mother, sounding very concerned. "You're probably still jet lagged with the time difference. I just wanted to check in. Say hello. And I love you."

Lexi nodded her head, since her mother could see the gesture. She took a deep breath, not concealing her agony. "Love you, Mom. Text you tomorrow to check in. Bye." She hung up the videocall.

This was one of those phone calls that happened at the exact right time, saying the exact right thing. It was as though the universe was sending out a lifeline, not when she wanted it, but precisely when her heart needed to hear it. This was that lifeline, and it was her trigger.

Every human had their own trigger — an event that touched deep down in their heart. An event that reached through all the everyday banality of life, reminding them what was truly important in life. Lexi's father's death was always her trigger. It reminded her of how precious life was and not to take a single moment for granted. Death and suffering change a person, and her father's death changed her. She missed him so much; her heart was sick.

The first year after his death was the worst. She would randomly break down and cry almost every day, for no reason other than heartache. Slowly over time, there were fewer tears, but the heartache never went away, it just came to visit less often.

It had been a while — six months perhaps — since she felt this deep heartache. The depth of this emotion always caught her off guard, reminding her of the great emptiness left behind from the death of a loved one. Did Monsieur Lapeyre have a daughter who was going through this exact feeling tonight? That broke her heart even more. Knowing a parent that you always depend upon, to always be there, was suddenly gone? No good-byes? No last words, just gone from existence. And you're left dealing with the hollowness, having no idea how to cope with a broken heart.

She couldn't let another person from the wall die, not if she could help. But how? How could she help? She glanced at the television and Monsieur Lapeyre. What if Monsieur Lapeyre was her father? And someone else realized what was going on with the wall. Would she want them to somehow warn him? Give him a "heads up, seven up"?

The answer was easy. Of course, she would. Perhaps she could alert the people from the wall? Tell them what's going to happen, give them the choice: live or die — well, maybe with a little less morbid vernacular. And if they chose not to listen, then that was their choice. She knew she couldn't save these people, like in some comic book; she was no superhero. But she could warn them. Maybe this would alleviate the guilt of the three deaths on her conscience.

She would have given anything for her father to have had this choice: live or die. He would have chosen to live. So, she guessed, would Monsieur Lapeyre, Louis Calendrier, and Georges Martin, too.

Lexi turned back to the television. Monsieur Lapeyre was still on the screen. "I have to warn them," she said to the image, hoping he would approve. "It's penance for walking out on you."

CHAPTER 14

Waiting

GARE DE LYON, PARIS. EARLY MORNING.

Saturday

The next morning, visibly exhausted, Lexi was back in
Gare de Lyon. She had a restless night with hardly any sleep and
plenty of crying. It had been a long time since she had a night like
that. It reminded her of how deep grief could be: even if years
passed, which they had for her, grief could still feel as fresh as
the day of the death itself.

Everyone always said that in time things get better and
the feeling goes away. In reality, she doubted grief ever truly
went away. Instead of suffering every day from a broken heart,
she found the hard days came fewer and farther between, but the
grief remained. It would probably be there 'til the day she died,
then hopefully she would see her father again. That's how she'd
know she was dead. Her dad would be the one to greet her on the
other side. She imagined him, eyes full of love, huge smile on his
face, standing there waiting, excited to resume the discussion
they were in the middle of. The topic was life after death, oddly
enough. That morning he had asked her what she thought

happened after people die. Was there an afterlife or anything? She paused for a moment and asked for some time to really think it over. It was a hard question to answer honestly. She needed to search her soul for the answer. He died that afternoon. She wondered if he knew, subconsciously. Probably.

Standing in the back of the train station, near her usual entrance, Lexi had her head down, looking only at the floor. She didn't have the strength yet to lift her face up and see the wall. She barely had the strength that morning to get dressed and walk into the station, hence her very casual attire of jeans, button-up shirt, and jacket.

The sounds of the station filled her ears. It was a busy morning in Gare de Lyon: people were coming and going all around her, while she was perfectly still. Slowly, she took in a deep breath, closed her eyes, and lifted her head, eyes still closed. She waited a moment, taking in another deep breath. Her eyes were puffy, with deep black circles underneath. It was obvious the damage done by a night without sleep and filled with crying. She waited a few more seconds, building up courage, and opened her eyes.

The wall was empty.

Lexi exhaled. It was sweet relief, if only for a moment, to have the wall empty. Casually, she walked over to the row of benches, halfway between the exit and the wall, to sit down. It was safer to sit among the crowd of passengers. She didn't want to get closer to those men, who were stationed at their regular position at the bottom of the wall.

After sitting, Lexi took a moment to look around the train station. She saw two policemen walking through the main terminal toward the men and the wall. She held her breath for a moment as they walked by, waiting to see if they were alerted to the men at the bottom of the wall. But the policemen only gave them a passing glance, then kept walking toward the exit.

Lexi had considered going to the French police last night. Or should she run up to the policemen right now? But her French was abysmal. And most importantly, she didn't want to draw attention to herself in front of those men. If they were capable of killing three men, who's to say they wouldn't come after her?

Right now, her best advantage was going incognito. She needed more time and information, so she would not be the one implicated in the deaths. She wanted some hard proof that the killings were being done by an assassin, not her. She was not going to jail while they continued on this murdering rampage. No way. Not on her watch. She was going to figure this out so their asses could go to jail. Forever.

To give the illusion of belonging in the station and being occupied, Lexi pulled out her old-school e-book reader and placed it on her lap. She took out her glasses and placed them in the middle of her shirt, securing them to her bra, and then put the pen and notepad next to her e-reader. Now she was ready.

She glanced up at the wall. It was still empty. She realized for the first time that it could take a little while for the next face to appear. There seemed to be no rhyme or reason when the face appeared. She could be here for hours waiting like those men. It didn't matter either way. She had no intention of visiting any tourist sights now. Not while all of this was going on. So, she had time to kill. Ha! That was all the killing she would ever do, and may she slaughter it!

Looking around the station again at all the people going about their daily lives, bothered by nothing but their own worries, Lexi was suddenly envious of them. She envied their lives, envied their ignorance at what was going on right underneath their noses, thinking their own problems were the end of the world, caught up in their bubble. She missed that bubble. She never even realized it existed. But her bubble popped at the sight of Monsieur Lapeyre's dead body.

How nice it would be to get caught up in the crowd of people having somewhere to go, somewhere out of here. She guessed there was a reason for the old adage "Ignorance is bliss." Truthfully, she had always abhorred ignorant people, and tried her best to stay away from them. Now the ignorant were the preferred company. But who was she kidding? She'd take knowledge any day over ignorance. Especially knowledge she could act on, using it to help other people.

A steady flow of people walked by her as another train emptied, making the same river of bodies she was caught up in only a few days earlier. She wondered how many of these people, if they knew what she knew, would even care. Would they take the time to help the people on the wall? She suspected it would hardly be one in a thousand that would — and she was that one in a thousand. Sometimes it was hard to be in the right place at the right time.

Assassins' Wall: Gare de Lyon

CHAPTER 15

Woman

GARE DE LYON, PARIS. MID-MORNING.

Over the next few hours of waiting, Lexi became more and more grateful that she brought her e-reader. It gave her the perfect cover as a passenger waiting for a train, and it filled her desire for the familiar. *The Count of Monte Cristo* proved to be a worthy companion. It was exactly what she was looking for, being one of her favorite books. It always gave her great comfort in a strange place to read a beloved story. It made her feel at home.

Every few sentences Lexi picked up her head to check on the wall, then gazed back down at the *Count*. She was really getting good at the rote action of looking up, then reading, then eyeing the wall. The Count somehow made the wall feel less menacing, foreboding, and frightening, and he gave her strength. She wasn't sure why. Maybe it had to do with the novel's theme of a person in a strange place, on a mission that only he knew about. Granted, the Count's rationale was revenge, while hers was the opposite. Yet the Count was more relatable now than at any other time in her life. But wasn't that a sign of great literature? No matter the time of life, be it youth, adulthood, or old age, there was always a new revelation in the story from the different perspective, making it fresh and timeless.

Looking up for what must have been the millionth time, Lexi stopped in her rote motion. Another picture was up on the wall. What took her breath away this time, wasn't the depth of the picture itself, which was very familiar to her by now, but the fact that it was a *WOMAN*! It never occurred to her that it would be a woman. She was expecting another older man, like Monsieur Lapeyre.

The woman had dark brown hair and looked a bit older than Lexi, but it was difficult to tell her exact age because of the pastel hues of the hologram: She was maybe in her late fifties. The hologram didn't define wrinkles or age lines too well. It probably had to do with the three-dimensionality of the picture. It lost the finer details needed to determine such things. But none of that matters in the big picture, as long as she found the right woman.

Frantically, Lexi put on her glasses and wrote the name and address in the notepad. She read over what she just wrote. The address wasn't in Paris. It was in a place called Fontainebleau. "Lord only knows where that is," she sighed to herself.

She quickly gathered her belongings, put the Count away, and swiftly walked toward the back exit. As she was about to enter the hallway, she turned around to check on the men. All three were still loitering around the bottom of the wall. The same guy glanced up to the picture on the glass.

"You take your sweet-ass time, buddy," she said silently, and started picking up her pace down the hallway. She typed the address into her phone map to get a better idea of where she was headed. She was going to get there first and warn this woman.

Assassins' Wall: Gare de Lyon

PART 2

The human brain had a natural ability,

inherent in its mechanism, to work on many

levels, in a process of constant promptings, in a

type of self-preservation.

If only humans understood.

Most ignore it.

Assassins' Wall: Gare de Lyon

CHAPTER 16

Number One

Marise Louise André

COTTAGE, FOUNTAINEBLEAU, FRANCE. MID-MORNING.

Marise André didn't sleep well last night. She never did after she had one of her "heart feeling" dreams. They always felt so real, so deep, and so heavy that it was hard to get back to sleep. And unfortunately, last night she didn't.

The worst part about these dreams was they always stick with her. Sometimes the heavy feeling would pass in a day or two, sometimes not for a week. On one occasion she had a dream that felt so real, the heart feeling lasted for almost three weeks. What a nightmare that was, both literally and figuratively!

It was hard to place the exact time frame when these dreams really started to take shape for her — probably when she hit puberty. She remembered being a kid and telling her three older sisters all about her dreams and the fantastic things they entailed. But in the André household, she was far from exceptional. It seemed every person, excluding her dad and third sister, Claudine, had the same ability. Marise's mother would often walk into the room knowing full well what the day's events were going to be, and when a child would run in hurt after falling off a bike, she would just nod her head in silent acknowledgement, having the bandages ready on the kitchen counter.

Marise's second-oldest sister, Annette, on the other hand, didn't have the same level of intensity as everyone else, but she would often get useful tidbits of information. Like who was going to win the next election or if another family member was secretly dating a new person. This was how they found out about the girlfriends of their only brother, Olivier. Marise's mom used to laugh and say, "Good luck keeping a secret in this family," and she was right. Every major life event was seen coming, not by only one family member but usually by two members of the André household.

As with all things in life, these dreams always came with a price. Marise knew before anyone else that her grandmother was going to die. She finally fessed up to her mother at the funeral, and not surprisingly, her mother admitted to dreaming about the passing as well. She didn't want to upset everyone in the family. Sometimes it was hard to share bad news.

At family gatherings on Sundays everyone would sit in a circle and ask if anyone had any new dreams they weren't sharing, which often brought on blank stares and slight giggles from the grandchildren. It got to a point where Marise's aunt

Bernadette would call the house and, rather than say hello, would ask, "Are there any new dreams to report?"

So last night's dream was hardly anything new for Marise Lousie. But this "heart feeling" was more intense than anything she had ever had before. She silently prayed the feeling from last night's dream wouldn't last long, but her prayers for such things often went unanswered.

Once, years ago, after another particularly intense dream, Marise checked into the hospital to have her heart monitored because of the heaviness. But her heart was perfectly normal, and she already knew it. Her trip to the hospital was what the dream was about. And she knew as soon as the dream "came to fulfillment," the heavy feeling in her chest would dissipate. It was a cruel irony. She had to go to a cardiologist and have him perform an EKG, among other tests, already knowing full well that the heavy "heart feeling" would dissipate *AFTER* she was examined by the doctor and completed the dream.

And these dreams weren't just random tidbits of information for her to have at her leisure. She realized a very long time ago there was always a reason she had them. The dream where she checked herself into the hospital was how she met her husband, well, now ex-husband, who was the cardiologist.

Her dreams were funny that way. They never told her what was important. Perhaps that was up to her. The dream never revealed that her cardiologist was going to ask her on a date on the check-up visit and within a year they would be married. The dream only showed her in the hospital having her heart examined.

And after her dreams "came to fulfillment" was she capable of having some perspective, asking why she had the dream in the first place. There were hundreds of other dreams where she understood the real reason she had the dream only after the events were completed; time brought the perspective.

Marise's dream last night was a doozy, and her heart felt like a lead brick — no, a cement block. She could feel every beat. If only her ex-husband could be here now with a stethoscope. The heaviness of this "heart feeling" made the hospital episode look like an easy walk in the park. She knew by this point in her life the best thing to do was just give into the dream and patiently wait until it "came to fulfillment."

Only once did she not listen to a dream, and the results were disastrous. She was in a terrible car accident and broke her leg and wrist. It could have been much worse; it should have been much worse. At the last second, not being able to deny the dream any longer, seeing the truck from the dream heading toward her, she turned the wheel and hit a fence. Had she not turned, the dream showed her paralysis from the collision. It was hard to deny a dream as it came rolling straight in your face.

After that accident, she promised never to take a dream lightly again. It was a promise she also made to her mother before she died. She had been in the hospital sick at the time of Marise's accident, and not surprisingly, her mother had the same dream as Marise. But the real reason Marise chose to ignore the dream was because it showed her mother passing away after the accident. It was easier to ignore both warnings and hope her mother would survive. She and her mother ended up in the same hospital and, with a little maneuvering, in the same room. Marise's mother told her late one night, while they were lying side by side, "Don't ever turn away from what God gave you, Marise. I have always lived my life with an open heart, prepared for what the good Lord had for me to do. It would be a shame for you to turn away from him because you didn't like what he had to say." Marise recovered; her mother didn't.

This morning Marise called into work to take the day off; she had thirty-five days left of vacation time for the year. Ah, the glory of the French employment restrictions. She put her purse by the front door and waited.

Assassins' Wall: Gare de Lyon

A

For every two separate points there is exactly one *line* that connects them.

Assassins' Wall: Gare de Lyon

CHAPTER 17

Warning

STREET, FOUNTAINEBLEAU, FRANCE. MID-MORNING.

In front of a beautiful little cottage outside of Paris, Lexi jumped out of a taxi and ran up the sidewalk to the front door. It was hard to believe she was just outside of Paris, but cities sometimes were that way. Walk a block and the city transformed. New York was the same — go an hour outside the city and you would think you were in rural America. It seemed Paris was like that, too.

At the front door, Lexi looked up and down the street at the small houses on the tree-lined avenue. It was a pristine neighborhood. No one was milling about or causing any problems. The whole street looked very well-tended, and that was a good sign the owners took pride in their homes. She turned back to the small brown and white cottage in front of her, looking at the numbers, making sure they matched what she saw on the glass wall.

The cottage and its surroundings were bucolic. It backed up to an enchanting little wooded area that was like something out of a fairy book. The perfect landscape made her think of Cinderella and Sleeping Beauty. Didn't those stories originate in

France? There probably was a reason. Only there was no fire-breathing dragon or evil stepmother here ... she hoped.

Lexi knocked on the front door and waited, looking both ways down the street, which was empty. The peaceful silence was deafening. The man from the wall could be here at any moment.

She knocked again, even more loudly. "Come on, be home," she moaned desperately. What if she got the address wrong? What if this wasn't the right woman? What if she wasn't home? Worst of all: What if this man saw me helping this woman? Her cover would be blown, and she wouldn't be able to help anyone else on the wall.

Lexi knocked again even more frantically, "COME ON!" she hollered, hurting her knuckles.

The door opened. A woman, in fifties with brown hair, stood in front of her. She was dressed in elegant pants and a top, with a clean sharp look that seems to be achieved only by French women. And most importantly, she had kind brown eyes.

Lexi took a deep, hard, long look into her eyes, and it changed everything. This woman looked just like Lexi ... this could be her in fifteen years.

"MARISE? Marise Louise André?" asked Lexi a little desperately.

"*Oui*," Marise answered with a slight smile in her eyes.

A wave of relief brushed over Lexi. She was the right woman. *"Parlez-vous anglais?"* She started sounding more and more frenetic.

"Oui."

"Oh, thank God! I was so worried you wouldn't speak English and I wasn't exactly sure what to do if you didn't, ..."

"Oui. I do. And what exactly do you have to do?" responded Marise matter-of-factly.

This paused Lexi for a moment. What an odd way to ask a question. In fact, Marise said it more as a statement than a question. What *did* Lexi have to do? Warn Marise? No. A warning wasn't enough. In theory a warning was all she intended to give; she didn't plan on getting involved. Tell Marise about these men and get the hell out of there, fast. If Marise wanted to stay at this address that was her choice, but now seeing those kind eyes ... they made Marise a living, breathing human being. And she looked just like Lexi. What if this was her? Would she want just a warning? No. That was not good enough. She couldn't walk away now and take the chance that this woman might die. If Marise did, she couldn't live with that. Her heart twinged again, saying, "No." It won't allow that.

Lexi imagined watching television that night with Marise's face all over the news, the broadcaster announcing she died. And Lexi stood in front of her only a few hours earlier, able to help. No... So, *Plan A* was out and on to *Plan B*. What was Plan

B? She had no idea, but the warning in Plan A was no longer enough.

"We have to leave right now!" Lexi grabbed Marise's arm and began pulling her out of the house. Marise reached inside the door and snatched her purse. She stopped to lock the front door. Lexi squealed, "No time for that NOW!" She checked up and down the street for signs of the man.

Holding tight onto Marise's arm, Lexi began to run, not in the direction of the street, but around the side of the cottage toward the wooded area in the back. Once they reach the side of the cottage, she picked up the pace, taking Marise's hand, pulling even harder. "Hurry... I don't know how fast he gets here. In fact, I don't know *HOW* he gets here..."

Marise quickened her pace right alongside Lexi.

Lexi guided Marise deep into the woods behind the cottage. She was almost talking to herself. "Hell, for all I know he could just appear from a plane, or a helicopter or something ... it's weird. Somehow, he gets way ahead of me ..."

Lexi turned to see if the man was coming down the street. She dragged Marise a little farther into the woods. The cottage was still visible. "Here., I hope this is far enough in." She stopped their trek and looked back at the cottage. They were about sixty feet away.

Marise stood looking, not at her house or the road, but at Lexi.

Lexi turned to Marise. "You're being very nice about it all. I always thought most French people never spoke English, if they don't have to, and hated Americans."

"And I always thought Americans were rude, pushy, and full of their own superiority," said Marise kindly.

Lexi smiled a little. "It seems you got me there, at least the rude, pushy part. Not feeling very superior at the moment."

Turning back to the cottage, Lexi felt her stomach drop. "He's here!" Marise turned to look.

Walking up to the front door was the lone Arab man from the train station.

"Did you see how he got here?" questioned Lexi anxiously.

"No. I was looking at you," replied Marise, now with a worried look on her face.

The man walked straight up the sidewalk to the front door, opened it, and then walked inside the cottage.

"Damn, I should have let you lock the door." Lexi began slowly stepping backward, like she did in Monsieur Lapeyre's house, deeper into the woods. She spoke in a hushed tone. "Maybe we should get a little farther back. I've never seen what happens when someone wasn't home."

Following her lead, Marise slowly creeped backward, moving into the forest. They were careful not to disturb the brush and leaves around them; the soft forest floor absorbed their sounds. "What happens when someone is home?" asked Marise, whispering.

The sound of breaking glass came from the cottage. Both women turned to look. Through the side windows the shape of the man was ransacking the house, moving furniture around, and breaking what sounded like china.

As Lexi and Marise continued to backtrack slowly into the woods, Lexi becomes panicked. "I'm sorry... I'm kind of new at this, and honestly, all I want to do right now is just throw up."

The man kicked down the back door, leaving the cottage to look around the backyard.

Lexi and Marise dropped to the ground, making as little noise as possible. Lexi quietly leaned over to Marise. "We need to get out of here."

"*Oui*. Follow me." On both hands and knees, keeping as low to the ground as humanly possible, Marise lead Lexi through the woods.

CHAPTER 18

Standing and Staring

STREET, PARIS. LATE MORNING.

This was not the plan. This was *NOT* the plan, Lexi repeated over and over in her head. And what did she do now? She turned to her right to stare at Marise, who was still beside her. They made it back to the heart of Paris and stood in the roundabout near her hotel. She had the taxi drop her and Marise off in a busy public place, figuring it would be the safest spot for them to part ways.

Lexi kept waiting for Marise to bolt, but she didn't. They hadn't spoken for the last half-hour, and she wasn't sure what to say to Marise. Sorry those guys destroyed your house. Or how about, you know you could be dead right now? No, she would sound like a lunatic. Sometimes it was best to start at the beginning.

"I'm Alexandra Peters, by the way. But my friends call me Lexi."

"Hello, Lexi. I'm Marise. But you already knew that."

"Marise Louise André," Lexi smiled, "You look just like your picture." Marise was surprised at the word "picture."

Lexi kept waiting for Marise to turn down the street and walk away, but they both stood in silence, waiting for the other person to move first. It reminded Lexi of her favorite childhood story, *The Zax*. The two Zax stared at each other, waiting for the other one to move first, but neither did. Years passed, neither Zax budged. And the world moved on without the Zax. What if the wall moved on without her? She couldn't stand around here forever, staring at Marise, waiting for her to leave. She needed to see if Marise was still up on the wall, or if it had moved on.

So it was, the south going Zax moved first. "I know you'll probably want to leave soon," Lexi said. "I didn't intend for you to stay with me or in fact be with me at all, but now that you are here, I want to make sure of something before you go. Would you mind if I go check on something first?"

"Where, Lexi?"

"The place with your name, but first I must stop by my hotel to change, if that's all right with you. You can wait downstairs in the lobby or in a café around here." Lexi pointed to the shops in the roundabout. "Whatever makes you feel more comfortable, just please, don't leave Paris and go back home until I check."

"*Oui*, Lexi. I'll go with you," Marise said calmly, almost lovingly.

They started walking toward Lexi's hotel. Marise was by her side.

This whole turn of events surprised Lexi. It made no sense. Why would Marise stay with her? For all Marise knew, Lexi was a crazy killer who intended to assassinate her ... no, wait ... that's exactly what that man was doing. A normal person would run away, and never go off with a complete stranger. Why was Marise following her?

Lexi stared at Marise. But she did just watch a random man tear up her house, and Lexi warned her about that. Maybe that garnered some trust. But as Lexi's dad always said, "Never look a gift horse in the mouth, Lexi bear." Maybe Marise was thankful she helped her out. Or more probably, and this was highly likely, Marise was just as crazy as the men under the wall. It was a toss-up.

Assassins' Wall: Gare de Lyon

CHAPTER 19

Changing

LEXI'S HOTEL ROOM, PARIS. LATE MORNING.

Bursting into her hotel room, Lexi walked straight over to her suitcase, took out a fresh shirt and jeans, and began to change clothes. Marise followed her into the room.

"Do you want to stay here for a bit or go downstairs and wait in the lobby?" asked Lexi.

Marise walked over to the bed and sat down. "What are you doing, Lexi?"

"I figured to be safe I should wear something different, just in case one of those men recognized me." Lexi pulled her shirt over her head. "You can stay here and relax until I get back. It won't take me long."

"Where are you going?"

"Back."

"To my house?"

"No, no back to the wall to see if your name is still on it."

"The wall?"

Lexi paused and took in a breath. "There is a glass wall in Gare de Lyon that had your picture, name, and address on it. That Arab man reads the name and goes to the address on the wall."

"And what happens if someone is at home?"

Lexi stared at Marise. "Well ... they die. It sounds crazy, doesn't it?"

"*Oui*, a little. And my name?"

"Marise, I have to be honest with you." Lexi paused for a moment. "I literally just got to Paris a few days ago, and since then I've seen four faces on this glass wall."

"And the three other people?"

"They're dead." Lexi continued dressing. "And the fourth one is sitting here with me."

Marise got it. There were only two people in the room, not five. "That man would have killed me."

"I wasn't willing to find out. My plan was just to warn you, but I panicked and kind of kidnapped you instead. I'm sorry." Lexi finished dressing and looked around at her stuff. "OK. I'm going. You staying in here?"

Marise stood up. "No, I'm coming with you. I want to see this wall."

Lexi hesitated for a moment. "Fine. But change first." She handed Marise one of her button-up shirts. "It may not matter and I'm not Agatha Christie, but it doesn't hurt to cover you up just to be safe." She reached into her suitcase and pulled out a baseball cap, handing it to Marise. "In case your picture is still up, the hat will hide your face a bit."

Marise put on the Mets baseball cap with a smile in her eyes.

Assassins' Wall: Gare de Lyon

A   M

A ∪ M

A *union* is the combining of members belonging to two different sets.

Assassins' Wall: Gare de Lyon

CHAPTER 20

A Twofer

GARE DE LYON, PARIS. NOON.

There were many different ways to get into Gare de Lyon. At last count, there were at least five exits out of the main terminal, thirteen sets of escalators, and thirteen sets of stairs leading up to the main floor from the metro station below. Lexi figured she and Marise had as many options as they needed to make their way toward the wall without ever taking the same route twice; it would just take a little legwork. The last few times she came in using the same entrance near the wall. This time was different. She was bringing along Marise, and a new approach was in order in case these men were keeping an eye out.

Using the doorway on the opposite side of the station, Lexi and Marise walked into the main terminal. Marise paused to look around the station. "Gare de Lyon. I always loved this train station: the green color, the architecture, the open space, and the natural light. It was built in 1900." She observed the main floor of the station. "Where is the wall?" Nothing seemed out of place on this side of the main terminal.

Lexi motioned her head. "It's over there on the other side of the departure board. It's hard to see from far away because it's glass. You have to get close to see the steel frame."

"*Verre?*" said Marise confused. "That is not what I was expecting."

Lexi started walking toward the opposite side of the station. Marise was a few steps behind her, using Lexi as cover.

Hundreds of people were walking around Gare de Lyon. It was much busier now than it was earlier this morning. It made it that much harder to pick Marise out of the crowd if they were looking.

Stopping right next to the small pastry and sandwich shop that made its happy home underneath the departure board, Lexi looked over to the glass wall. The second pane of glass was empty. But only one man was standing there just as he was before, staring out toward incoming trains.

Marise caught up to Lexi, standing right behind; her head was right above Lexi's shoulder, and the bill of the baseball cap was next to Lexi's face. Lexi took a quick glance over her shoulder at Marise and then turned back to the wall. "You're not up there anymore, and the second guy is missing as well. There are three men in total."

Marise's eyes started at the top of the glass wall and slowly investigated it all the way down to the bottom. They stopped on the lone figure standing there at the base. "Who are these men?"

"I have no idea. Unfortunately, it took me a couple of days to realize they were behind the killings. I'm ..." Lexi stopped mid-sentence. The second man from before, not the one from Marise's house, walked up to the wall and started talking with the other man at the bottom; the two of them formed a huddle.

"I wonder where he went or who he killed?" she said half-heartedly. "I can't even think about that right now," she added, sounding a little defeated.

"Have you ever seen what happens when they return to the wall?" asked Marise.

"No. I'm not even sure that your face won't pop up again since they didn't find you. I have *NO* idea how this works."

"You mean them or it?" Marise nodded toward the wall.

"Both." Lexi turned around to face Marise, creating her own little huddle. "Marise, I'm worried you may go back up on the wall again. I need to stay here and see what happens next."

"How long can that take?" inquired Marise.

"Could be five minutes or up to the two hours I waited this morning for you to pop up. If you want, you can leave the station and wait somewhere else. You can give me your cell number and I will call you if you come up again." Lexi pulled her phone out of her bag. "Just don't go home yet, not until it's all clear." She looked down at her phone, pressing the screen to get into her contact information.

"No," said Marise tersely.

Lexi looked up. "No, you don't want to give me your number?"

"No. I am staying with you," declared Marise matter-of-factly. She peeked around Lexi toward the wall. "I think we should sit in the Express café and wait. I don't want to get any closer to them," she said, eyeing the men.

"OK," agreed Lexi, a little shocked.

At about where they were standing, next to the destination board, was a small Express café that was sectioned off from the rest of the main floor. It had a bunch of tables and chairs for people to sit and eat while waiting for a train.

They passed two perfectly placed trees at the entrance of L'Express Bleu Café. Lexi and Marise walked in and sat down at a table on the edge of the café. Lexi sat facing the wall, while Marise sat with her back to it. Also, conveniently, there was a little green shrub blocking Marise from most of the station.

Once seated, Lexi took another look up at the glass wall. "God, I hope another person wasn't up on the wall while I was out getting you. I'll feel guilty about that."

"Deal with what is in front of you now, right now, Lexi. Not what you have no control over in the past," Marise advised sternly, like a mother to a child.

Lexi looked at the wall again and the second man who just returned to the wall. "I bet he did. Another person must have been up on the wall while I was gone." She faced Marise. "It was probably just pure luck that you went up on the wall while I was here."

Marise stared at Lexi for a moment. "*Merci*, Lexi." She said it with all her heart and truly meant it.

"I shouldn't be thanked." Lexi took a quick glance back at the wall. "I feel that if I were a more intelligent person, I would have put the damn pieces together sooner and maybe they would all still be alive."

"What is your profession, Lexi?"

The question again surprised Lexi: The day, it seemed, is full of surprises. She had always heard how Europeans were keen on *not* defining people by their job, but rather by using books, philosophy, or some other form of existential intellectual comparison. It was always the Americans whose first question is about your job.

"I'm a materials engineer for a government subcontractor called E.S.C.O.T."

"What does that stand for?"

"Exploration of Science and Communications of Tomorrow. I think the C.E.O. who started the corporation was a bit of a Disney junkie who went to EPCOT one too many times." She smiled.

"Well, you obviously aren't too intelligent," teased Marise, smiling back at her.

"What about you, Marise?"

"I'm a physicist at Université Paris Diderot — Paris 7."

"Wow! Obviously, you're the dummy here." Lexi howled and quickly glanced to her left. She suddenly jumped. "No!"

"What, Lexi?"

"Another person just popped up on the wall." Lexi began quickly scrabbling through her bag. "And it's not you."

Marise casually, so as not to draw attention to herself, turned around and looked at the wall. At first, she stared intensely at it, then slowly she becomes more and more confused. "Where is the picture, Lexi?"

Lexi covertly points to the wall's second pane. "On the second pane of glass, on the right-hand side of the wall." She frantically dug through her bag, pulling out the notepad and glasses. "Damn it, I wasn't ready yet."

Marise casually turned around to look again and stares at the glass wall. "I don't see any picture, Lexi."

This stopped Lexi. She snapped her head up. "What? Tell me what you see!"

"A glass wall with steel support beams. No picture on the second square. No picture, nothing at all. The glass looks the same as it did a minute ago. Perfectly clear and empty."

Lexi stared directly at the hologram. "Right there, in the middle of the glass, I see a picture." She was a little forceful with her words. "To the right of the picture is a name and below that is an address." She saw the giant holographic face as clear as day, staring out into Gare de Lyon.

Marise surveyed the wall again. The glass appeared empty, perfectly transparent, as glass should be. "Really? How can you see that?"

Lexi paused for a second to ponder what Marise just said. "I don't know. In fact, you're the first person I've spoken to about it. No one else has looked up at the pictures but me." She nodded slightly toward the men, "and them."

As she started to get up, Lexi put on her glasses. "I have to get a little closer to read the name and address clearly. Stay here for a sec." She picked up the pen and notepad and walked out of the café toward the wall.

Marise watched Lexi from the table, turning her chair just a bit to get a better view of the wall. Was it crazy to believe this stranger who could see pictures on a glass wall that no one else could see? That was a hard question to answer. Lexi did manage to get her address and name correct. She couldn't look up her address on the internet. Marise was renting that house from a friend, and it would be in the owner's name, not hers. And the Université website only gives a faculty email and the phone number only rings in her office. But she made a promise to both her mother and herself; she would stay with this until the "heart feeling" from the dream dissipated. And her heart was still heavy; it had its own gravitational pull.

Marise sighed, not out of exasperation at the situation, but as a method to try and relieve the heavy weight of her heart. It was going to be a long while before all of this was over.

As Lexi approached the wall, she gazed up. It was definitely a man, and not Marise. Thank God. She was both grateful and filled with dread: grateful that Marise was no longer in the crosshairs and full of dread because the cycle was about to begin all over again with someone new.

On the wall the long name caught Lexi's attention first. She glanced up at the picture. The man looked younger than the previous men, and if the pastel palette of the hologram wasn't playing tricks on her eyes, he had blond hair. Bright blond. It looked canary yellow in the hologram, next to the pinks, blues, greens, and oranges. She quickly wrote down the name and address, which were only visible and readable once she was within twenty feet of the wall.

As soon as she finished writing, she turned around to walk back to the table and Marise. There was no need to get any closer to those men.

Walking through the main entrance, directly in front of her, was the man from Marise's house. He was bolting toward the wall and directly toward Lexi. Despite herself, she froze dead in the middle of the station, staring at the man.

Marise, who was watching Lexi, saw her standing still staring at something straight ahead. She turned to see the man from her house walking across the train station, past the benches, right toward Lexi. Marise stood up about to shout, when Lexi finally caught herself and started moving, pretending to preoccupy herself with writing something in her notepad.

The man walked past Lexi, passing within a foot of her, never looking at her, intent only on the wall and his companions.

Quickly hustling back to the table, Lexi saw that Marise was already standing up. "We have to go now." She stopped right in front of Marise. "He leaves right away. We have to get there before he does."

The man joined the other two on the opposite side of the wall.

Marise turned her back to the wall and the men, looking directly at Lexi. "Why didn't you move, Lexi?"

As Lexi watched the men huddled together, she seemed removed, as though she had blinders on. "My mind," she said, half listening to Marise but mostly concentrating on the men. Her mind was racing with questions: Did he give up on Marise? How long did he wait? Was there a time allotment they were given to wait for each person on the wall? Or was it a one-time-only thing? Did they have to come back to the wall? What were they saying to one another right now? Was he telling the other two that he didn't find Marise? Had this ever happened before? If not, what did they do next? Go back to Marise's house? Or do they focus on the man currently on the wall?

Lexi was lost in thought, and she couldn't stop watching the men. It was, present location excluded, like watching a train wreck in a train station. She needed to witness the reaction of the other men when they found out the man didn't kill Marise. She had to know, and it couldn't be good. Their reaction could tell them a lot.

"Marise," uttered Lexi, still staring only at the men huddled together at the bottom of the wall, "my mind was too busy asking questions to tell my feet to move. I had to catch myself from asking him my questions directly."

All three of the men, for the first time, turned and stared up at the picture of the man currently on the second pane of glass. The gesture was in perfect unison and eerie in appearance.

"Oh, that can't be good," guessed Lexi as they huddled in together again. Then suddenly, instead of the one lone man who ransacked Marise's house, *TWO* of the men left the bottom of the wall together. So that was what they were discussing. Sending along more than just the one man.

The two men quickly stared up at the picture one last time and left the same man alone at the bottom of the wall.

"Oh, my God, Marise!"

"What, Lexi? I don't want to turn around or they may see my face," Marise responded with a little panic in her voice.

"They are sending two men!"

Marise couldn't help herself. Slowly, pretending to pick up her bag, she turned around and watched the man from her house, along with the second man, walk across the station toward the exit. "Is this the first time they have sent two?"

"Yes. Well, at least for the two times I saw, they sent only one person."

"I think it is because of me," declared Marise.

"I agree. They must have never missed one before. We'll have to hurry, then. I want to make it a twofer ..." Lexi began walking out of the café with Marise by her side. She handed the notepad to Marise. "Do you know where this is?" Lexi pulled out her phone and began typing the address into the map.

"*Oui*. It's a hotel."

"A hotel? That's new," said Lexi, a little surprised.

"It's very close to here." Marise handed the notepad back to Lexi.

"Really? Then we'll have to hustle to beat them there." Lexi picked up the pace once they were out of the café, running toward the exit on the opposite side of the station. Marise was beside her. "Can you lead the way, Marise?"

"*Oui*."

When they both reached the main exit, they broke out into a full sprint.

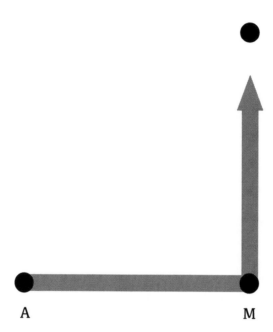

A *right angle* is an angle measuring 90° and in a circular rotation it makes a ¼ turn.

CHAPTER 21

Number Two

John Michael Edward Stanton Barry

JOHN'S HOTEL ROOM. PARIS. NOON.

John Michael Edward Stanton Barry was doing what every tourist would do on a weekend trip to Paris: unpacking his bag in his hotel room. He was quietly singing to himself an old Beatles tune, but he changed the words slightly. Instead of octopus's garden, he sang, "I'd like to be under the sea, in a jellyfish's garden ..."

But why he came to be in Paris was more unusual. A few days earlier, he was walking down the street minding his own business when something happened that hadn't happened in a very long time — years, in fact. It had been so long he almost forgot this could happen. He had a flash. No, not a flash of the body like some middle-aged perimenopausal women, but a flash of the mind. An image took over his sight for the briefest of moments in the position of the third eye.

It used to happen to him all the time when he was a child. He would have a flash of an uncle who was about to walk through the door, or he would get a flash of the kid down the street who wanted to go outside and play. He knew at age six there was something to it because during the Christmas holiday, whenever he saw a Santa Claus, the image of his dad would flash into his mind. It wasn't until he was almost nine, and his parents sat him down to talk about where "Father Christmas" really came from, that he put all the pieces together. The flashes would tell him what was about to happen, or important information he needed to know. Not that the real identity of Father Christmas was paramount in his mind.

The most intriguing fact about these flashes was that he had no control over them. He had no idea why he saw the images he saw or when he would see them. It seemed to happen randomly, and as a child he never questioned why.

During his youth, the flashes started becoming a usual occurrence. He could tell if his brother was about to hit him for stealing something or if he was going to get in trouble with his parents for lying about schoolwork. And by the age of twelve or so, John took all these flashes for granted. He began ignoring them and saw them as a burden. Why did he care if his grandparents were surprising the family by coming over for dinner? Why did he care if his brother kept secret naughty magazines under his bed? And the burden of these flashes got heavier and heavier until John wished he wouldn't see them anymore. What's a twelve-year-old kid going to do about it?

Ignore it all, naturally. But there was always an opportunity cost, and he paid it heavily.

A few months later, at about the age of thirteen, John got a flash one afternoon while walking home from school. It warned him that the neighborhood bullies, who wanted to beat him up, were hiding in an alley, ready to come after him. Ignoring the flash and taking it for granted that he could outrun anyone, he didn't change his course, go back to school, or go get his brother. Instead, he went forward as if nothing had been shown, and of course the neighborhood bullies were waiting for him in the precise spot he saw in his flash.

They promptly ran after him and beat him severely with sticks. He was in the hospital for weeks with broken bones, a broken nose, a fractured skull, and a concussion. He often thought, while lying in the hospital waiting to heal, that if the flash had shown him what would have happened *after* the kids chased him, he would have listened. But he couldn't choose what the flashes showed him or what would happen afterward, so he made a promise to himself while in the bed recovering. He would never ignore or take lightly a flash again. *EVER*! And he didn't.

The flashes came less and less frequently as puberty eased and John attended Cambridge University. By the time he reached his mid-twenties, the flashes rarely popped up and were all but a fond childhood memory, except for the brutal beating.

Now in his late thirties, John had gone almost ten years without a flash. That was until Tuesday. John was on his way to work and the image of the Arc de Triomphe flashed in his mind. It had been so many years since he had seen a flash, the sight stopped him in the middle of the sidewalk for a full five minutes.

For the next hour or so, he questioned whether or not the flash had happened, trying to remember if this was what it was like seeing flashes as a kid. The image of the arch was so faint in his mind's eye when he saw it, and it must have happened in a millisecond, he thought he could have been daydreaming. As a kid he remembered the images being larger than life, burnt into his mind. But this flash was so faint and fleeting, he almost didn't believe it had happened, thinking it was maybe his imagination. That was until later that evening when he saw it again.

He was sitting at dinner with friends and the image flashed into his mind. This time it was clearer, sharper, more defined.

Flash: The Arc de Triomphe, Paris, France.

What should he do with this information? Go home and do some research on the Arc de Triomphe? Or go and see the arch itself in France?

He found out the answer at dinner. He had his third flash while looking at his best friend's fiancée. She was from France and spoke English with a very heavy accent.

"Françoise, I've never asked you," said John. "Where in France are you originally from?"

"Paris."

He knew what it meant. He needed to go to Paris. But why? He never asked that question as a kid, but now as a fully cognizant adult, the question was the first thing on his mind. Why Paris? There was no use expecting the answer now. He assumed the reason would be in Paris when he got there.

In an odd way, John was thankful. It was one of the few times he appreciated being an adult, and having the consciousness to ask the question, Why? As a kid, he was reactionary toward life and these flashes. He never asked the question: Why did he have these flashes? But now as an adult, he felt more equipped to deal with the flashes and what was about to happen in Paris. His knowledge and experiences had made him ready for battle, not that he expected anything of the sort. He guessed there was something or someone waiting for him at the bottom of the Arc de Triomphe. Whatever it was, he knew it would be there. The flashes were never wrong.

When John got home from dinner that night, he jumped on his computer, made a few travel reservations, and was ready to set off to see the Arc de Triomphe by the weekend.

Back in his hotel room in Paris, John finished the lyric of the jellyfish's garden: "... in the shade." He left the closet, where he just hung up his jacket, walking over to his suitcase lying open

131

on the bed. He reached into his bag, but suddenly halted singing and looked out blankly. Another flash occurred.

Flash: A street was thick with buildings in a dense urban area. The road was dirty and dark. John was a young blond kid about thirteen, walking down the street by himself. A noise came from the long dark alley he was passing. It was the dinging sound of an elevator. The noise made him turn. He saw two bigger kids emerge from an elevator opening directly into the alleyway. The kids had a rough look about them from their clothes to their hair. They headed toward the blond boy. When he saw the two bullies coming toward him, John began running at full speed down the street away from them. The bullies chased after him, turning out of the alleyway onto the street. He ran at a full sprint, turning down another street to get away, but it was no longer kids pursuing him. It was two full-grown men. And the boy was now John, fully grown. He heard a word as clear as a bell. "Run!"

Coming out of his flash in the hotel room, John's ears were still ringing with the word *RUN*, almost as though his ears did just hear the word. He realized what he had to do, and this time he would heed the warning.

In this flash, the boys were the same bullies who put him in the hospital when he was a kid. They were hunting him, but they changed, and so did he, which means the time was now. He needed to *RUN*!

Without another thought, John quickly grabbed his phone and his wallet. He put on his jacket and ran out of the hotel room.

When he was out the door and into the hallway, John turned toward the hotel elevator. It was next to his room. He heard the elevator ding. The sound froze him in place for an instant. The ding was a knife through his body. Another flash was before his mind's eye.

Flash: He was standing next to the elevator in the alleyway. The doors opened and the bullies walked out.

Snapping out of the flash, John realized it was this elevator. He rotated around, in the opposite direction, to run down the long hallway.

The elevator doors opened, and Lexi was standing in the middle of the elevator. She saw John, a striking man with golden blond hair, for the briefest of moments as he turned and sprinted down the hallway. The hair was the giveaway. It matched almost exactly the vibrant pastel yellow from the hologram. She caught his profile. It was definitely him, but she wasn't expecting him to be so tall. The sight of John running away, down the hallway, momentarily startled her. She never expected that she'd have to pursue him to warn him.

She stepped out of the elevator, confused. Not sure what to do next, she took a few seconds to think. Maybe he would be OK since he wasn't in his room. But what if those guys sat and waited for him, the one man waited at Marise's house for a while.

And since John was the second person they missed, maybe they would give him a little more time. But how long? There were too many unknowables.

In Lexi's mind there was only one option: Try and catch up with John and tell him not to go back to the hotel room. Then a most important fact hit her. The men from the wall would be here any second. *She* had to get out of there.

Immediately Lexi, like John, began running down the hallway. She passed John's hotel room right next to the elevator, noting the same number from the glass wall.

John never glanced back to see who came out of the elevator. He disappeared around the corner at the end of the hall, opened the door to the stairs, and ran down.

A few seconds later, Lexi heard the elevator dinging. She reached the end of the hallway and dodged around the corner, peeking back to check who was in the elevator. She saw the two men from the wall walk up to John's hotel room door. Quietly, she tiptoed backward, just as she did in Monsieur Lapeyre's apartment. It was becoming a too often used tactic to get her out of trouble. Soon it wouldn't work. She opened the staircase door and closed it, hardly making a sound. She sprinted down the stairs at full speed.

Waiting in the lobby of the hotel in an inconspicuous spot, pretending to read a magazine, was Marise. She kept one eye out for Lexi and anything else suspicious. It was against her better judgment to let Lexi go upstairs on her own, but Lexi convinced her it would be better if she went to find John alone. If one of the men showed up, Lexi pointed out, they wouldn't know Lexi's face. And Lexi was right: it was for the best. The two men just passed Marise and never took notice. Whether it was because of the baseball cap or because they were focused solely on their new target, she didn't know.

Marise wanted to pace the lobby while she waited. It took all of her self-control to stay seated, out of the way, pretending to read.

A swift movement caught Marise's eye. Looking up, she saw a tall blond man dressed in nice gray pants, a vest, and a jacket run through the hotel lobby and out the front door. "*Cela ne peut pas être un bon signe*," she said to herself, intuiting that man had something to do with the wall.

Marise stood up, waiting for whomever was coming next: the men from the wall or Lexi. Whatever it was, she was ready.

Running through the lobby, exactly as the blond man just did, came Lexi. She saw Marise, already on her feet.

"They're here, upstairs," warned Marise, hurrying up to Lexi.

"I know. I just saw them. They went to his room," replied Lexi, dashing out the front door of the hotel with Marise right beside her. They made it outside. Lexi halted for a second to catch her breath. "John was running away before I could speak to him."

"I just saw a blond man in gray pants and a jacket running out the door." Marise looked up and down the sidewalk, and in the distance, she spotted a bright blond head bobbing down the street. "There he is, running away!" Both Lexi and Marise turned, without a word, and began to run after him.

John sprinted down the sidewalk, then suddenly turned right at a street corner, continuing down another street. The last time, the bullies caught him. This time, he was going to make sure they didn't. He glanced back down the road. He didn't see two men following him. Maybe the flash was wrong? But the last time he thought that he ended up in the hospital for weeks. And wasn't it better to be safe than sorry? He could have a good giggle about all this later. Looking back again, he saw the sidewalk filled with normal people walking to and fro: No men were running after him. He slowed his pace down to a jog.

When Lexi and Marise, still at a full sprint, finally made it to the street corner that John had just turned down, Lexi saw him much farther down the road, going a little bit slower. "There he is," shrieked Lexi, as they continued the chase. Thank goodness he was tall and had such blond hair, because otherwise they would have lost him by now in the crowd of people. He was easy to follow, but catching up to him would take a lot of effort.

A few blocks further down the road, John took another swift left turn, crossing a street that flowed into a roundabout. He glanced back again. There didn't seem to be two suspicious men following him, but his flashes were never wrong. He must have out-run them or, by listening to his flash, avoided their presence altogether. But he had to keep moving. Just in case. He slowed his pace down to a brisk walk, crossing another street that made up the circle.

Finally reaching the roundabout, Lexi and Marise spotted John walking at a reasonable pace on the other side of the large circle. They slowed their pace from a full sprint to a healthy run, trying to keep him in sight.

John crossed another street, making it to the top of the roundabout. Before entering a café on the corner, he gave another glance down the sidewalk. The two men were nowhere to be found. No one was going to be beating him up today.

Lexi and Marise were not far behind, running across the streets of the roundabout.

Walking into a café that was empty, John paused a second at the door to catch his breath. He looked around at the beautiful café and noticed an empty table in the back, a perfect spot to take a moment to collect himself and perhaps have a cup of tea. He sat down and tried to slowly pull himself together: flattening his golden hair neatly back in place, adjusting his shirt sleeves, putting his collar back inside his vest, and tucking his shirt back into his pants. It was a hell of a run.

At the entrance to the café, Lexi and Marise almost stumbled through the door. They had maintained their fast pace throughout the roundabout and looked disheveled. They glanced around the café, spotting John in the very back. At the sight of him, Lexi and Marise turned to each other and smiled. They tried to catch their breath. The race was over. They found him.

The women gave each other the once-over. They appeared to be a mess, like two robbers who ran away from the police. Before they took a single step farther into the café, just as any woman would do, they tidied themselves up. Lexi tucked her shirt back into her pants, pulled out a tissue to wipe the sweat off her face, then pulled out a compact from her bag and re-applied some makeup. She handed Marise a fresh tissue as Marise straightened her shirt and fixed her hair. When Marise was done she tried to fix Lexi's hair as well. They took a moment and examined each other again.

"OK?" Lexi asked, holding her hands out wide so Marise could see her entire outfit.

"*Oui*," approved Marise.

Lexi smiled pleasantly at Marise. It could have scared off John, if they looked like two crazy, disheveled women off the street. They had to look presentable to convince him that they weren't lunatics, and that the information they had wasn't crazy either. It was their best shot at saving his life.

"I think you should go first, Marise," suggested Lexi, motioning in John's direction. "I really don't speak French very well."

Marise smiled at her and took the lead.

Pulling a handkerchief from his own pocket, John wiped his forehead. He was still sweaty but looked a little more put together than before. He was looking down, checking out the zipper of his pants, when he heard a voice.

"*Pardonnez-moi. Pouvons-nous s'il vous plait nous asseoir?*" questioned Marise, standing at the opposite side of the table from John.

John jumped a little at the first sound of her voice. He looked up at Marise and then around the empty café. "*Oui,*" answered John, confused. Why would this woman ask to sit down when the café was empty? It was not uncommon in Europe for complete strangers to share a table when there was no other seat in a busy restaurant, but more than half the café was wide open.

Marise sat down in a chair, then Lexi stepped in behind her, taking the other empty seat. John seemed even more surprised at the second person sitting down at his table. Marise turned to Lexi.

"*Parlez-vous anglais?*" wondered Lexi, trying not to sound nervous.

"Yes, I speak English, and I am English. You're in luck, a two-for-one today." John smiled at her. He stared at Lexi for a moment and with his eyes on her face, he had a flash that lasted for an instant.

Flash: A beautiful girl about thirteen with brown hair and brown eyes laughing on a sunlit day in a perfect meadow.

John blinked a couple of times, returning from his flash. He couldn't remember the last time he had this many flashes in one day. When he was nine maybe?

"Are you John Michael Edward Stanton Barry?" quizzed Lexi.

The sound of his full name brought him back into the present. "Yes, I am." He sounded very surprised, "Do you know me?"

"In a way, Mr. Barry," replied Lexi.

"Please, call me John."

Lexi inhaled a deep breath. "OK, John. I honestly don't know how to do this lightly so ... It would be extraordinarily dangerous for you to go back to your hotel room." She hesitated a moment. How do you explain all of this, so a person didn't think you were crazy?

Seeing Lexi's reticence, Marise stepped in. "There are two Arab men after you. We believe if you go back to your hotel ..."

"... they will kill you," finished Lexi. She waited a moment. How was he going to react? Think they were lunatics or get up and walk away?

John stared ahead, blankly.

Flash: He was a young blond boy caught on a city street by two bullies, who were beating him half to death with sticks.

Watching John stare at her was an odd experience for Lexi. He was looking at her, but he wasn't there. And the silence was a bad sign. She'd seen it before when a child was really hurt and they scream silently for way too long, only to come out with the loudest yell anyone had ever heard. John's silence felt like this. How long before he screamed?

"Mr. Barry, I'm not sure if I can make you believe us — if this were me, I know I wouldn't believe two strangers in a café. But please, for your own safety, do not go back to that hotel room or something will happen to you," pleaded Lexi sincerely. This one was going to be harder than she thought.

John finally blinked, coming back to the present. "Please, call me John. And you are?"

"Alexandra Peters."

"American?"

"Yes. Very. And it's Lexi."

John turned to Marise, who said, "Marise André, French."

"It is nice to meet the both of you." John grinned at them. "Thank you. I do believe you."

Lexi turned to Marise, giving the faintest of smiles and raising her eyebrows in triumphant surprise.

"And I will not be going back to that hotel room anytime soon," promised John.

It was such a relief to hear. Lexi looked at John. Really looked at him. She noticed that he had a slight aura around him.

She realized she forgot to put on her sunglasses when they went running after him. It was the solar retinopathy again. The sunlight from the brief run must have caused another relapse. She looked away for a second, blinked her eyes, then turned back to test her vision. The aura was still around him and within it were mini shooting stars darting around, kind of like what she saw when she stared at the sky at La Grande Arche. Also, his aura was light blue; usually they were white. The metamorphopsia and chromatopsia were obviously still affecting her eyes. They should have gotten better since Thursday. Now she really had to go see her ophthalmologist when she got back to New York!

Lexi blinked a few more times, pulling her sunglasses from her bag, and securing them to her bra so she wouldn't forget to put them on when she left. "Do you need a place to go and make some arrangements for your belongings?"

John stared at Lexi.

Flash: The young brown-haired girl's hair blew in the wind.

John was staring at Lexi, but he seemed to be tuned out again. "Or should we leave?" asked Lexi very loudly, hoping the sound of her voice would tune him back in.

Flash: A young thirteen-year-old blond boy leaned in and kissed the girl with the brown hair.

Marise started getting up out of her chair. She touched Lexi's shoulder, motioning for her to follow.

"Please, whatever you do, don't go back to your hotel. At least for today," said Lexi even more loudly, praying her words penetrate his brain. Maybe this was his way of blowing them off? Making it clear the two crazies should shove off, and leave.

Lexi and Marise were out of their chairs, walking away, when John finally came back to the present. "Excuse me, please." He took in a long deep breath, blinking. "There is *soo* much to think over." He started to get up as well. "Yes, I will take you up on your very generous offer. I do need a place to go and make arrangements, thank you." He abruptly got up and followed Lexi and Marise out of the café.

CHAPTER 22

Arrangements

LOBBY, HOTEL, PARIS. EARLY AFTERNOON.

Lexi entered her hotel lobby with Marise right beside her, while John held open the door. She headed over to the couches and sat down. Marise sat down beside her, and John plopped in the adjacent chair.

Lexi turned to John. "I've been thinking ... Maybe the best thing for you to do is to call your hotel and tell them the concierge from my hotel is picking up your suitcase and items from your room."

John nodded in agreement. "Yes. That may work," he said. "Do you think those men might have left it a mess?"

Lexi glanced at Marise. Given what happened at Marise's house, the chances were high that John's room was a disaster. But why upset him? Maybe his room wasn't as bad as the house? Maybe they were too focused on finding him to destroy the room?

"Well, if they did, the hotel staff can just pick up all your belongings. For all they know, you had a party in your room last night," Lexi assured him.

"I just checked in."

"Oh. Well, maybe you got an early start for tonight. What do they know?" Lexi smiled. "I'll tell my hotel you're staying with me for the night and bring your stuff here. I'm sure they won't question a liaison."

John raised his eyebrows.

Lexi caught the unintentional subtext. "Or what they *think* is a liaison going on. They're used to it. They're French." Lexi caught herself again expressing an unintentional stereotype. "No offense, Marise."

"No, you're probably right," agreed Marise. Lexi returned to John. "Once you have your stuff, you're free to go home, or do whatever you want to do, just not at that previous hotel address."

"I think that should work," he said. "May I ask how you knew they were after me?"

Lexi looked at Marise for a second, then back at John. "Your picture, your name, and your address at the hotel were on a wall."

Flash: A train pulled into a train station.

John paused for a second. He looked lost in thought when he spoke. "It will take the concierge a while to go and collect my belongings at the other hotel. A few hours, I think. I want to see this wall."

"What is it with everyone wanting to go see the wall?" scorned Lexi, "If someone told me a wall is the source of information that could lead to my demise, and if I went to go see

146

this wall, I could, potentially, be recognized by these assassins, who are working toward that end ... *MY END*!" Lexi paused for a moment to gain control of her emotions. "It'd be the last place on earth I'd want to go." She huffed.

John was unmoved and remained silent, waiting.

"OK, fine. But you must cover up first. I don't want those men recognizing you," insisted Lexi.

"Neither do I," replied John very seriously.

Lexi got up, with John right behind her, and started toward the front desk. "Let's go speak to the clerk."

Assassins' Wall: Gare de Lyon

CHAPTER 23

Underdog

LEXI'S HOTEL ROOM, PARIS. EARLY AFTERNOON.

Walking into her room followed by Marise and then John, Lexi headed straight for her suitcase and started digging through it.

"I was thinking," said John, stopping next to Lexi. "Do you think it will be safe for the clerk to go into my hotel room? What if those men are still there?"

Lexi stopped searching through her bag for a moment. "I'm assuming it's OK. The clerk wasn't up on the wall, but you're right, C.Y.A. We should have told the guy downstairs you were staying alone in your room. We can on the way out."

"C.Y.A.?" repeated John.

"Cover Your Ass." Lexi continued digging through the side pockets of her suitcase. "I could have sworn I packed it!" She stopped, looking up at John, who was hovering over her. "Maybe it's a sign I can't find it." She closed her suitcase. "John, I really don't think that you and Marise should go back to the wall. It would be safer if you both wait here for your bag. Give me or Marise your phone number in case your name goes back on the wall."

"Can it do that?" John was surprised by the suggestion.

"I don't know. But it seems best to think of all the scenarios right now." On the front of her suitcase there was something poking out of the front pocket. Lexi unzipped it and pulled out a foldable hat.

"Where is the wall exactly?" asked John.

"Gare de Lyon."

"Where's that?"

"It's a train station. *Gare* is 'station' in French," answered Marise.

John flinched at the word *train*. "A train station?"

"Yeah. Why? Have you been there before?" wondered Lexi. "No. I flew to Paris, but I need to go see this train station," he said forcefully.

"All right," agreed Lexi in a resigned tone. She handed Marise the hat from her suitcase. "It isn't pretty, I know."

Marise unfolded the hat, fluffed it up a little, and made it look fashionable, as only a French woman can do. She handed John the baseball cap, and he slowly put it on. The cap didn't quite fit in with his neat outfit or with him. Maybe it was his posture or the fact that the hat wasn't on straight, or his hair peeking out underneath the cap, but he looked ridiculous.

Lexi smirked at John, who looked uncomfortable, "Go, Mets," she said, half-laughing, hoping a little ra-ra cheer would encourage him.

"Where do they play?" he wondered, not being an aficionado of most American sports. Rugby was his sport of choice.

"New York City, slugger," she said, truly laughing now and heading toward the door. Marise grabbed her bag and was right behind her.

John, generally not a vain man, was busy looking at himself in the mirror. He tried to adjust the baseball cap, so he didn't look so silly. "I thought the baseball team in New York was the Yankees?" he said, then sighed, finally giving up on the mirror and the cap.

"They are, but this is New York City's other team. They are the underdog. I like an underdog." Lexi beamed at him as she walked out the door.

"Obviously," muttered John under his breath, just loud enough so both women could hear him. He hustled out the door to catch up with them. He knew they were speaking not only about the team, but also about him. It was obvious she rooted for the underdog. He was one. They all were the underdogs in this game. It was sheer luck they hadn't lost yet. He had never watched a game of baseball in his life, but he silently prayed that the underdog in this game would win. Or at least that this Mets team had enough good luck to share. He decided this would be his new lucky cap, and with it on he wouldn't lose this game.

"Go, Mets," he said quietly, almost pleadingly, to himself. They would need all the luck they can get.

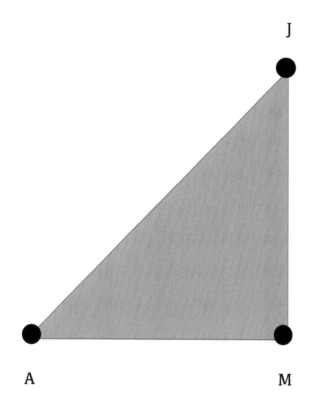

A *triangle* has three points and three sides joining together to create a shape.

Assassins' Wall: Gare de Lyon

CHAPTER 24

Full Circle

GARE DE LYON, PARIS. AFTERNOON.

Walking into Gare de Lyon had become a familiar action by now for Lexi. It was an action most people would take for granted, kind of like walking into an office every day for work. The only difference with this work was every time she entered Gare de Lyon, it was a gamble. What was going to happen next? Who was going to be up on the wall? Would the men be at the bottom of the wall? Had she missed more people on the wall while she was out getting the others? The stakes kept getting higher and higher.

There was a part of Lexi, deep down inside that hoped when she walked into the station, the wall would be gone. Poof! It would simply disappear, which would end her worries, her frustration, and her responsibilities. And now with both Marise and John in tow, she had the additional worry of them being recognized by the men. No, it was not your usual day at the office for her. Every entrance was a whole new gambit, and no moment could be taken for granted or someone could die.

Lexi, Marise, and John entered Gare de Lyon by a new entrance, one that Lexi had never used before, on the far-left side of the station. Lexi and Marise, together, walked into the main terminal.

John followed a few feet behind. He scanned around at the station: the light, the beams, but especially the trains. He turned to his right. A train was slowly pulling into Platform M. He was transfixed by the sight. It was exactly what he saw in the last flash. Then it dawned on him: All these flashes for the last few days had been a whirlwind. He couldn't remember the last time he had so many flashes, so close together. It was as if his mind was on overdrive. It gave him the odd feeling of being in the exact right place at the exact right time.

There was a fleeting sense of accomplishment for John: He trusted, and he followed. Not that he was proud of himself or feeling any type of hubris, but knowing what was ahead was a humbling feeling of a lesson learned. He listened to his flashes and he learned. Completing the full circle. Now he understood why he had to get beaten up so long ago. It was the only way to be ready for this moment. He knew he was supposed to be right here, right now.

Then there was a new thought: Where were all these flash images coming from? How was he able to receive the information exactly when he needed it? For him it denoted a life beyond what human beings acknowledged as reality. He had never taken the time, as an adult, to ask the deeper questions concerning the flashes. As a kid he didn't think, but now he was *thinking*—

deeper than ever. And the question was: if he was able to pick up these flashes, what was making it all possible? Who or what knew what was going to happen ahead of time and to warn him through the flashes?

Marise and Lexi approached the large winding staircase in the back of the station. Marise stopped, turning to Lexi. "I have an idea. Instead of John and I waiting down here where those men could potentially see us together with you — one person is easy enough to hide — the two of us would be more difficult. We can go upstairs and wait inside Le Train Bleu."

Lexi checked out the second-story windows of the restaurant towering above the station, with neon signs beckoning visitors to come up. "That's great, Marise. I totally forgot about it up there. And to be honest, I was fretting about you and John being in the main part of the station. Last time we were here I was so worried they would see you, even with the hat on." It never occurred to Lexi to go up to Le Train Bleu to wait. The wall was on the main floor, therefore so was she.

Lexi watched John lagging behind, staring at a train coming into the station. She thought better of calling out his name. John was a very common name, but it's best not to tempt fate. His name was one of the few pieces of information those men had and yelling it out across the station might be the lure and fishhook they needed to turn around.

Marise and Lexi slowly began walking up the curved stairs leading to Le Train Bleu. A few moments later John turned around, looking for them. The station, fortunately, was not very crowded and Lexi gave him a little wave. John promptly joined the two women on the stairs.

The entrance to Le Train Bleu beckoned in bright neon blue and red lights, almost like the red-light district in Amsterdam or Las Vegas, or any other type of lurid, sinister establishment. Lexi's hopes weren't high. Back home, neon lights often indicated a lower-class establishment.

On his way up the stairs John paused on the first landing, taking a moment to look around the train station from a higher perspective. He couldn't see any wall or any wall besides the four walls holding up the building. He continued, following the ladies up to the main landing in front of the revolving door of Le Train Bleu.

In a grand panoramic view of the whole station, John could see, passengers were mulling about or standing around, waiting for a train. The hum of the station sounded different up there, fuller. He saw, on the left side of the station, the large glass wall towering above the crowd. "Is that it?" asked John with a little disbelief in his voice.

"Yup," answered Lexi, who had her face down, not looking at the wall.

John appeared almost confused. "I wasn't expecting it to be glass."

"*Moi non plus*," chimed in Marise, stepping beside him, looking at the wall.

"When you said 'wall,' I thought it would be concrete or brick or something else, but glass?" said John, staring intently at it. "I don't see anyone on it."

Lexi huffed a little. There was no getting away with it any longer. She was going to have to look at the wall, whatever the consequences. She lifted her head up, glancing at the wall, checking the second pane of glass. "Nope," she said with a huge sigh of relief. "No one is on it, now."

She dreaded looking at the wall. It created a pit deep in her stomach to even look up. When she walked up the stairs, she had purposely not looked at the wall, and by not looking, she avoided being responsible for the people on it. Eventually, she knew she had to do it, but she felt it was all right to give herself some respite here and there from the duty of watching the wall. Her heart, and now her stomach, needed a little break from it all, especially after chasing John.

At the bottom of the wall Lexi saw the lone man standing at his post. Thank God he never looked up. He only stared out toward the oncoming trains, almost like he wanted to pass as a normal onlooker. Too much glaring and checking things out around the station would flag him to the authorities. He probably thought watching the train tracks made him look more convincing as a passenger waiting for a train, rather than the killer he was. But his culture knowledge was way off. People hardly ever stared at the empty train tracks for more than a few seconds, unless a train was coming into the station, like when John had just watched an arriving train. Staring out at blank tracks for hours on end looked very suspicious.

Lexi perused the ceiling of the station, knowing there were security cameras somewhere. No modern culture seemed to do much anymore without them. So maybe that man thought making as little movement as possible would make him less obvious to the cameras. If these guys were smart, they would carry a suitcase, roller bag, or something with them to look like a passenger waiting to board a train. Then again, a suitcase or bag sitting at the bottom of the wall for too long would alert the authorities. They would think they had a bomb, and a roller bag would get in the way when they went to assassinate someone.

John touched Lexi's shoulder. She searched for Marise, who was already in the restaurant. John waited, acting like a gentleman as he prompted Lexi to step through the revolving door first.

Around she went and once inside of Le Train Bleu, Lexi gasped. It was not anything like she expected. It was a feast for the eyes and one of the most beautiful places she had ever seen. But wasn't that the truth of life? The most beautiful places were never where you expected them to be, especially in a random train station in Paris. She wished she had stepped in here before and spent an hour or two just to look around and take in all the grandeur of the restaurant. It replicated a room out of Versailles or another era of grandeur long since forgotten.

The restaurant's long main room was lined with carved arches — well, carved everything: the walls, the ceiling, the doorways, and the windows. In places like this, Lexi always wondered what the bathroom was going to look like. The main ceiling was curved and almost twenty feet tall. There were paintings on every available inch of the walls and ceiling showing different scenes: a woman by the sea, sailing boats, and cliffs next to the seashore. They seemed to portray everything under heaven; all she had to do was look up to see angels and saints painted along the ceiling like the Sistine Chapel, although she was sure Michelangelo was long gone when this place was built. There was no doubt many talented artists left behind their craft for all to see. There were cherubs, naked ladies with shields, and faces in the molding, on the ceiling, and in every corner of the restaurant. Booths ran in rows with brass bars along the top. Coat hangers adorned the end of every booth and were topped with a crystal ball, like a cherry on ice cream. Wooden floors, red seats, and red carpet were rolled out, as though leading to a movie premiere. But what caught the eye immediately was the lighting.

Chandeliers shaped like large blossoms ran throughout the restaurant, as well as flower-shaped lights all along the walls.

And if that wasn't enough, at the far end of the restaurant a beautiful wooden clock floated on glass above a wooden bar. For a moment Lexi forget about the wall, the men, even John and Marise, and lost herself in the beauty. Paris, she had to admit, despite everything she had been through, was full of beauty like this: a normal façade on the outside and then, once you walked through the door, true elegance. Her heart sank for a moment. This place reminded her of Monsieur Lapeyre's lovely apartment. It had the same type of grandeur and beauty on the inside while looking deceivingly ordinary, or in this case unremarkable, on the outside. She was brought back to the present and to the glass wall downstairs.

Instead of sitting in the main restaurant, Marise lead the way to the left, past tables and wooden barriers, some with etched glass dividers, toward a large arched hallway. As John and Marise walked ahead, Lexi lagged behind, still taking in the magnificence that was Le Train Bleu.

In front of the arched hallway, there was a large round wooden bar sitting in the middle of restaurant with waiters busily picking up or ordering drinks.

They passed the bar and walked through the arched opening, down a hallway with red carpet, deep red chairs, wooden tables, and red curtains. It reminded Lexi of the Haunted

Mansion in the Magic Kingdom Park in Walt Disney World. All they needed was the floating candles to make it complete.

There was a sign etched into the mirror above the first doorway that said, "Big Ben Bar." The name caught Lexi's eye. Wasn't it odd? In the middle of Paris to find a restaurant on the second floor of the train station that looked like a mini recreation of Versailles, only to then have the bar named after a British clock? John was probably proud.

They turned right into another room filled with red couches and seats underneath the same flower chandeliers. This was supposed to be the more informal room. As if that was possible.

Marise sat down on one of two long red couches by the window. John followed, sitting across from Marise, and finally Lexi plopped down next to John on the couch. There was a long wooden table between them.

It took a few more moments of browsing around the room before Lexi brought her attention back to John and Marise. "I think you two should be all right in here, waiting for me. Those men wouldn't think you'd be here, right under their noses. Well, at least I wouldn't think of it."

"Who do you think those men are, Lexi?" questioned John, picking up a menu to have a quick look.

"I've been asking myself that same question for two days." Lexi paused for a moment. "I have to be honest. I really don't know. But my best guess would be some extremist terrorist off-shoot cell funded by an Arab state that was trying to kill off what they believe are key personnel assets in the West."

John raised his eyebrows and turned to Marise, who was also staring at him, in wonder.

"Random, I know," said Lexi. She realized as soon as she said it that it sounded a little too conspiracy theoryish to believe. But all of this was crazy, wasn't it? Maybe they needed crazy to explain crazy?

"And maybe a little out there," added Lexi.

"Then why can you see the pictures on the wall?" asked Marise. She had purposely kept quiet this whole time, not expressing her opinion or conjectures, only reacting, and speaking when she needed to. She wanted to sit back and observe this woman and try to figure out the truth. There were many different layers of the truth. The first layer was the visual, veneer, observational truth — the kind politicians count on. Perception was reality truth. But that was only the beginning. The second layer of truth was your what, when, and where's of life. Most of the time you were lucky if you found the answers to questions on the second layer. And finally, there was the third layer of truth, the layer few people ever got to see in their lives. This was the layer that explains the veneer of the first and the rationale of the second. The true explanation and motive were the third: the real truth, the whole truth, the *WHY* of truth. And

Marise wasn't sure if they would get down to level three with these men. Right now, they were struggling to see the basic veneer of the first.

"To be honest, Marise, I haven't exactly figured that one out yet, either. I don't know why I'm seeing the faces. And maybe John can see them, too, but I don't want to risk bringing him downstairs yet to find out." Lexi quickly glanced over at the table a few feet away to see if the people were listening to their conversation. "But I'm wasting time here. Someone could be up on the wall right now. You both should order some food. This may take a while." Lexi stood up and turned to John, who looked surprised. "I had to wait hours this morning," she explained, then continued straight out the door.

Walking down the stairs from Le Train Bleu, Lexi had a satisfied look on her face. Upstairs were two people she helped today, about to eat; they were alive and well, and she had something to do with it — everything to do with it. And she had to admit, deep inside her heart, so no one else could see, it felt a little good. Very good.

At the bottom of the stairs, she stopped at the exact spot on the floor where she was this morning. What a difference almost eight hours could make. She was defeated, hopeless, and hanging by a thread this morning, not sure if she could do anything with her knowledge and help the people on the wall. But now, looking at the wall, she had come full circle. She knew she could help these people; she knew she could do this, she could beat these guys and the glass wall, and get these people out of harm's way.

Lexi smiled to herself and headed over to the benches to sit, but not in the same spot as before. No, it was best to mix it up. She sat down a row back and a few seats over from where she was earlier. She looked up at the wall. It was empty. The one lone man was still at the bottom, waiting. She pulled out her e-reader, glasses, and notepad from her bag. It was back to *The Count of Monte Cristo*, and she was ready for it all to begin again.

CHAPTER 25

Police

LE TRAIN BLEU, GARE DE LYON, PARIS. MID-AFTERNOON.

An hour later up in the Big Ben Bar, John and Marise were eating a light meal at the table.

"May I ask you a question, Marise? What would happen if we went to the French police with all of this?"

Marise stared a John for a moment. "I have been contemplating that as well," she replied, taking another moment. "But what proof do we have? Only Lexi can see the people on the wall; therefore, she would be the only suspect."

"And you can't see what is on the wall."

"No," replied Marise.

John took another bite of his food and chewed it, brow furrowed. "We could try and call the police anonymously. Leave the name and the address that Lexi sees on the wall."

"*Oui*, we could, but by the time they got around to checking the call the person would be long deceased," said Marise, sounding a little discouraged.

"All right, then," said John, furrowing his brow even deeper.

"Lexi and I barely waited a few minutes to run and go get you. If we hadn't run, I think you would be dead right now. I know I would be." Marise took a ladylike bite of food.

"Wait," said John, confused. "You were on the wall as well?"

"*Oui*. She was referring to me when she said she waited hours this morning." Marise looked out the window, taking a few seconds to herself. "How can we prove the content of the wall? What would we say to the police?" She turned back to John. "That there is a picture on a glass wall you can't see. The people end up dead, by unknown nameless men, and the only person helping has no way to verify her innocence. It would not stand up in a court of law in France."

"Nor in England," interjected John.

"If we turn this over to the police we could, most likely, lose Lexi." Marise shook her head no. "I am not willing to sacrifice her. Also, they trace the phones."

"They do in England as well."

Marise paused a moment, taking another bit of food. "Also, I'm not going to sacrifice anyone else from the wall, waiting for the police to arrive. We shouldn't sit back and watch all these people die when Lexi can do something about it. Not until we have more information about these men and what group they are working for."

"We don't know their names, where they live, or who is behind all of this," said John. "What would we say to police — just go look in Gare de Lyon for a few Arab men standing around, near a wall? Thirty percent of this country are Arab immigrants, not to mention the ethnic profiling."

"They'd probably laugh at it all. And we don't even know how they kill the people, John," responded Marise.

"Have you both found anyone dead?"

"No. Lexi did. I'm the first person she saved. You were the second."

"And she's down there, waiting for the third." He stood up, thinking about Lexi and all the responsibilities she was carrying for people she didn't even know. "I'll be right back. I'm going to go check on her."

"Please don't go downstairs, John. The men may see you," warned Marise, looking concerned.

"Don't worry. I'll look down from one of the windows inside the restaurant." He winked, smiled, and walked off.

John quickly passed through the bar and over to one of the windows looking down on the main terminal. It took him a minute to find Lexi in the middle of the train station. It reminded him a little of those old *Where's Wally* books from when he was a kid. Where's Lexi, he wondered? It was hard in the crowd of people to recognize the brown hair, but he finally recognized the back of her head. She was close to the wall but not too far away from him.

John watched her for a moment, admiring her courage. She knew that a few yards away are men who were extraordinarily dangerous, and she continued to put herself in harm's way for perfect strangers. There's a lot to be said for that. He wondered why she was doing it.

His grandfather had always spoken about the American fighter pilots he knew and flew with during World War II. They had no inhibition with how they approached the enemy, feeling they could conquer anything. The Americans had a deep level of optimism and courage. Lexi had this. Maybe it was that optimism that helped win World War II. What about their current war? He hoped so.

CHAPTER 26

Coincidence

GARE DE LYON, PARIS. MID-AFTERNOON.

Lexi was knee deep in *The Count of Monte Cristo* reading and occasionally staring at the wall for more than an hour. And still nothing. There was only the one man and the wall. The other two men still hadn't come back. With Marise, he came back right away. Obviously, they hadn't given up on John, yet. Maybe he was right about not sending the clerk upstairs to his room. What if the men were just sitting there, in the hotel room, waiting? Would they kill someone not on the wall? It put another pit in her stomach.

She didn't have that answer, and prayed they wouldn't kill anyone else. In truth, she had too little information to make any kind of judgment. The last thing she needed was to have another person's death weighing down her heart. She decided to check back at the hotel and make sure the person who was sent out came back, alive. Maybe the men were waiting downstairs in the lobby for John to come back, and the clerk wouldn't be killed. Sometimes it was better to think about things from a positive perspective.

The light had changed slightly by mid-afternoon. It gave the station a warmer feel. The crowd of passengers had filled out again. As the afternoon neared evening, commuters returned in a steady stream. The benches had slowly filled to capacity while Lexi waited for the next face to appear on the wall.

She was thankful for the crowd. It was easy to get lost among all the faces. She was worried that maybe the men would start looking around the station. They would be in full alert mode by now since they missed two people from the wall.

Looking over to her right, checking out the station, Lexi saw the other two Arab men cross the main terminal, back to the wall. It was the first time the men used the entrance on the right-hand side of the station. So now they were mixing it up, too — something was up. She watched them make their way to the wall.

"Good. You've given up on John," she whispered quietly to herself, quickly peering up at the wall, which remained empty.

When the two men got back to the bottom of the wall, they joined the third in a huddle and began speaking intensely. They're probably putting together some ideas as to why they didn't find John, asking themselves why two people from the wall were nowhere to be found. The first time something happens it was by chance, and the second time it was a coincidence. And the question was: Are these men thinking it was a coincidence? Entering from the other side of the station might be an indicator they thought otherwise.

Lexi looked back at Le Train Bleu, hoping the men wouldn't get hungry any time soon and go up there for some food. But they weren't dressed very well. They probably couldn't afford such a fancy place. It was a superficial assessment, but hopefully a correct one. They had yet to leave their duty of the wall. They took no lunch breaks or bathroom breaks — or come to think of it, never even sat down to give their feet a rest, well, not that she had seen. They were machines. Maybe they stopped for bathroom breaks on the way *back* from killing someone?

She returned her attention back to the wall and the huddled men. "That's two in a row, boys. Battin' kind of sloppy today. Third time, you're out!" Lexi's voice was barely audible; there was no chance the men could hear her. The station's ambient noise made a constant hum from the people to the loudspeaker. For a voice to reach farther than a few feet would require a good shout.

"Go, Mets," she cheered, her words immediately absorbed by the ambient noise. The Mets made her think of John and the awkward way he wore her hat. She smiled ever so slightly to herself. Her satisfaction at saving the two people upstairs was quelled by the sight of the three men intensely plotting together in a tight circle at the bottom of the wall. The next person was going to be even harder to save. They knew something was up. As with any baseball game, the third time you miss, you're out;

perhaps there was even a change of innings. And those assassins didn't want to miss again and strike out.

CHAPTER 27

Reasons

LE TRAIN BLEU, PARIS. LATE AFTERNOON.

After another hour, Marise examined her empty plate while sipping some coffee. "We should get some food for Lexi. I don't think she's eaten since this morning."

"I think that's a wonderful idea," said John, pulling out a small notepad from inside his jacket pocket. "I'm ashamed, I should have thought of that as well." He flipped open the notepad and began to draw. "A sandwich should be nice."

Marise glanced at her watch and then around the restaurant.

John started drawing what resembled a jellyfish, and he hummed for a few seconds about the jellyfish's garden again, never taking his eyes off the paper. "I've been thinking. Why would these men want us dead? The only natural assumption I can come up with is our professions. So may I ask, what is yours?" He looked up, still occasionally humming the old Beatles tune.

"I'm a physicist at the Université Paris Diderot — Paris 7, Materials and Quantum Phenomena Laboratory."

"Impressive," said John, half drawing, half listening, kind of humming. "And may I ask if you are doing anything at the

University that would be of interest to these men? Any new projects?"

Marise paused for a moment. "No, not at all. I work in a research laboratory as well as being a professor at the Université. We have been conducting the same superconductivity experiment for almost three years. Even the students participate and know about the labs. I'm far from the only person who has the information."

"Do you have any new research or ideas that these men may not want you to have?" asked John, returning his full attention to drawing and humming.

"No ..." Marise thought for a minute.

John managed to slip in a few words from the tune. "Jellyfish's garden in the shade."

"The only new idea I've had that's related to a new work experiment," she said, "came to me very early this morning."

John became concerned and stopped humming. "Is there any way these Arab men would know about it? Have you told any of your students or colleagues? Posted anything online about it, or on your social media?"

"No! *Pas du tout*! You're the first person I've spoken to about it. I haven't written it down yet. There hasn't been time."

"Oh." John became deflated. He thought he was on the right track, but since she had told no one, then that was a dead end.

"And what about you?" wondered Marise. "Can you think of any reason they would want to kill you?"

"None whatsoever. I have absolutely no idea why. I'm one of the most boring individuals I know." Marise laughed a little. "I barely go out to pubs, I work the most ungodly hours, I've had the same chums since university, my family has owned the same home for years, my brother is a little weird, but otherwise I live a very ordinary life. I get up, go to work, and come home, day after day. Boring." He laughed at himself. "I'm bored even saying it."

"And where do you work, John?"

"I'm currently at the London Research Institute at the Lincoln's Inn Fields laboratories."

"Anything in your work that would spark the interest of these men?" questioned Marise.

"Not that I can think of. I'm currently leading a research group at the Institute focusing on naked mole rats."

"*Pourquoi* naked mole rats?"

"They don't contract cancer. We've been studying their molecular biology for years to try and find out why. But why would these men want me dead over mole rats?"

"*Je ne sais pas.* Maybe they want the cure for prostate cancer." She laughed.

Assassins' Wall: Gare de Lyon

CHAPTER 28

Pattern

GARE DE LYON, PARIS. EARLY EVENING.

Calmly reading a passage from *The Count of Monte Cristo* on her e-reader, Lexi stopped to take a quick look at the wall. No one was on it and the men at the bottom were still speaking intensely, probably hatching a new plan of attack on how to kill their next target. She wondered if there were any consequences for them if they didn't. Who was putting the people up on the wall? She never really thought about it before, but now it was all she could think about. Who was in charge? Was it the assassins or someone else?

If the assassins were in charge and they missed their target, would the people behind the wall just go ahead and put up the next person? They moved on swiftly. Were they keeping a list in the back of their heads with names and addresses "to be resolved later"? She didn't know, but time would reveal the answer. If a new face appeared on the wall, that would make it three times. And three was a pattern.

Maybe, hypothetically, the assassins were given a certain amount of time to kill their target and, if they didn't, move on to the next target. Maybe the men at the bottom of the wall weren't the ones in charge. And maybe the people in charge figured the men do their jobs in an orderly manner, completing their task in time. That made the most sense.

If a new face did appear on the wall, for the third time, one conclusion was clear. The men probably weren't in communication with the people who put up the faces, the people behind the wall. If they were, they would tell them to stop putting up new people until they killed the previous ones. Because, what was the point of an assassins' list if you didn't *assassinate* everyone on it? You were supposed to check off one person, then move on to the next one. But they didn't do that with Marise and John. The wall and/or the people behind it moved on to the next person. The steady stream of faces seemed to be more one sided. Was there a way for these guys to say to the people in charge, "Hang on, we missed one? Or two?" Lexi shook her head, trying to figure it all out in her mind. It was hard work to think like an assassin. Her brain didn't function that way.

Looking up at the wall again, she found it still empty. She sighed and continued on her e-reader, changing the page. Edmond Dantes, or the Count, as it were, said, "I was restored to light and liberty, and became the possessor of a fortune so brilliant, so unbounded, so unheard-of, that I must have been blind not to be conscious that God had endowed me with it to work out his own great designs. From that time, I looked upon this fortune as something confided to me for a special purpose."

Lexi stopped reading with a start! What were the chances of that? Reading this exact passage at this exact time: Something being endowed for great designs and a special purpose. She felt that way about the wall and helping out these people on it. She had long believed there was a certain order to the universe, a pattern. Everyone had their own saying to go along with her hypothesis. There was the old favorite "everything happens for a reason." Or the eternal "what is meant to will be" and "there are no coincidences" and so on ... It was not an accident she happened to read this passage at this precise time.

It was a marker — reminding her of the pattern, telling her to keep moving forward with what she was doing. She always thought these markers just scratched the surface of how the universe worked: It was a giant organic complex machine, one could say computer, with such intricacy within its workings that it was well beyond human comprehension. From a human perspective, we only caught glimpses of the pattern in this complex machine.

She was not sure if any human could understand the whole pattern of the organic machine called universe. Our brains couldn't have enough space or computing power to comprehend the whole. The machine was the size of the universe, so to ultimately comprehend the inner workings, it would take a cognizance the size of the universe. Humans were just a small cog — on the giant wheel — turning only a miniscule section —

making up one tiny portion — of the entire universal organic machine. Maybe she should have been a cosmologist instead of an engineer.

Lexi reread the passage from *The Count of Monte Cristo*. It filled her with hope and purpose; with a slight grin she looked up at the wall — and then the grin was gone. Another face was already up. How long had it been there? How long had she wasted daydreaming on the nature of the universe when back down here on Earth another person was up on the wall? Was it John or someone new? She scrutinized the face and suddenly looked bewildered. She put on her glasses, raising her eyebrows, even more surprised.

Lexi chose this seat because at this distance she could see both the name and the address on the wall without getting any closer to the men. Using the same notepad, she wrote down the information. The name began with an S.

As she was about to get up, she watched the lone Arab man, who was usually left behind, climb up high on the steel frame of the wall. Without any effort or struggle, he reached the second pane of glass and touched it with his index finger; the face and information disappeared.

Lexi let out an audible gasp. The man sitting next to her on the bench turned and stared at her. She turned to the man. "Excuse me," she said, aware of the double meaning, while jumping out of her seat. She quickly walked — not ran as her heart wanted to — over to the stairs leading up to the restaurant. She didn't want to bring attention to herself, since she already caught the attention of another passenger. Lexi knew she had to keep her emotions in check while on the main terminal floor. Too much attention could potentially be very bad.

As Lexi was about to climb the stairs up to Le Train Bleu, she froze mid-step. There was a decision to be made and there were two choices. One: Go off and find the next person from the wall on her own, call John and Marise later, tell them they were off the hook, not to return to their addresses on the wall today. Tell them that was nice meeting them, but it would be safer away. Or two: Go upstairs and get them.

It was an obvious choice. Number one would be the safest. But she knew deep down in her heart that she needed their help. She wanted their company, not physically per se, which was a benefit, but she needed them mentally: to prove to herself that she was not crazy about what was happening. She needed to share this with another human being. It made her feel safe to be in a group of people. She was not strong enough to do this alone. She was no lone wolf. She was a pack animal, or more eloquently — a social butterfly. She needed people. She needed Marise and John to make it through this situation.

Lexi turned to her left, seeing all three men in a deep discussion at the bottom of the wall. They hadn't left yet. She turned and stared up the curved staircase in front of her. If the assassins had three, she wanted three.

She began running up the staircase toward Le Train Bleu.

Quietly sipping her coffee in the first room of the Big Ben Bar, Marise was staring out the window, lost in thought, while John was busy humming and drawing more jellyfish on his notepad. He spoke without looking up. "You think so?"

"*Quoi?*" Marise turned away from the window toward John.

John glanced up from his drawing. "Didn't you just say, Lexi's coming?"

Looking very confused, Marise started shaking her head, only getting a single sound out of her mouth, "N..."

Lexi ran into the room, out of breath, over to the table. "We have to leave now. Another face just popped up. And they haven't left the wall yet. There's still time."

Dropping money on the table, John and Marise quickly stood up.

"And so much for my ridiculous extremist terrorist theory," said Lexi, quietly leaning in as they all head out.

"*Pourquoi?*" inquired Marise, who was right beside her, jacket on, purse at the ready.

Lexi walked ahead, about to sprint. "The new person on the wall," she said almost in a whisper, "He's Arab." She took off running down the hallway and out the door of Le Train Bleu.

John and Marise glanced at each other, then swiftly followed Lexi out of the restaurant.

Assassins' Wall: Gare de Lyon

CHAPTER 29

Number Three

Saif Ullah Muhammad

APARTMENT, DEPARTMENT 93, SEINE-SAINT-DENIS. NIGHT.

Saif Ullah Muhammad sat with his face to the wall, typing away on a computer in one of the most dangerous suburbs of Paris, Department 93. Next to him was another man, also sitting at a desk working on a computer. Their shabby desks ran along the wall of a dilapidated apartment, which had hardly any furniture in it but a few scattered shelves and a saggy mattress in the main room. The faded walls were not painted any special color of a comfortable home, and noises from the adjacent apartment could be heard through paper-thin walls. It was government housing at its best, or worst.

Saif looked like he was in his late forties, and he was not dressed in traditional Middle Eastern attire but wore a pair of dark pants and a button-up shirt. He stared intensely at the computer screen while typing very fast. He suddenly stopped, paused for a moment to take in a breath, and ever so slightly leaned over. He waited a moment, slowly taking in a few deliberate breaths. It didn't help. He leaned over even farther, clutching his stomach, breathing in short then long breaths, acting like a pregnant woman in labor.

The feeling dissipated. Saif sat up straight about to return to his computer when the stomach pain came again in a wave. It felt like a combination of a stabbing, a stomach cramp, and nausea all at the same time. Another wave flowed in, and he hunched over his desk even farther than before.

Saif quickly shut down his computer and turned to the man sitting at the next desk, speaking in Farsi, "My friend, I need some fresh air for a minute. I do not feel well. I will be right back."

The man nodded silently, never taking his eyes off the computer screen.

Another wave of pain hit Saif and he leaned over almost completely, taking in a huge deep breath. He then grabbed his jacket and walked out of the apartment.

Saif remembered having a stomach pain like this many times before, a little over ten years ago. He was in Iran, in a plain room with nothing but a chair and bloodied walls, being tortured. It wasn't all his blood, either. The Iranian government wanted him to retrieve classified information from another government's computer systems, specifically targeting Western nations like the United States, England, and Germany. But Saif wouldn't do it. He had his heart and integrity. It felt wrong to use his cyber security skills to spy on other countries.

The Iranians thought a little torture was sure to change his mind about helping them out. After a month of constant beating and burning, Saif would not relent. He held onto that deep spark within his heart and refused to let go. What they wanted him to do was wrong. They would use that information to harm others, whether it was more men like himself or the Western governments.

Saif naively figured, after enough time, the Iranian government would let him go because he was more valuable to them alive than dead. What he was not expecting was the psychological torture as well. And he should have. The Iranians imprisoned his wife and young eight-year-old daughter in an attempt to sway him. That was when the pain started in his stomach.

The first time he felt the pain was when the Man came into the room to inform him that his wife and daughter were imprisoned. And if he did what the Iranian Public Security Police wanted, they would let them go. But Saif would not relent. He knew deep down in his heart his wife also knew this fact. They were of the same mind and heart. That was why he married her.

A few days later the same Man came in again. The stomach pain started at the very sight of him. He showed Saif pictures of his wife and daughter's beaten bodies, but Saif still would not be swayed. This pattern went on for weeks. Every time this Man entered the room to give him new details about his family, the stomach pain returned. The amount of beating, torture, and raping his wife and daughter went through, he could only guess. It got to a point where he almost knew when the Man was coming because out of the blue his stomach would start shaking, in preparation for his entrance and the horrific news. And within a few minutes, inevitably, the Man would enter. Saif never learned his name. That was also part of the torture, making him feel truly powerless and sub-human.

How much time passed after that, Saif wasn't too sure. They started constantly keeping the lights on in the room to distort his circadian rhythm. Soon thereafter the Man showed Saif pictures of his wife and daughter's burnt appendages and other unmentionables that a father should never have seen done to a young daughter. His stomach pain was so intense he vomited all over the Man and the pictures. It was a fitting end to the disgusting images they held.

Every new visit brought a new level of human depravity, not to Saif, of course — he had to be healthy enough to do the work they intended for him to do — but to his helpless family. And as their torture progressed, so did the stomach pain, which was at a near constant by now. On the day the Man came in to tell Saif his family had been killed, after emptying his stomach onto the floor, Saif literally passed out from the stomach pain. The Man left him unconscious on the floor, lying in his own vomit.

The Iranian capturers didn't realize the final act of killing his family didn't break Saif. It cemented his resolve. It became his anchor stone. He would not let his family's death be in vain. His wife shared his beliefs, and had their daughter grown up, she would have lived by them as well.

Back in Department 93, Saif closed the door to his apartment and stopped in the hallway to take in another deep breath, trying to ease the stomach pain. The thought of his wife and daughter brought tears to his eyes, but he had to keep moving. He knew the only way to make this pain subside was to get outside, walk, and take in some fresh air, mentally remind himself that he was no longer in a small prison cell. He had the freedom to do what he liked, to help only those he deemed worthy — not some corrupt government looking to gain an advantage on the world stage.

These panic attacks were a reminder of a life long ago lost, and a sense of helplessness long since conquered. He wished these psychological reminders would stop popping up. He researched post-traumatic stress disorder, which obviously he had, and the diagnosis stated that a person suffering from P.T.S.D. often replayed the life-and-death event over and over in their mind. They also could have panic attacks and feel the emotional reverberations of what transpired during the traumatic event.

Saif hadn't had a panic attack in the last four years. To him, it always seemed that just when he had moved on with life, his mind and stomach would give him a little reminder of what he went through. As though he could truly forget. This episode was another reminder: Don't forget his wife, don't forget his daughter, and most importantly, don't forget all he had suffered to be where he was.

This panic attack was probably the worst Saif had ever had, besides the actual torturing event itself.

Another wave of pain hit his stomach and he hunched completely over, releasing an audible groan. He clutched his stomach, holding onto the wall so he didn't fall over. His face was bright red, and it took every fiber of his being not to vomit in the middle of the hallway. Saif took in a few shallow breaths, pushing the vomit back down into his stabbing stomach. He gradually returned to a standing position. Tears ran down his red face, not only tears of remembrance, but also tears of pure agony.

Once upright, Saif took in a few more calming breaths and began walking down the hallway, hoping that with each step to get outside the pain in his stomach would subside.

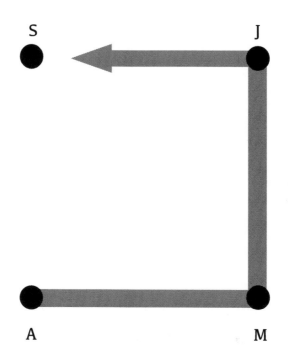

A set of points is *coplanar* if there is a unique plane containing all the members of the set.

CHAPTER 30

Panic

STREET, DEPARTMENT 93, SEINE-SAINT-DENIS. EVENING.

It happened in many industrialized nations: The area around a large metropolitan city was where the disadvantaged live. And in these disadvantaged areas, unfortunately, came crime. Crime committed out of necessity, survival, or the social opportunity to move out of the area. Usually, the people who lived in these disadvantaged areas were the minorities, delineated by race, economics, or religion. Name the country and there was probably a dangerous area, and France was no different.

Department 93, as it was locally known, a northeast suburb of Paris, was one of these neighborhoods. It slowly popped up when a large Arab population immigrated to France from North Africa. Without work or knowledge of the culture, and in need of financial assistance, the immigrants found the government housing was a miniature version of the country they just left. Sometimes these areas unofficially took on Sharia law. Department 93 was probably one of the most perilous places to be if you were not Arab or male.

Lexi, Marise, and John were almost speed-walking down the street. They stuck out like sore thumbs, kind of like Le Pouce

195

statue on La Grande Arche plaza. Maybe that was what the statue meant? Don't be a sore thumb, but the group was. Lexi looked around at all the Arab men walking around, with only the occasional woman. She knew they were a sore thumb in this neighborhood, but that couldn't be helped right now. They had a job to do, and they must do it, location be damned. They were the only non-Arabs on the sidewalk, and Lexi and Marise were the only women who are not covered from head to foot. Men kept staring at them as they passed by.

The light was dimming, and darkness meant danger in neighborhoods like these. Lexi kept her eyes on her phone, following the directions. They had to get there before the men from the wall. At least *they* wouldn't stick out like sore thumbs around here. More men ogled the women as they passed.

John noticed the looks from the men, so he took a position close behind Marise and Lexi. Not that he was any great expert on Arab culture, but what he did know was their derogatory views about women, especially women acting independently. He didn't share these views, but it would be best to stand behind Lexi and Marise, like a father would over his children, giving the *illusion* of a male chaperone. Maybe, he hoped, they could make it safely through this part of town without incident.

"How far away is it?" asked John, sounding a little anxious, as they walked by another group of men who stared at Lexi and Marise.

"Another block or two." Lexi looked around at the 1960s industrialized style buildings. "This area doesn't look *too* bad."

"As with any place, it is not the area that makes it unsafe, it's the people," replied John. He stepped in a little closer to the women, hovering over them.

Marise kept an eye not only on the neighborhood but the people as well. "Department 93 is dangerous, Lexi. It is on a government list of No-Go Zones: *les zones de sécurité prioritaires*. You couldn't have walked through Seine-Saint-Denis neighborhood alone. There is a French government website with a map showing you where not to go here."

"Really? Wow. I don't think America has that. We probably should. Oh, I almost forgot. We may have a problem, you guys."

"What?" demanded John, stepping in closer, waiting for the onslaught.

"I think the men may suspect that someone else is reading the wall."

"*Pourquoi?*" questioned Marise, looking worried.

"As soon as the face popped up, one of them climbed up the wall and touched the second piece of glass. When he did, the name and face disappeared off the wall. They have never done that before. If someone else reads the names, they could ..."

"Help prevent them from being killed," finished Marise. She thought for a moment. "You're right, Lexi, they know or at least suspect someone else is reading the wall. That is why they haven't killed their last two targets."

"Well, they are right! We can read it!" Lexi turned, grinning at Marise.

"*YOU* can read it," reminded John.

"I bet they have never missed one before. They're smart. And quick," said Lexi, almost with an inch of admiration. "Which makes what we are doing now even more difficult and dangerous. They know about us ... Or me." She turned, looking at Marise then back at John. "I shouldn't have asked you both to come."

Lexi realized she had chosen the weaker of the two options. The guilt of her choice reached the bottom of her stomach with the realization that the men knew someone was watching the wall. She had, for her own sense of security, brought John and Marise along, putting them both in danger. Not like they weren't in enough already. It was selfish of her to bring them.

NOTE TO SELF: STOP BEING SELFISH.

"No," said Marise, feeling deep down exactly what Lexi was feeling. "You couldn't do all this by yourself. It is our responsibility, too. We are the ones up on the wall. Not you."

The irony was that Lexi could walk away at any moment. What did she care? She wasn't up on the wall. She could just go home and never think about these people or Marise again. But Lexi wasn't that kind of person. Marise knew it in her heart, which was feeling slightly less heavy since this morning, but far from fully normal again. Marise knew a lot more than she was willing to say at the moment. But she was slowly learning to trust Lexi ... Alexandra. Doesn't that mean helper or something to that effect? How befitting. "Alexandra. I will not leave you alone while you do this."

"Nor will I," said John, who had his own reasons for staying. He was having trouble bringing himself to admit *why* to the women. Not yet. Not 'til he knew them better. He got a pang of guilt in his heart walking behind the ladies. Was he any better than these Arab men? They didn't trust women to be able to take care of themselves, and the first rule of any healthy relationship — be it friendship, romance, or a relationship with a relative — was to *trust*. Rule number two was communication. Once he trusted them, he was going to communicate.

Lexi stopped and looked at Marise and John. "Thank you. I know I couldn't do this alone." She glanced down at her phone and picked up the brisk pace down the street. "Almost there," she said, turning a corner.

Saif reached the courtyard of his apartment building and breathed in a giant deep breath of fresh air, then released it. He still had his hand on his stomach and the pain was far from over, but he knew the air and a walk would soon ameliorate his condition.

As he walked slowly through the courtyard and onto the sidewalk, each step brought Saif an inch of relief. When he was only part way down the street, away from the building, there was a noticeable difference in his stomach. The stabbing feeling of a knife piercing his stomach slowly dissipated but was not completely gone. Every step brought a more upright position, until finally his gait was a little more normal.

Looking up from her phone's map, Lexi was worried. "Marise, I have to be honest. I'm not sure what to say to this man to convince him to come with us." She looked back at her phone and at the map. They were almost there.

"I don't think we will have to convince him," Marise answered confidently.

"What do you mean?" Lexi looked up for a second, catching a glimpse down the sidewalk. She stopped walking. "Oh, my God, Marise, that's him!"

Farther down the sidewalk, walking straight toward the group, was Saif. He was about thirty feet away, walking with his head down, slightly clutching his side.

John and Marise stopped, turned, and stared at the man walking toward them.

Saif didn't notice their presence up ahead.

When he was only a few feet away, Lexi spoke up. "Excuse me, Mr. Muhammad. Mr. Saif Ullah Muhammad."

Saif was startled, hearing his name. He stopped ahead of the group, looking upset. "How do you know my name?" he said forcefully.

"Ummm. Well, that's a bit complicated," said Lexi. "I'm so sorry to upset you and disturb your walk, but ..."

"Lexi, they're coming," interrupted Marise, who was staring further down the road.

Approaching in the opposite direction, on the same side of the road, were the two men from the wall.

John watched them enter the courtyard area of a building. He took a step closer to the ladies.

"Who is?" questioned Saif angrily, grabbing his stomach. It was shaking now, about to release another wave of pain.

"Those two men," John nodded, only slightly moving his head, toward the two.

Saif quickly turned around and saw the two men walking through the courtyard. The sight of the two men brought it all back again, but with more intensity than before. A giant stab of pain cut into his stomach; instead of a knife it felt like a sword. His face turned red, his eyes teared up, and vomit surged up his esophagus.

"They are going into my building," said Saif. He could barely get the words out without getting sick. He turned around, facing Lexi, horrified.

"Yes, I know," she said. "That is why I stopped you. Those two are ..."

Another stab of pain hit Saif's stomach. It hit with such force that it was reminiscent of the day he learned his family had been killed. It took such control, the likes of which most humans do not possess, for him not to pass out right there on the sidewalk. He ground his teeth together, trying not to scream, as tears rolled down his face.

"Who do you work for?" he asked, trying not to lean too far over in agony, not showing these foreigners his weakness.

"I'm sorry?" Lexi was confused by both the question and his behavior. She took a little step back, bumping into John.

Hunching over slightly, grabbing his stomach, Saif took in a deep breath. "Do you work for the American government?" He had long suspected an American government agency, like the NSA or CIA, had been secretly keeping tabs on him and his work.

"Yes, well, it's a government subcontractor ... but ..."

"Lexi, time!" pressed Marise, harshly but quietly.

"Please, Mr. Muhammad. Can we speak at another location?" Lexi said calmly. It was obvious to her this man was barely able to keep it together, for whatever reason.

"Away from this neighborhood," interjected John.

"Yes," answered Saif, quickly beginning to walk ahead of the group.

Lexi, Marise, and John all stared at each other in bewilderment.

The second Saif passed the group, and they could only see him from the back, he grabbed his stomach and hunched over, letting out the pain with a deep breath. His face was red as an apple. He took in a massively deep breath, then turned around to the group, straightening himself. "This way," he said forcefully so as not to vomit. He turned around, now allowing the tears to flow down his face. And they did.

What he needed was fresh air and distance from those men. Saif continued walking away. He didn't look back to see if Lexi, John, and Marise followed him. All he wanted to do was keep moving and quell the pain.

Lexi hesitated for a moment. It was a gamble. Saif acted just as crazy as the men underneath the wall. Maybe they were connected? But he was on the wall, not at the bottom of it. And she was not ready to let a little odd behavior be the rationale for ending a man's life. He needed to know the other men were after him. They had his address and were potentially going to kill him. He, at least, deserved to know that, and then she could let him be. But a little precaution didn't hurt, just in case.

Lexi turned to Marise and John, thanking her lucky stars they were with her. Without them here — and with Saif's odd behavior — she probably would never have followed him deeper into Department 93. Not alone. She started walking. When she was a step ahead, she turned back to John and Marise. "We just have to *warn* him," she said, sounding as if she was trying to convince herself and not the others. She stepped forward. "This way," she mimicked Saif's forceful tone.

Marise stepped to her side, and they began walking together.

John followed behind the women, like before, intending to keep up the illusion of his chaperone role at least until they were out of Department 93. He was ready to leave Saif behind. He felt that Saif's ailment wasn't physical. It was clear that Saif was suffering from some type of physiological trauma since he wasn't clutching a bloody stomach or showing any type of actual physical trauma to his abdomen. Saif was clearly about to void the contents of his stomach, had heavy breathing, sweating, and tearing of the eyes, which meant he was probably in the middle of a panic attack. John was not sure if Saif was in the right state of mind to hear a warning from Lexi. He could have a psychological breakdown at the word "death."

Marise had guessed it. Saif knew something. Why else would he be out and about walking? Like John knew something. Why else would he be running away earlier? Like Marise knew something. All three of them *knew* something beforehand that put them out of harm's way. But Marise kept asking herself. *HOW?*

Further down the street, as they turned the corner, Lexi stopped, put on her glasses, and quickly glanced down the street toward Saif's building. She muffled a quiet chuckle to herself, wondering what those men would do when they discovered their latest prey was not at home. The third time was definitely not the charm for them. What would they do? Ransack the apartment like Marise's house? But would they want to draw attention to themselves in an apartment building filled with people? Or will they just wait it out longer than they did with John, not wanting to go back to the wall and admit they missed their mark yet again, for the third time.

"Saif is lucky number three," Lexi murmured to herself. She wondered if Saif meant lucky in Arabic. It probably should.

Assassins' Wall: Gare de Lyon

CHAPTER 31

Surprise

STREET, PARIS. NIGHT.

All three followed Saif, who was now only ten feet ahead, not looking back. He hadn't spoken to them or anyone for a very long time. It felt like they had walked through more than half of the city.

Lexi leaned over to Marise. "Do you think he forgot about us?"

Saif turned around. "No. We are almost there." He was surprised they were still following him. He figured that if he walked long enough and far enough, eventually they would give up. But whatever they had to say was probably important, and they were persistent enough to continue to tail him for more than an hour. Most people would have given up after thirty minutes. It was a test. And they passed it, or at least this portion of it.

Saif was finally composed. It took almost thirty minutes of fresh air before the stabbing pain finally subsided, and this attack was the longest he had had in a long time. His face was no longer red, the tears had dried up, and his breathing was back to normal. Now walking with a normal gait, he had stored his wife and daughter back into his memory bank, and he was ready to listen to what these people had to say.

Following behind, Marise wondered if he had purposely taken them all through the city to get to this destination, which was in a neighborhood she usually didn't traverse. She was sure there was a quicker way to this location, but she didn't want to scare Saif off with too many questions in the beginning, especially questions about his intentions. She didn't know how he would react, after his strange behavior earlier. The best way to save his life was by keeping quiet, at least for now.

John could tell Saif was in a better place physiologically. His demeanor had changed, and by the looks of it, the panic attack was over. If Saif's erratic behavior had continued, he was ready to sway Lexi and Marise not to warn him, and he probably would have won that argument. Calming himself down saved Saif's life.

After turning a final corner, Saif headed down a long dark hallway off the street. He walked through a door deeply embedded in a building. There were no markings above the door or on the building to indicate where he was headed. It was hard to see in the dark. The whole building was spray painted with graffiti, another wonderful neighborhood.

Lexi, John, and Marise stopped and gazed around at the rough-looking building and then at one another. "We have to warn him, then we can leave," Lexi announced nervously.

"Agreed," said John.

"*Oui*," Marise nodded.

Lexi was the first to step forward down the long dark hallway. Marise and John were right behind her. She opened the dilapidated door. It led to a flight of stairs going down. The lighting in the staircase was ominous, just a single off-color bulb. It had the feeling of an excessively dangerous location, like a crack den or a human trafficking facility. Hopefully it was neither.

The atmosphere put Lexi on high alert. She silently prayed to God, as she walked down the steps, that this warning didn't cost them their lives. At the bottom of the stairs was another door. Lexi slowly opened it.

To say she was surprised was an understatement. Lexi gasped audibly as she opened the door. Paris kept shocking her. The room was the antithesis of what she was expecting. Before her was a dimly lit, beautifully decorated hookah bar.

Marise and John stepped through the door a second later, and both of them looked shocked as well. They were no longer in Paris. They had walked straight into the Middle East, thousands of miles away. The walls of the hookah bar were bright red, with a gold filigree border around the edges. Framed artwork, not drawings or images but Arabic words, written in gold and silver, hung along the walls. Warm-colored long couches with long, circular, ornate fabric pillows were arranged around the most intricately carved wooden tables. The lighting in the room felt warm, like candlelight, and the floor was covered in Persian rugs.

Lexi had never been to the Middle East or inside a hookah bar before, but this was what it must feel like to be transported into *The Arabian Nights*.

Saif noticed his entering guests; it was hard to miss them and all the noise they made. He was surprised that they had followed him all the way down here. They passed another test. What they had to say must have been important.

He continued speaking with a Middle Eastern man, Farid, behind the carved wooden bar. He said in Arabic, "Farid, my friend, the usual, please." Without even a glance back to the group or to the door, he walked to the back of the establishment and sat down on an empty couch. It was not accurate to say he was sitting; in reality he was more lounging on the couch.

All three, still at the door, slowly looked around the bar. Marise was in awe of the place. "I thought they passed a law in France making it illegal to smoke inside a bar."

John scanned the place, and his eyes stopped on the few Arab men smoking hookah pipes. Not a single woman was in sight. "I don't think they are worried about the laws of France in here, Marise."

They began to make their way across the bar, toward Saif. They passed sparsely populated couches with men smoking hookah pipes. All the men stared at Lexi and Marise as they walked through the bar. Both Marise and Lexi noticed it immediately.

Lexi gingerly took a position down the long U-shaped couch. "Is it all right that we are in here?" she asked Saif as she sat down.

He didn't even glance at the other men in the establishment. "No," he said matter-of-factly, "but they will survive. There is no written law in this country forbidding a woman from coming in here. But an Arab woman would never step in here. Sharia Law."

Marise sat down next to Lexi.

John, whether consciously or unconsciously — Lexi was not sure — took a seat positioning himself between Saif and the women. The better position would have been between the other men in the bar and the women. Saif was the only man in this whole place who seemed somewhat at ease in their presence.

Farid, the bartender, brought over a large hookah pipe and placed it on the wooden table in front of Saif, ignoring everyone else on the couch. He quickly left, making no eye contact with anyone but Saif.

Ignoring Farid's indifference, Saif turned to the group. "Would you three like anything to drink, or smoke perhaps?" He grasped the pipe and started smoking.

"*Oui, un café, s'il vous plait. Merci,*" answered Marise.

211

"Please, one for me as well. Thank you," said John. He still wasn't sure how Saif was going to react to Lexi's warning, so placing himself between Saif and the women was the only thing he could think of to do. That or get ready to run. He took a moment. No, he hadn't had a flash that they needed to run. Come to think of it, he hadn't had anything to warn him about Saif. And he trusted his flashes; he'd learnt that much. He wondered, probably for the first time in his life if the absence of flashes was an indicator: No warning about Saif. No warning about this place. Nothing. Maybe Saif could be trusted? But that wasn't a reason *NOT* to be cautious. The flashes didn't tell him everything, only some things.

"Coffee's fine, thank you," replied Lexi, pretending to look around at the splendor of the place, but checking it out to see if the three men from the wall were around. They passed a few men on the way in, and it was hard to get a good look at their faces. All they needed was to literally walk into the lion's den. She surveyed the whole bar. The men from the wall weren't there, thank God.

Saif called over to the bartender, speaking in Arabic. "Farid, my friend, three coffees please, and one for me as well." He began to look calmer and more relaxed as he smoked his pipe. He took a moment, and a few more puffs from the pipe, to observe the oddly assembled group on his couch. "It would seem you know my name, but I do not know yours." He turned to Lexi.

"I'm Alexandra Peters." She gestured to her right. "This is Marise André," who smiled politely, "and John Barry." He slightly nodded in acknowledgment.

"And the American government has sent you to assist me?" probed Saif, suspiciously.

Lexi glanced at Marise for a moment and then back to Saif. "What if I said yes? Would that make what I am about to say seem more plausible, if it came from the American government?"

Saif took another very long drag from his hookah pipe. "Yes, it may," he said while exhaling smoke. "So please." He raised his hand, palm opened graciously, for Lexi to begin.

It was such a joke. Lexi quickly thought about how most people believed the American government was efficient and helpful in a timely fashion. Those people had never actually worked for the government, and they probably never dealt with the American government. It was anything but efficient. In fact, it was slow: slow and laborious. She always found it amusing to see all those movies about how the American government was on top of all problems in a flash of an eye, knowing what everyone was doing at the exact moment they are doing it. In truth, it took a lot of time just to fill out the paperwork required for anything, and then receiving the correct paperwork in response could take even longer. And the French government wasn't any better. Just add more wine.

Lexi drew a deep breath. Maybe she should have ordered a hookah pipe as well. It seemed to be working for Saif. Because this was the part that always scared the hell out of her. What if Saif didn't believe her? Take that leap of faith. Marise and John's belief in her and in what she had to say was the key to saving their lives, and without believing, they would die. She had seen enough death in the last couple of days. The guilt of not being able to help those people was eating away at her heart. She should have put the pieces together sooner. Warned them. Given them at least the option to live. Monsieur Lapeyre. Saif would have that option, like Marise and John. They took it. She only hoped Saif was ready to take this option and a leap. No matter what, he was gambling with his life. She exhaled the deep breath.

Lexi leaned in and spoke softly, so no one else at the bar could hear: You never know, maybe one of these men knew the assassins at the bottom of the wall. "I'm not really sure how to tell you this gently. Those two Arab men that were walking into your building were going to assassinate you."

John braced himself for the impact when it hit Saif. He stiffened his body, ready to react.

Lexi waited for what seemed like an eternity for Saif's response. Would he take the leap with her? She expected Saif to be shocked, or destroyed, or as emotional as she was when she realized the truth about the wall, but what she got was quite the opposite.

"Yes, I see," said Saif calmly. He was not taken aback, didn't flinch or jump or stammer. He looked as cool as an autumn day.

"You don't seem to upset or surprised by this information," remarked John, surprised at Saif's tepid reaction after the near psychological breakdown John had witnessed just an hour ago at the mere mention of Saif's name.

"No. It wouldn't be the first time," explained Saif, again speaking as though it was just another ordinary day. He gently took another long hit from the hookah.

John couldn't believe Saif's reaction. He seemed more surprised than Saif. He turned to Lexi, eyes wide open in astonishment. What kind of person did they — no, did *she* just save? Saif must be mentally unbalanced; before he was a crazy lunatic on the street who panicked at his name being uttered aloud, and now he was cool as ice with the news of his death and potential assassination. It was not right. John was the one on edge, not Saif. He kept waiting for the flash to get the hell out of there. But none came. It was blank in his third eye, with only ocular sights to be seen.

"And had we ..." Lexi began.

"No, Lexi, you ..." Marise interrupted her.

"No, *WE* ..." Lexi shook her head at Marise. She realized she wouldn't have come this far into the hookah bar without them by her side. "Had *we* not intervened you would most likely be dead right now." Lexi's concern reverberated in her voice.

Saif took in another long drag of the pipe. "Yes, I see," he said more calmly than before.

It aroused a curiosity within John, wondering what exactly it was that Saif's smoking in the pipe. He leaned forward a bit and sniffed the smoke Saif just exhaled. It smelled like some sort of tobacco, but he couldn't be too sure. He was never into drugs at university, or any substance that allowed you to lose control.

"And do you know who they are working for?" Saif asked Lexi.

Lexi hesitated for a moment. This was the question she avoided asking, even to herself. The answer might be too horrible. Who would do such a horrible thing? Who was behind the wall? She didn't know. She turned to Marise, searching for what to say.

Seeing the angst on Lexi's face, Marise answered for her. "No. We do not."

"Do you have any idea? Since this wasn't the first time for you, then?" said John with a hint of accusation in his voice. Maybe Saif was worse than the men at the bottom of the wall.

John was growing angry. Not with Saif, but with himself. He wished he had some control over the flashes. That he could will them into being to find out something, anything really, about this man. His lack of flashes right now was even more maddening than constantly getting them.

Farid, the bartender, walked over with the four coffees and placed one in front of Saif and the others in the middle of the wooden table, not in front of any particular person. Saif turned to Farid, speaking in Arabic. "Thank you, my friend."

Farid glanced at Saif and nodded, making eye contact only with him. The gesture was not lost on the other three, especially the women.

Saif waited a few seconds until Farid was gone. "It could be anyone, really, a new branch of ISIS, another terrorist cell from any country: like Iran, Syria, Yemen, Afghanistan, Lebanon, Palestine, or the northern territories of Pakistan, just to name a few."

"Then why are they after us?" questioned John forcefully.

Saif was a little surprised. "*Us*? What do you mean '*us*?" He turned to John. "You?"

"Both John and I were on the wall," Marise answered quietly.

This truly concerned Saif. He took in another lungful of smoke. It was one thing for another Middle Eastern man to be after him, even the Iranians. But why these Westerners? He was a high-value target. As for them ... He didn't know them. They could also be inconspicuous high-value targets. "I cannot say why exactly." He exhaled the smoke. "It could be a myriad of reasons."

Saif paused for a moment, then turned back to Marise with an even more surprised and confused look on his face. "You said a *WALL*?"

"Yes. It's in Gare de Lyon," replied Lexi.

Pulling the pipe away from his mouth, Saif leaned forward, taking a sip of his coffee. "I have never heard of that before, in such a public place for everyone to see. But a train station is good cover, lots of people moving around, it's easy to get lost in the crowd if anything goes wrong and everyone is carrying a bag. And you two were on this wall?" Saif eyed both Marise and John.

"Yes," said John and Marise in almost perfect unison, slightly nodding.

Saif then studied Lexi, who had a pit in her stomach ... *Here it comes.*

"And what about you, Alexandra Peters? Working for the American government ..."

"Lexi," was all she could mutter.

"How are you involved with this wall?"

"Well, I'm the one who saw their names on it." Lexi smiled slightly at Marise and John.

Marise smiled back, hoping it would offer Lexi some visual comfort. She knew how hard this was for her. It was very easy for

Lexi to approach another woman, or even John, because they were Westerners, but she felt the apprehension in Lexi with Saif. Not that she was prejudiced; it was more fear of the unknown, like a fish out of water. And Lexi was out of the water right now, a fish in the air trying to catch its breath.

"I see. And I ..." Saif said slowly.

"... was on the wall," said Lexi.

"When?" Saif asked so forcefully he almost yelled.

"Right before we came to meet you," Lexi said nervously.

Saif jumped up so quickly it startled everyone, except for John, who was waiting for it. John sprung to his feet, positioning his body between Saif and the ladies, expecting the blow to come, but it didn't.

Instead, Saif threw down the pipe and put some money on the table. He turned to Lexi. "I must see the wall. NOW!" He stormed out of the hookah bar.

Assassins' Wall: Gare de Lyon

CHAPTER 32

Taking Matters in Hand

GARE DE LYON, PARIS. NIGHT.

It was time *again* to enter Gare de Lyon. This made seven — or was it eight — times that Lexi entered this train station in the last four days. It was so many that she'd lost count. She decided to use the original entrance from when she first arrived. It was a simple idea, but a good one. The men seemed to be using the other entrances across the main terminal as well, so this time it was probably best to go back to the beginning.

Walking in first, Lexi reached the main terminal floor from the small hallway. Following a few feet behind her was Saif, who was now wearing Lexi's hat that was formerly on Marise's head. John and Marise waited a few feet farther back down the hallway in full disguise. John was still wearing the Mets baseball cap, refusing to take it off when asked — not that he meant to be ungentlemanly about removing his hat, but why change their luck? Marise was now wearing Lexi's scarf over her hair, á la Audrey Hepburn. They all were in another round of musical disguises. The hats and scarfs probably didn't help the cause, but they couldn't hurt, at least from a psychological standpoint.

Stepping onto the main floor, Lexi turned back, looking at John. She realized that until this was all over, that baseball cap probably wouldn't leave his possession. Which was fine with her. It did, she had to admit, give her a bit of a giggle to see a foreigner, especially an Englishman, willingly wear such an American symbol. There was nothing more American than a baseball cap, except, maybe apple pie.

Saif stopped right behind Lexi. He understood he looked just as silly as John, if not more so wearing a woman's hat. It worried him a little; his whole outfit might turn more heads out of pure ridiculousness than if he just remained hatless. But Lexi was insistent, and everyone had changed their head coverings, that was, except for John. But Saif couldn't blame him. If he had something that brought him luck, or he felt it brought him luck, then he shouldn't change it.

Curiosity got the best of Saif, and he took a few steps past Lexi into the main terminal. Lexi touched his arm as he passed. "Don't go in too close. You were just on the wall. It's straight ahead." She gestured toward the large structure that was, in truth, hard to miss. "And it's glass." That seemed to be a stumbling point for everyone.

Walking farther into the station by only a few feet, Saif scanned the main terminal. His eyes stopped on the giant glass wall, which was triumphantly standing directly in front of him.

He took another step closer and saw a single man at the bottom of the wall. His stomach jumped.

Saif turned back to Lexi, who was still standing at the entranceway of the main terminal. He got very close to her so no one else could hear. "There is a man standing at the bottom of the wall."

"Yes. He's with those two men we saw at your building."

Saif rotated back to the wall. It was empty. There were no names or faces on it. All he saw was transparent glass. "I do not see this list on the wall."

"Well, it wasn't a list, really. It's more a single picture with a person's name and address next to it." Lexi squinted her eyes a little without her glasses. "No one is on it right now." She smiled. Her relief was visible.

Saif looked at her with a very concerned expression on his face. "Yes, I just said that." It made no sense. Why would she repeat what he just said, and what he could clearly see? *Or not see* ...

Saif glared at the wall, which remained empty, and then turned back to Lexi. She had an expectant look on her face. He glanced past her shoulder, seeing both John and Marise still standing down the hallway. Why weren't *they* trying to look at the wall as well?

"I see," he said very slowly, being both ironic and literal. "Can those two not see what's on the wall?" He motioned only with his eyes toward John and Marise.

Lexi hesitated a moment and shook her head no. "Marise can't. John may, but he hasn't seen the wall yet when a picture is on the glass."

"So only you can?" wondered Saif.

"Yes, theoretically, and those three men. But maybe you'll be able to see it too when someone else pops up on the wall," she said with a little optimism in her voice.

Saif slowly turned around and took a long hard look at the train station hustle and bustle: This was not what he expected. Nor were these people. This was different than anything he had ever been through before. Something was wrong with this whole situation. He finally turned back to Lexi. "Did your government send you to do this?"

Lexi looked hollow. "No, I'm sorry to say. It would help add some credibility to this incredulous situation. I know. It's a little crazy. Trust me, I understand completely."

"I see," said Saif. "Did your government send you to save me?"

Lexi shook her head. "Well, no."

Saif turned around again to look at the man standing at the bottom of the wall. "There is only one way to find out who they work for, and what they are doing."

"OK. What?" wondered Lexi.

"We must ask him." Saif thundered off toward the wall, leaving Lexi standing alone at the entrance looking stunned and speechless.

Saif walked boldly through the busy train station toward the wall, ridiculous hat, and all.

"Oh, my God!" said Lexi a little too loudly.

From farther down the hallway, John and Marise watched as Saif walked across the station floor. They quickly moved in behind Lexi. "What's he going to do?" asked John.

"He's going to ask him," answered Lexi, dumbfounded, pointing toward the wall and the man standing at the bottom of it.

All three watched, the human train wreck that was about to take place in the middle of Gare de Lyon, and without any trains involved whatsoever.

As Saif approached the wall, a slight stabbing pain started in his stomach, just like before. The pain made him think again of his wife and daughter, and the Man holding the pictures of their dead bodies. What if this man at the bottom of the wall was him? It could happen. It was a very small world.

Saif tried to get a better look at the man, even though he was only halfway to the wall. The man at the bottom of the wall had kind of the same build and hair as the Man from the prison cell, but he could only see his back from here. What if it was him?

A stab fully hit his stomach. Could he handle it? And what would he do? He wouldn't kill that man right in front of an entire train station full of people. Or maybe he would.

As all this sunk in, Saif's stomach pain became even worse. Nowhere near as bad as it was in the hallway of the apartment building, but it took his stomach a little time to get wound up. He hunched over slightly, grabbing his stomach. He paused for a second to take a deep breath.

"*Oh, shit*," said John, watching Saif hold his abdomen. The women probably took his expletive as a protestation of Saif walking to the wall, but he knew what that meant, and that this doesn't end up in a terrible mess for them, and for Saif.

The station was fairly busy. Saif started walking between people, their bags, and benches to get over to the wall. His eyes swept around to check on the other people in the station. The activity was good cover. It gave off a high level of background noise so no one would hear what he was about to say. And it was easy to blend in with such a large group, if he needed to, hat discarded of course.

Saif also noted the strategic error the man made by standing on the opposite side of the glass, facing the incoming trains. He wouldn't see Saif coming, and another wave of pain hit Saif's stomach. He took another deep breath.

Casually, Saif walked up to the wall, then around it, pretending to take a keen interest in the train tracks. He turned and viewed the Middle Eastern man's face for the first time. It wasn't him. It wasn't the Man from the prison cell. He quietly thanked Allah Almighty. He was not sure if he could have handled it. He probably would have passed out in a pool of vomit on the floor, or killed the Man.

But seeing this man's face changed something for Saif. His stomach immediately stopped the stabbing pain, although it still hurt, and he was able with one deep breath to stand up straight and directly approach the man.

Saif stomped up to him and stopped. They stood facing each other, staring for a few seconds. It was a game of chicken. Who was going to move first? Saif smiled, stepped in closer almost to the man's ear, speaking Arabic in a low whisper. "You are going to come quietly, gently with me right now."

The Arab man made a move to step forward, but Saif stopped him, arm on his shoulder. "Run and I will cut you from your gut to your head so everyone in this train station can see your insides."

Looking down, the man saw the knife in Saif's hand that was partially concealed by the long sleeve of his jacket. Only a small portion of the blade was visible. It was pointed directly at the man's stomach. He leered at Saif, then turned to his right and left, looking around the train station.

"They aren't coming. They're busy." Saif smiled and paused. "Looking for me." He put his arm fully behind his back to guide him. "Move slowly," he said, pushing him forward. "I am not afraid to cut you open." Saif pressed the knife in closer, hitting skin but not cutting it. He moved his arm up to the Arab man's shoulder, like a buddy, always keeping the hand with the knife pointed at his side.

"This way," said Saif, guiding the man back around the wall.

Once they reached the corner of the wall, and the main floor, Saif faked a giant smile, laughing and speaking in French. "Good to see you as well, my friend," he said very loudly so the other people near him will hear. "Tell me how have you been? I've been ..."

Side by side the two men slowly walked across the floor toward the group. They walked in between and around people who didn't even take notice of the two. Saif kept leaning in, talking, and smiling with the man from the wall. From a distance it appeared as though Saif was picking up an old acquaintance at the train station. If it weren't for the stone-cold look on the other man's face.

When they reached the halfway point, while in the middle of a large group of people, the man tried to step away, but Saif laughed and grabbed his whole body tighter. Saif was a slender man, but apparently able in the body.

Lexi watched the scene in disbelief and horror. It was her worst nightmare and then some. Bringing this killer — this assassin closer.

As Saif headed toward to the group, John could see he was no longer suffering from a panic attack. His face looked normal, no sweating or tearing, and he wasn't clutching his stomach anymore. Saif was truly a scientific enigma. What could trigger a normal person's panic attack — a life-and-death situation, like walking across the station with a killer — caused Saif no trauma whatsoever. Watching how he smoothly handled the man by his side, John had to hand it to him. Saif had courage. Crazy, he-didn't-care-if-he-died courage. To obtain that type of courage, a man had to have been on the brink of death before, lived through it, and redefined the meaning of death. Soldiers had it. But John didn't. He still cared too much for life. He had known fear before, but not death. Saif had tasted death, and it no longer held any fear for him.

As Saif and the man were about to walk up to the hallway, Marise realized whatever the Arab man had said wasn't a good enough answer for Saif. And to get the answer Saif wanted, they would have to talk further. Gare de Lyon was not the place for that, but where then?

Saif passed by the group huddled together in the entranceway; he sauntered down the short hallway toward the exit. He only slightly turned his head as he passed Lexi, John, and

Marise. "Follow me," he said inconspicuously so no one in the station would realize they were together. He continued walking with the man down the passageway toward the exit.

Lexi, John, and Marise stared at each other in pure astonishment. "Who is this guy?" Lexi finally blurted out.

"I'm worried he's more trouble than they are," warned John.

"*Amicus meus, inmicus inmici me*," said Marise.

"*Oui*," agreed John.

"What's that mean? My Latin is non-existent," said Lexi.

"My friend, the enemy of my enemy," replied Marise.

"Yeah, right, or just another enemy. Maybe there is a reason he was up on the wall," countered Lexi, looking at Marise and John. "I'm sorry. That's not fair," she said contritely. "We don't know why *any* of you were up on the wall."

"No, don't apologize, Lexi. I was thinking precisely the same thing," admitted John. "He's trouble."

From farther down the hallway, Saif looked back at the group, who were still huddled together talking. He knew they are deciding whether or not to come along and follow him. He didn't care if they came or not. He half expected them not to, and that was understandable. It was their decision. The average Westerner wasn't used to getting their hands dirty to clean up a mess. Their world was very orderly, without many messes. They have people in their governments to clean up messes, like the police, or FBI,

CIA, MI6, GCHQ, and DCRI. But in his world, he was the one who had to get down and dirty. He had to find out who these men were before it got any dirtier.

All three watched Saif walk out the door. Marise understood this was the moment; they could let Saif go off on his own and take care of this. But it wasn't a final solution. There were still too many unknowns. Who were these men? Why were they killing the people up on the wall? How did the names get up there? And what was the wall? This assassin was just one piece in the puzzle. And the puzzle couldn't be put together with four, now five pieces, not without finding out the second layer of truth. All of this would just keep going on and on. And the people behind the wall could easily replace a piece or pawn like that Arab man. Just because one assassin was gone didn't mean this ended. What he could provide was truth. And to stop the wall they needed the second layer of truth: the what, when, and where. At least Saif was brave enough to find out the truth. She was not. Maybe Lexi and John were brave enough, but Saif was the one person who could do it.

Marise took a few steps down the hallway, looking back at Lexi and John. As soon as she did, her "heart feeling" was a little less heavy. She realized this was the path forward. Her heart no longer had the heaviness of the sun's gravitational pull, weighing it down like it did this morning. But the feeling still hadn't fully dissipated. There was more to be done.

Lexi realized something about Saif. He was forgetting that he was up on the wall, too. She didn't have the courage yet to tell him the first three people up on the wall were now dead. And there was still a chance that he could die in the company of the assassin. They didn't know how they killed those people. What if the assassin tried to kill Saif? She couldn't let that happen, not after meeting him.

"OK," Lexi said hesitantly, joining Marise. John stepped in directly behind the women, and they all moved to the door.

Oh, the irony. Lexi thought Saif was the one who needed to take the leap and trust her; yet here she was taking the damn leap herself.

NOTE TO SELF: J....U....M....P.

"How many languages do you speak, Marise?" asked Lexi as they reached the exit.

"Four, not including Latin, since it's only the official language of the Holy See."

"Wow. And you, John?"

"Three."

It made Lexi feel stupid. She only spoke English, and American English at that. She did speak "ob" but that didn't really count. It was a secret coded gibberish language her best friend taught her when she was a kid. She put "ob" before the vowels in every syllable of a word, but after consonants. Like: "H*ob*ell*ob*o. H*ob*ow *ob*are y*ob*ou?" It was a convenient secret language that

232

only they spoke fluently. Even today, in her late thirties, her best friend will break out in "ob" in the middle of a crowded room, asking to leave the party or commenting on a person, all while everyone around had no idea what was being said. Yes, she may not know Latin, or even French. But "ob" was hard to master, and even better since very few people can understand it when it was spoken quickly. She recalled many a confused face hearing "ob" spoken at full speed. But Lexi could only listen fluently; she hadn't quite mastered speaking it at break-neck speed, even after twenty some odd years. But there was always the future.

Assassins' Wall: Gare de Lyon

PART 3

"Where is everybody?"

- Enrico Fermi

Assassins' Wall: Gare de Lyon

CHAPTER 33

Interrogation

BASEMENT, DEPARTMENT 93, SEINE-SAINT-DENIS. NIGHT.

Saif opened the door and turned on the light in a dark basement. It was filled with random stuff: storage boxes, furniture, bikes, and books, but mostly electronics and other odd computer parts. It wasn't your usual wet dark basement, but a dry cool storage space underneath a building, without windows. At Saif's side was the man from the wall, who still had a stone-cold look on his face, despite the knife pointed at his body.

Toward the back of the storage area was a pile of furniture from an apartment, all stacked up. Saif grabbed an old-fashioned chair with sturdy wooden arms from the pile, turned it on its feet, and sat the man down. Using the duct tape sitting on top of a pile of boxes next to the furniture, he taped the man's arms to the chair and his legs together to restrain him. The man continued to stare coldly at Saif, even while being tied up.

Lexi, John, and Marise reluctantly walked through the basement door. This was much more than they have bargained for. They were back in the dangerous Department 93 neighborhood, in an unknown basement, with one man

237

brandishing a weapon, and the other man an assassin. All in all, it was a pretty mixed bag.

John, at this point, was hoping to make it out of there alive. They all watched from across the room as Saif finished taping up the assassin. He checked each appendage for the durability of the duct tape and the man's ability to move out of his binding. The tape was secured, and the man wasn't going anywhere.

Saif stepped back; a slight pain started in his stomach. He clutched his side, taking in a quick short breath. He looked at the Middle Eastern man in restraints and that was when it hit home. He had gone about as far as he was capable of going. His stomach reminded him of that. He realized *he* couldn't be the one who tortured this man in order to get information out of him. It reminded him too much of his past and what was done to him. Secretly he was thankful the others had come along with him. Maybe one of them would do what needed to be done? Bringing himself into this situation, which was the exact opposite of what he went through in Iran, wasn't his best idea. And this other man looked the sort that wouldn't breathe a word without some type of incentive, be it physical or psychological torture to break his silence.

Turning around to face the group watching from the doorway, Saif walked over, knife in hand, straight up to Lexi, and proceeded to hand her the weapon. "Here. You're the American. You should be the one to torture him."

"WHAT?" Lexi was shocked by this presumption. "Torture him? I didn't know we were going to torture him, just because I'm American? Are you kidding me?" It was ridiculous. Yes, she came from a country that was known for waterboarding, and other types of coercive information-gathering methods, but that didn't mean *SHE* knew how to do this or wanted to be any part of harming anyone. For any reason! Information gathering or not, she didn't have the heart for this.

"Well, how else do you think this works?" asked Saif, pointing with his knife to the man in the chair. "He won't talk otherwise."

Lexi and Saif both look over at the man in the chair. He seemed about as uncomfortable as someone sitting on a beach lounger by the pool. He watched them with a slight smile on his face, which put both of them off guard for a moment.

Saif again tried to hand the knife over to Lexi, who stepped back, hands held up. "I'm not some secret special ops commando, Saif. I am *NOT* torturing him!" She pushed the knife away from herself, back to Saif. "You do it! This was your idea in the first place!" She lowered her voice to sound like Saif inside the station. "Let's ask him."

Saif didn't move. He looked crestfallen. He thought maybe she would have the courage he lacked. Do what he couldn't do. The American was the logical choice: she seemed to be the leader of this group, she looked sturdy and strong, and she did have the courage to come warn him. But if she wouldn't do it, then he went through all of this for nothing.

Desperately, Saif turned to John, knife held out handle first, hoping he might take it.

John simply shook his head no.

And Marise spoke up even before Saif turned to her. "No, Saif."

It was all on Saif. But could he bring himself to do it, to torture this man? He should have thought through this plan better. Saif took a deep breath and tried to ignore his stomach. He took a step forward toward the man, knife held up, ready to cut.

"You." The man looked directly at Saif, speaking in Persian. "Stay away from me." His voice was so cold it cut Saif in two, no knife needed.

The minute the man spoke, his words make him real, not some object to be cut up like a paper doll. Maybe if he hadn't spoken and made himself human by asking Saif to stay away, he could have done it. But the words put an end to it, for him.

Saif stepped back in with the group across the basement. No one moved forward toward the restrained man. All four stood in complete silence for a minute, staring at one another to see who would act first. No one made a sound or moved for a while.

"It seems no one is up for torture," said Marise with a little glee in her voice.

"Some fearless group we are," said John, half joking and half annoyed with the situation, and with Saif for putting them in it. "Ready to fight for our lives if need be." Why did Saif go through all this trouble to bring the man here if he didn't have the stomach to interrogate him? The irony hit John at once. Of course, Saif didn't have the stomach for it. He probably expected one of them to get information out of the man. He guessed the only person, besides the man about to be interrogated, who had seen anything resembling torture that wasn't in a movie was Saif. And he backed out, not that John could blame him. He couldn't do it either.

"Well, at least we all have risen above," said Lexi, who was quietly grateful that her companions could not stoop to such measures. Why lower their dignity to the level of the assassins? It would make them no better. Granted, she had no idea how they were going to get any information out of the man, but at least they all keep their humanity and their integrity. And that was worth something — no, *everything*!

Lexi turned and smiled at the group, even at Saif. It said a lot about his character that he wouldn't do it. And she knew immediately she could trust him.

The restrained man stared at the group, disgusted. "You weak humans," he said in English, his tone almost accusatory.

All four turned in unison toward the man tied up across the room. They all had, in their discussion about torturing him, almost forgotten about the soon-to-be-tortured.

"You mean '*WE*,' don't you?" demanded Saif. The man's statement shook him to the bone. Something was not right.

"No. I mean *YOU!*" replied the man, looking at the group as though he was the one in control, not the one duct-taped to a chair about to be tortured, well, almost tortured.

Marise, John, Lexi, and Saif all turned and stared at one another, confused. What the man was saying made no sense.

Just because he was an assassin didn't mean he wasn't a human being. Marise wondered if this was his coping mechanism to detach himself from his prey. And everyone here, but for Lexi, was his prey. She had never taken the time to research the psychological state of insane psychopaths and how they referred to their victims, but this was probably pretty close to how they deal with their victims. Removal.

Lexi thought the man's words insinuated that he felt superior to them. Didn't Hitler view the Jewish people as an inferior race? He used that as a justification for killing millions of people. They were animals, in the Third Reich's eyes. Throughout history, people had executed or exterminated those who were labeled inferior or different or animals. Not human beings ... but wait ... that was *not* what he just said. If *they* were the weak humans, then what was he?

John stepped toward the man. They had him talking, without torture, and he didn't want it to stop. "Who do you work for, then? Which government or terrorist organization?"

"You are all so small-minded," answered the man, softly laughing at John.

Saif couldn't discount what he just heard. It made no sense. "Who are you?" Saif asked sternly, like a father would a child.

"I am a member of the EVO squad."

"EVO squad?" repeated Marise, her voice dripping with curiosity. "What country ..."

"Or religion," Lexi interrupted.

"Is that under?" Marise finished.

"Must be some new type of environmental action group. I've never heard of it," interjected John. Not that he was an expert in extremist groups, but he did keep up with the news, and this was a new one.

"It doesn't matter," stated the Arab man, looking at John, Marise, and Saif. "Soon you three will be dead anyway." The mention of death silenced all three. The man's voice was certain. He meant what he said.

Lexi's heart dropped. These words were her greatest fear. It seemed that nothing, even being restrained, quenched his thirst for their deaths. He was an assassin to the end. And she guessed torture wouldn't work either. It would only strengthen his resolve. Somehow, she had to change his mind in order to get him to stop this pursuit. But how the hell did she do that? How do you make a man NOT want to kill? It was beyond her armchair psychology knowledge.

"Why do you want to kill us?" grilled Saif. "What have we done worthy of being killed?"

All of a sudden, the man tried to get out of his duct tape restraints. His elbows and shoulders roll forward, his arms made a backward V shape. He tried to pull his arms free of the duct tape by pulling in the opposite direction of his body.

Everyone jumped at the sight of his elbows bending at the wrong angle. It was not humanly possible.

"What the hell!" cried Lexi.

The man pulled his hands even harder, trying to get out of the duct tape. His hands gave just an inch, then stopped moving. Luckily Saif had done a proper job of securing the hands, and the man went nowhere.

"*C'est impossible*," shouted Marise, in total amazement.

"... for a human," the man said slowly and deliberately, so everyone could watch as he rolled his elbow and shoulder back to a "normal" position. He sat and waited patiently, watching in expectant happiness at their confusion.

"Are *you* human?" questioned John, not quite buying into the acrobatics show they just witnessed.

The man was silent for a moment before answering. "No."

Lexi was having a hard time catching her breath. Her heart was racing, and her mind was going a mile a minute again. What the hell was happening here? The cognitive leap needed to accept what this man... no, *being*... was saying was too much for her. She had always believed there were other life forms elsewhere in the universe. Always! Scientifically it would be improbable for there not to be. But not here, not now!

"What is the EVO squad?" questioned Saif, who seemed to be keeping it all together very well, in spite of what they just learned.

"We are the Evolution squad. It is our objective to stop humanity," answered the man.

"From what?" asked Marise.

"From evolving." The man waited for a moment for it to sink in. "And we are supposed to kill any human being who will move humanity's evolution forward."

"And you see who to kill from their picture on the glass wall?" inquired Lexi.

The man growled at Lexi. *"How do you know that?"*

Lexi spoke too hastily. She was always had the bad habit of speaking before she thought things through. And now it was too late to take it back. Now this assassin knew she could see the wall. He knew she had uncovered a trade secret. And that was very, very dangerous. They were killers.

John always tried to take the scientific perspective toward any uncertainty in life. This man seemed to believe what he was saying, but it was hard for John to suspend disbelief to the level of accepting that the man was not human. The only way to discount what this lunatic was saying was to get more information. He stepped in closer to get a better look at this *MAN*. He was a molecular biologist, and he wanted a closer look at this person who claimed not to be human. Sometimes people could perform great feats with their bodies that wouldn't normally seem possible. In a delusional or hysterical state of mind, people could lift up cars, walk on fire, pierce themselves and not bleed, or perhaps bend their arms and elbows in what looked like an impossible way.

"Why? What is humanity evolving to?" wondered John.

"Our objective is to stop humanity from coming into The Great Connection," replied the man.

"What's The Great Connection?" questioned Marise.

"If humanity comes to The Great Connection, they will surpass the evolution of us all!" wailed the man angrily.

"All?" repeated Lexi, completely surprised. "How many are there?"

The man ignored Lexi and her question. He was above such ignorant offerings. "In 500 years, if humanity continues forward on its current evolutionary course, you will take over this galaxy and beyond."

"You are killing us for what may happen in 500 years?" tested Marise angrily.

"It will happen," he said coldly.

"So, by killing us you think you will stop the evolution of humanity," said Saif.

"You couldn't stop evolution," insisted John.

"We will slow it down long enough to give us enough time to get ready," said the man, a little smugly.

"Ready for what?" quizzed Lexi.

"The End." The man sat there with a satisfied look.

Marise, Lexi, and John stared at each other. There was almost nowhere to go from there. What was left to ask after "The End?" It seemed futile to continue the interrogation. The man was only making sense to himself and speaking in a cryptic language with definitions that only had meaning to him.

Saif started pacing a little bit. He spoke to himself and also to the restrained being in the chair. "What I don't understand is how can humanity surpass you? It's obvious you have already exceeded our evolution, since we aren't on other planets killing an alien species."

Saif stopped and turned to the man. "Are *you* not able to evolve anymore?"

The man was silent for a moment, staring down the four humans in front of him. "You don't comprehend the depth of your own minds. The human brain is the most extraordinary mechanism in the known universe. You are so blind and ignorant, because it receives information all the time, uses it, and you aren't even cognizant of it. You are not worthy of it. You barely comprehend the depth of your own consciousness and this world. Stupid, Reckless humans," he added as an aside, like spitting out filth.

"We don't?" said John, laughing a little. He'd heard enough crazy ramblings from this lunatic man. "But *YOU* do?"

The man looked coldly at John. "You will be killed soon." Then turning to Marise and Saif: "All of you. I am done speaking."

Lexi and Marise stared at Saif. What had started as a leisurely walk around the room had now turned into nervous pacing, like that of a caged animal. He started breathing heavily and clutching his stomach.

John's eye caught the movement of Saif's hand going down to his stomach. He stepped back to the group, putting himself between Saif and the women.

"We need to leave. I need to leave NOW!" cried Saif as another more intense wave of pain hit his stomach.

Both Lexi and John looked at the chair and the individual sitting in it. "Should we just leave him?" asked John.

"YES!" Saif could barely get out the words. Another stab of pain hit his stomach. He bent over slightly and ripped off a piece of duct tape, motioning for John to put it on the man's mouth. "Here, tape his lips shut. No one will hear him."

John reluctantly walked over and put the piece of tape across the man's mouth.

Saif, half hunched over, paced the room. All he needed was fresh air. He had managed to remain in this closed basement, interrogating the man, for much longer than he had thought possible.

Once Saif saw the duct tape was in place on the man's mouth, he darted toward the door, breathing out heavily to help alleviate the pain.

The others reluctantly followed Saif toward the door. No one, besides Saif, seemed to be fine with leaving a person — or whatever he was — behind taped to a chair.

Lexi was almost out the door when she suddenly yelled. "Wait!"

Everyone stopped.

Lexi ran over to Saif, who was already out in the hallway. He was hunched over, gulping in long, deep breaths. She gently, without a word, put her hand on his knife.

Now she wanted it? On the way out, instead of the way in? Before, Saif had to practically force the knife into her hand, and still, she wouldn't take it. He looked at Lexi's face for a moment. It was time to trust her. He was in no condition other than to let go. He released the knife.

Lexi took it and ran back into the basemen. She approached the man, knife in hand. She paused for a moment in front of the chair. They both stared at each other. Without a single word, she walked over to him, and cut off his left index finger in one swift movement. The cut through the flesh was much easier than Lexi thought it would be. She figured bone would be impossible to cut through.

The man screamed through the duct tape, and there was an audible gasp at the door from Marise.

Lexi picked up the finger from the floor. An unusual yellow substance that had the consistency of mucus was dripping out of it, not red blood. She held up the finger, examining the substance. "Yup. He wasn't lying. He's not human."

"Thank you," she responded to him and truly meant it. She grabbed a random plastic bag from the floor and put the finger in it. She spun around and ran out of the door toward John and Marise. Saif was already ahead of everyone, speeding down the hallway.

CHAPTER 34

Arches

BOULEVARD SAINT-DENIS, PARIS. NIGHT.

Everyone was walking in silence along the sidewalk. There was a lot to take in.

Saif was still having a hard time breathing, but he looked calmer and wasn't clutching his stomach. The walking was more for him than anyone else. He needed at least a half hour to calm himself down, and they had been walking for almost an hour. He was walking ahead, and the group was following.

Marise was also quiet, walking alongside John and Lexi.

John pulled out a pack of cigarettes from his jacket and lit one up. He was worried. He had spent the last mile in silence, trying to put a pattern to the whole thing: no, not to the crazy man that claimed to be an alien. He had a handle on that lunatic. What really worried him were his flashes. The pattern of when he got them, leading up to what happened that afternoon, then nothing. The flashes had all stopped since he met Saif. And he couldn't remember a time when he wanted them more, needed them more. And the question was, why did he see those specific images? Were the flashes just a warning? But no, that's not right. All of the flashes were about a direction. Which direction should he go? He saw the Arc de Triomphe to get him to Paris. He probably would never have taken the trip here without it. He wouldn't have left the hotel room as abruptly as he did without the flash of him as a kid and the bullies. And he was indeed ready to leave Lexi and Marise in the café after their warning about the hotel room.

A pattern was beginning to emerge in John's mind: Every time he was at a crossroads about which direction to take, the flashes guided him to the choice he wouldn't have otherwise made. And without that intervention, he wouldn't be here now. No wonder he didn't get a flash about Saif or even the delusional man still in the basement. He never would have left Lexi or Marise alone in that neighborhood to deal with those men alone. That was never an option, so there was no need for a flash to change his direction. But why was he being led in this direction? With these people? John turned and looked at Lexi.

She was staring up at Porte Saint-Denis as they walked past. It was another old stone arch that was a miniature version of the Arc de Triomphe, but miniature wasn't the precise word since this arch was at least eighty feet tall, gleaming high above the evening lights. Paris seemed determined to keep giving her constant reminders of the glass wall in Gare de Lyon. That was all she can think about now when she saw any arch: the assassins' wall. Looking down from the arch, she watched John smoke.

"I'm not proud of it," he said, noticing her attention, "and I have been trying to quit, but it's the only thing that helps calm me down." John took a step back, allowing Marise and Lexi to go ahead. "I'll stay back if the smoke is bothering the both of you."

"No. I'm fine, John." Lexi looked back up to the Porte Saint-Denis as they continued walking by. "It's weird. I kind of knew there was something not right with those guys from the wall."

"How?" asked John, beginning to wonder if he wasn't the only one having insights, or dare he say "flashes" of intuition into this situation.

"Every time I got near those guys at the bottom of the wall my heart would go: No, No, No, No!" Lexi waved her hands in front of her chest, making an X with her arms, crossing them with the word "no".

"I thought I was just being prejudiced. Unfortunately, a lot of Americans are since September 11th, Afghanistan, and ISIS. We found ourselves skittish around Arab people, always waiting for the other shoe to drop, or bomb to go off."

John looked a little surprised at her admission, but not for the reason she thought. If she had come to this conclusion by some hard, observational scientific evidence, then he wouldn't have suspected this, but her "heart" told her. Maybe he was not the only one who intuited things. But Lexi didn't seem to be conscious of how or why her heart knew things.

"It's terrible, and it's very wrong. I know that," she continued, seeing John's surprised reaction. "Which is why I cognizantly dismissed how I felt around those guys. I told myself, you're better than making stereotypical judgments around ethnic groups, Lex. Rise above. So, I brushed it aside."

Saif, at this point, was only a few feet ahead of them. He turned around to look at her.

"I'm sorry, Saif, if I've offended you with what I said before. I didn't mean to. But there is just something about *those* guys ... beings ... non-humans ... that said No! No! No! No!" Lexi waved her hands, crossing them in a giant "no" gesture again. "They aren't right."

"Your gut instinct was correct, Lexi. Follow it," said Saif, never giving a hint one way or another if she offended him.

Lexi glanced up again as they approached another stone arch, Porte Saint-Martin. This one was further down the street and much smaller than the arch they just passed. But instead of one large arch opening through the center, like the Arc de Triomphe, this one had three. How many of these things were there in Paris? That made two in a block. *WILL PARIS EVER LET HER FORGET THE WALL?*

John exhaled smoke from his cigarette, turning to Lexi. "Do you believe what that man just told us?"

Lexi looked down from the smaller arch. "What, about him being an alien?"

"Yes," replied John.

"Well, I'm a science fiction junkie, John. So, yes, I believe it. Does it surprise me? I've been watching science fiction movies and TV shows since I was a kid. Also, I read a ton of science fiction novels. Alien beings are almost second nature to me now. I've often identified more with the alien character than the human ones. You could say I've been programed by sci-fi to be OK with intelligent alien life — expectant of it, in fact. But in my naiveté, I always believed aliens would be beneficent in nature. That they wouldn't try to kill human beings before we 'surpass the evolution of us all and take over the galaxy.'" Lexi's tone mockingly mimicked the homicidal being's insipid tone from before.

"I figured," she continued, "the level in advancement needed to technologically travel to Earth could only be achieved by a compassionate race, otherwise they would have annihilated themselves long before they got here." Lexi turned back to John. "Guess I was wrong about that one! But I have always, *always,* believed one day that humans would discover alien life. *ALWAYS!* Probably living in the Milky Way Galaxy or Andromeda, but we would see them through the Webb Space Telescope, or the Voyager 1 and 2 spacecrafts, *NOT* through a glass wall, in a train station, in Paris."

John took a giant drag from his cigarette. This was going to be hard for her to hear. "I do not believe a word of what he said."

"But how could you not?" questioned Lexi, confused. "You saw what he did with his arms. Its finger!" She swung the bag in front of John. "You heard him!"

"Yes, I'm very well aware of all that, Lexi," answered John calmly. "But I don't believe he is an alien species sent here to stop evolution. That is ludicrous." He knew she wasn't ready to hear the truth: Sometimes your eyes could fool you. He had seen a clinically insane person before, and this man was clinically insane, probably the reason why they picked him to be a killer.

"Do you believe him, Saif?" asked Lexi.

Saif barely glanced back, always keeping his eyes on the road ahead. "In Islamic culture, we have what are called Jinn. They are beings that can influence people for good or for ill. But they are not of this world. I grew up with my mother always talking about Jinn. Even men who are very influential in the Muslim world, from princes of Saudi Arabia to the current leader of Iran, believe in them. The Koran even speaks of the Jinn. I believe in these beings ... and that being is a Jinn."

Marise turned to Lexi, finally speaking. "I thought he was a government operative or part of a small extremist sleeper cell. But not human? No. Scientifically speaking, I couldn't believe what I just saw, what I just heard. It's all too much." Marise's voice became gentle. "I'm sorry. I'm not ready." She paused for a moment. "And you believe him, Alexandra."

"Yes, Marise. I do." The reaction of the group threw Lexi off guard. She at least expected John or Marise to get on board with what just happened. Not be in denial with what was going on. Maybe they couldn't rationally take it all in. Most people were comfortable with what they knew as reality. The minute anything shook that reality, denial became their coping mechanism. It would be hard shaking the old scientific view that we were alone in the universe. How hard was it for Nicolaus Copernicus to convince the world of the heliocentric model in the 1500s? Probably damn near impossible. But change took time.

After all this, Lexi expected there was soon to be a new model of the universe, like with Copernicus. They were no longer the only life forms in the Milky Way Galaxy. Humans were probably only a small part of a giant system of intelligent life, no longer able to be geocentric fools. Didn't that being say "us all"? John and Marise just needed time to adapt to this new way of thinking. It was oddly funny to her; they were supposed to have adaptations that moved humanity forward. Yet this new way of viewing life in the universe obviously wasn't it. Their adaptations must be something else.

Marise's "heart feeling" got heavier. She couldn't believe that "aliens" were the answer to the "who" in the second layer of truth. Or did she not want to believe this was the truth? This was the problem with her dreams; it was all up to interpretation.

"Saif, I need to go back to my hotel," said Lexi.

CHAPTER 35

Adaptations

LEXI'S HOTEL ROOM, PARIS. NIGHT.

Lexi entered the hotel room first. John, Marise, and then Saif filed in behind her. John dropped his suitcase, retrieved from the other hotel, by the dresser, and Lexi headed straight over to her suitcase.

"Thank God the clerk made it back here alive," said Lexi, opening her suitcase. "I was so worried."

"I think it proves they don't kill anyone who wasn't on the wall." John adjusted his suitcase on the floor to fit in the small space between the dresser and the door.

"*Oui.* It could. But he didn't see anyone in your hotel room, John. They were probably gone by then," said Marise, sitting on Lexi's bed.

Saif chose not to sit down. Lexi's room made him a bit uncomfortable. He felt it wasn't proper for him to be in here. Westerners always opened up their lives so easily. Laying everything out for the whole world to see, especially on social media. Their lives were an open book: Here is where I'm going to dinner, here are my kids, here is where we're going on vacation, here are my kids in the bathtub, this is the movie I just saw. Open books. That was dangerous in his world. And he feared in the long run, it would be dangerous for Westerners as well: on many levels. They gave up their private, personal information to complete strangers, corporations, and governments. People had to earn that level of trust and respect to be worthy of that information in his world; it was not just given away on a platter for everyone and anyone to consume. Westerners weren't cautious enough to know a little protection of self goes could go a long way.

Lexi pulled out a Ziploc baggie filled with toiletries from her suitcase, emptied it, and pulled out the cut-off index finger from the bag. "This thing is gross," she said, putting the finger in the fresh clear baggie. She set the baggie down for a moment on the dresser, and rummaged through her messenger bag to retrieve the notepad she used to write down names from the wall. She quickly scribbled on the pad.

John looked over at Lexi. "What are you writing, Lexi?"

"Oh, just an idea that I had," she answered, finishing her note. "It has to do with work, and the project I came to Paris for." She threw the pad back into her bag. She would need it later to write down the next name from the wall. "We have been having some issues with the aluminum beryllium alloy shielding for a communications satellite, and I've been trying to figure out a way to solve the problem. This idea may work."

She returned her attention to the clear baggie with the finger in it from the dresser, turning it around to examine the digit. A pool of the yellow mucus was filling up the bottom. "It sure isn't a human finger in here," she said, holding the bag high in front of John's face.

John took the bag from Lexi and began inspecting the finger through the bag. "So much for your no torture, and us rising above, Lexi."

"Well, we'll need it," she said, smiling slightly, "and he does have nine others to use. I did thank him for it, John." Lexi reached into her bag and pulled out Saif's knife. He was so far ahead of her in the basement hallway she never got the chance to return it to him in private.

"Saif, thank you for lending me your knife," she said, handing it back to him.

John continued to examine the finger through the bag, turning it around and around, looking at it from every angle. It looked real. He opened the bag and sniffed the contents. It didn't have the metallic smell of blood, but it did give off another acrid smell. And he did watch Lexi cut it off that man's hand, but there had to be a scientific explanation for what he just saw.

"The most important question to answer now is, why us?" questioned John, never taking his eyes off the finger. "Why were we on the wall?"

"That being said, each of you have some adaptation that will advance the evolution of humanity." Lexi looked around at the group. "So, what can you do? What's your adaptation?" She turned to Saif, who started pacing the room. "Saif." He stopped pacing with a jolt and stared at her. "What about you? What can you do?"

"Nothing. Absolutely NOTHING!" Saif proclaimed with absolute certainty.

John lowered the bag and took a step closer to Saif. Saif seemed to be on the verge of another panic attack again. Whenever Lexi brought up a certain topic. Or maybe it was Lexi who bothered him? Best to take a position between Saif and the women in case he lunged for her.

Lexi wasn't sure if Saif was angry with her or the situation, but she trusted him. She took a step closer to Saif, much to John's chagrin. "Look, we all know why I am here," she said pleadingly. "Obviously I can see the people on the wall. The holographic image must be outside the normal human visual spectrum. Otherwise, why can the *aliens*" — she struggled with the word — "God, I hate that word. Why can *they* see it?"

John turned and gaped at Lexi, in wonder. "Like a tetrachromat."

"A what?" wondered Lexi.

"A tetrachromat." John paused for a moment, waiting for an acknowledgement from the others. There was none, only blank stares.

"A tetrachromat has a four-colored visionary system. All humans, well, it seems except you, Lexi, have a three-colored system, a trichromat. Humans can see within the visual spectrum of wavelengths from about 380 to 750 nanometers, which is your normal violet through red visible light. A *tetrachromat* can see outside the human visual window and see ultraviolet light, which is 300 to 400 nanometers. Most reptiles, some insects, and birds are tetrachromats."

John smiled at Lexi. Finally, there is a scientific answer to a question. "You're a bird, Lexi!"

"Yes, thank you, John, I'm a bird," she said sarcastically, rolling her eyes without any amusement in her voice. "But *you* all were on that wall for some reason."

Saif stopped pacing and calmly, genuinely, without any anger in his voice, spoke. "Lexi. I have no idea why I was on the wall. Whatever evolutionary potential I have must still be dormant in me. I CANNOT do anything."

Everyone stared at Saif, then at one another. No one spoke or made a move for a long moment, as though everyone was waiting for someone else to move first. Just like in the children's book by Dr. Suess, *The Zax* popped up again. No one was willing to move north or south. They just stood and stared. John and Marise took a long, hard look at each other.

"Now, I know this is frightening," said Lexi. "Who would want to admit what they can do? Honestly, if you all didn't know that I could see what's on the glass wall, I don't think I would say anything. Come to think of it, I know I wouldn't say anything because it would just seem normal and natural to me."

"Like a person who is color blind," interjected John. "When you ask them what the color green looked like to them, they say green. But it's *their* green. They have always called it green. It is a normal color to them. But it's not what everyone else sees."

"Hell, I thought the holograms on the wall were some kind of new modern art sculpture," said Lexi, half laughing at her own ignorance. "Did you all know that the first time I saw the holographic picture on the wall, I thought it was so innovative and on the edge of science? That's why I remembered the first man's face so well. I was in *awe* of the wall."

"What happened to him?" asked Saif.

"He died." Lexi pulled out the newspaper from her bag and handed it to Saif, pointing at the front-page picture. "I saw his face the next day in the paper and went back to the wall to double check if it was him, but another man, Louis Calendrier, was already on the wall. But I know it was him," she said, pointing again to the paper. "Georges Martin." The regret dripped from her voice.

Everyone remained quiet for a long moment. Finally, Marise decided it was time. Someone had to go first. She was the first person Lexi saved. So, it seemed fitting, to her at least.

"Alexandra, let me ask you a question," Marise said kindly. "Did you ever find it odd that you show up on my doorstep, tell me to leave right away, grab me and pull me out of my own home, and I never put up a fight?"

Lexi was shocked for a moment. "My God. No, Marise. Now that you mention it, I never thought about that. It's all gone so fast and so much has happened since then, I guess there wasn't time. I'm sorry I never noticed. I was so focused on *NOT* finding you in the house dead. You probably thought I was some rude, crazy ..."

"American." Marise interrupted with a smile. "Actually no. That's not why at all. I think my adaptation, or little gift, as my family calls it, is dreaming. You see, the night before you came, I dreamt about you."

John and Saif both turned to Lexi, who was truly dumbfounded for a moment. "Really?" she finally said.

"Exactly as you are right now. In my dream you showed up at my door, weren't quite *AS* forceful and your clothes were a bit different, but you kept saying how important it was that I go with you. You were going to save my life and you had to show me something. You took my hand, and we walked toward a large cement wall, but the wall blocked our path. And in the dream, I knew you. I felt you were a good person, meant me no harm, and were there to help. You also told me that you needed *my* help to continue, that I needed to trust you. It was all in my heart when I woke up."

The room was silent for a moment.

"You were waiting for me, at the door?" posed Lexi.

Marise laughed a little. "In a manner of speaking, yes, I was. I figured you would show up. I have a very good turnaround with dreams. They usually come true within a day or two."

"Does it always happen? Do you have prophetic dreams every night?" questioned John.

"Oh no, every once in a while. But I can tell these dreams from others. They feel different, heavier. The heaviness is in the heart area, and they feel more real. I don't pick them. And I have no control over it. But I have learned in the past to trust these dreams and listen to them. And I do." Marise looked at Lexi. "And here you are. Exactly as I saw you." She beamed at Lexi. "And you did save my life."

Saif was beyond himself. "And that's your evolutionary adaptation? Worth killing for! Moving the human race forward? Dreams?"

"I wouldn't call myself or this ability anything special, Saif," replied Marise. "And I've had this all my life, and so do most of my family members. It was very normal to us all. Nothing special. We all talk about our dreams all the time. But is this adaptation, as that man said, worthy of being on the wall? No," she said flatly to Saif.

John was looking down at the floor, hands in his pockets. He had a decision to make. And the time was right now. He made it through the first two points of any good relationship with these people: trust and communication. It was time for number three: honesty. It had taken a lot of honesty for Marise to go first; now it was his turn.

John quickly looked up. "I get flashes."

Everyone reacted to John. "Flashes?" marveled Lexi.

"A quick flash of a picture in my mind's eye. Right here." John pointed to the middle of his forehead, above his brow. "A picture almost superimposes itself on what I am seeing with my eyes. It's as though I'm seeing two images at once. But the third-eye image takes over for just a millisecond, until I see what it is. Then it's gone. It flashes."

Lexi eyed Marise, then turned back to John.

"When I was a kid, I thought I had an active imagination, daydreaming and such. Seemed routine to me. As I got older, I noticed a correlation between what I saw and what was about to occur in my life."

"OK. And what can you do with this adaptation?" asked Lexi.

"I'd know who was calling before the phone rang, or if a person was coming to visit ..."

"You had a flash before we arrived," declared Marise, already knowing the answer.

"You must have! At the hotel. You were running out of there," said Lexi.

"Yes. I did in the hotel room. I had a flash of these two boys from when I was a kid. They beat me up and put me in hospital. When they flashed in my mind's eye, I knew I had to run out of there, or I would have been beaten up."

"More likely killed," insisted Lexi.

"And I ran."

"Thank God you did, John," said Lexi.

"But understand I have no control over when I get a flash or what I see. They just appear. And you all must know, before a few days ago, I hadn't had one in more than ten years."

Lexi walked over to the bed and sat down next to Marise, defeated. "Well, this wasn't the best start. We have a man who gets random flashes in his mind's eye, and a woman who every once in a while, has a prophetic dream. Ladies and gentlemen, I give you the future adaptations of humanity."

"Maybe they killed all the good ones last week," said Saif, half smiling and half serious.

"Speaking of." Lexi jumped up. "I have to get back to the wall. I can't have another person's death on my conscience." She opened up her suitcase and pulled out another shirt. "I'm going to run out of clothes pretty soon. They have seen me in almost all of these."

"I'm coming with you," Saif informed her.

"So are we." Marise and John speaking in almost perfect unison.

"... Birdy." John grinned at Lexi.

"Fine! I've given up on stopping all of you from coming. But please, for the love of God, stay hidden in the main terminal area in case the third alien ... being ... thingy managed to escape from the basement or if the other two are back at the wall."

"They won't be able to find him, the Jinn, that fast," said Saif.

"I hope you're right, Saif." Lexi grimly placed the baggie with the finger into her messenger bag.

Assassins' Wall: Gare de Lyon

CHAPTER 36

Worst Fear

GARE DE LYON, PARIS. LATE NIGHT.

Lexi strolled into the train station alone. John, Marise, and Saif had all gone to their separate entrance of choice. The group split up before they got to the station, figuring it might be easier for the other two "beings" to spot a large group of people whose faces had all appeared on the wall, rather than a single person.

It felt strange to Lexi to be alone with the wall again. It had an identity to her now and it was evil, with the intent to kill. Yes, it wasn't exactly alive like a person, but it felt alive. The information flowed like blood, and the glass was the brain: telling *them* where to go kill. The wall had lost all of the initial artistic beauty long ago.

Looking around the station, Lexi couldn't see any signs of Marise, John, or Saif. Wherever they were hidden, they did a pretty good job. She couldn't find them, which was a huge relief. She realized just how much she had come to rely on their companionship. She felt safer with them around. But didn't a true hero always go off on a mission alone? She was not a hero, in the traditional sense. Not just because she didn't feel as safe alone,

271

but because she didn't really save them like a hero. A true hero received glory. There was no glory in all of this. No parades or flowing over of appreciation from the people but that was not fair — Marise did thank her. Also, a hero wanted the job, and she did not. If it weren't for her guilt for the dead, she wouldn't be here at all: Guilt really did go a long way.

Gare de Lyon was familiar to her now: the sounds, the lighting, and the people. Yes, even the smell. Lexi had gotten a good idea of how many people would be in the station at a given time of day.

It was late at Gare de Lyon. The last exodus was about to occur. People were trying to catch the final train or arrive in Paris before the trains stopped running. There weren't too many people around, so she was able to see the wall from top to bottom from all the way across the main floor.

She usually judged how close she could get to the wall by the number of people in the station. The more people there were, the closer she could get to the wall without being seen by the men. She kept referring to them as "men." It was a hard transition to "alien." The word "alien" brought about too many comparisons: from illegal immigrants in the States to one of the many characters she grew up loving and watching. The word "alien" felt *alien*. It felt foreign, not real: like it belonged on a TV show or on the movie screen. These beings were all too real. And the word "alien" didn't quite describe the ineffable feeling of fear they instilled or the true sense of reality of the situation. "Alien" felt made up and fictitious compared to the corporality of these beings. She thought she should reserve the right to judge the nomenclature of what to call them until a later date, but for now, to keep it real, she decided on "sentient beings."

The glass wall stood there by itself, alone for the first time: no picture on the glass and none of the beings at the bottom. It was an opportunity Lexi couldn't pass up, even though there weren't enough people in the station to give her cover. Hopefully, the other two sentient beings — there, she said it — were still looking for Saif or for their companion, who she hoped was still duct-taped to a chair back in Department 93.

With all the beings gone, Lexi could get close to the wall. Really close. See how it worked, at least from an engineer's standpoint. Maybe there were light diodes on the side of the glass to illuminate the faces? It could be a new type of holographic projection system, for only people who can see ultraviolet light. That made no sense. But there had to be a way for the image to appear in the glass. Not *ON* the glass but *IN* the glass like a hologram. She had always loved holograms, but she never took the time to scientifically investigate how they worked.

NOTE TO SELF: Next time you find something interesting that intrigues you, take the time to find out how it works. You never know how that knowledge could come in handy in the future.

Slowly she ambled over to the wall, passing the benches. She paused for a moment in the middle of the station to look around, making sure the sentient beings weren't coming. She continued on, stopping directly below the glass wall.

It was much bigger than she thought it would be up close. The wall, itself, was impressive. From the back of the station, it was hard to appreciate just how large the wall really was. The single sheets of glass were huge; each pane was taller than her by almost three feet. When the being climbed up to the second piece of glass, he made it look so easy and effortless. She would have to work hard and struggle to get up there. It was going to be difficult. She hadn't done a pull-up since high school.

Lexi took another step closer, checking out the bottom piece of glass and the steel structure. First, she quickly glanced around the station again to make sure no one other than human beings were coming. The coast was clear. And John, Marise, and Saif were still out of sight. No doubt they were keeping an eye on her. The thought made her feel safer, in a strange way. They were watching over her as she watched over them.

Lexi touched the metal support of the wall. She was, after all, a materials engineer; granted, her field of expertise was aluminum alloys. The metal appeared to be a steel compound, quite common in manufacturing and building, probably A36, low carbon, nothing special there. The metal showed no signs of protrusion from of any type of device that could explain how the faces were illuminated.

She ran her fingers all around the metal square of the bottom portion of the wall, never touching the glass. They touched the glass to remove the faces, which meant there was likely something in the glass to detect heat or an electrical charge. She was afraid that her finger on the glass might trigger an alarm or sensor. Carefully she made her way around the bottom square. It appeared that the steel skeleton only supported the glass. There was no projection system requiring wires for a light source or fiber optics hidden along the inside. She stopped, holding her hand on the steel for a moment, feeling for a heat source that could potentially reveal any type of mechanism underneath the thick beam. But the metal was as cold as ice. It appeared to be steel, nothing else.

Seeing nothing that seemed out of the ordinary, Lexi glanced up to the second piece of glass. That was where the faces appeared anyway. But first, she quickly took another look around the station to see if anyone was coming. No one was.

The second piece of glass, like the first below, didn't show any signs of technology that would explain how faces were being projected into the glass. No drilled holes along the steel where a fiber optic could sneak out. No wires, no lighting. No nothing. She took her time, so not to miss a scratch, going visually from corner to corner to corner, inspecting every square inch of the glass and steel. It was smooth and clean.

But this made no sense. She had been damn near positive that she would see something upon on closer inspection. *SOMETHING!* Even the glass was perfectly clear and unscratched. Her own logic aside, she half expected to find a face 3-D lasered into the glass and illuminated by some light source below, kind of like those etched crystal cubes she saw at all the tourist traps back home. But that wouldn't fully explain the images. The faces on the wall were different every time. Also, if they were lasered into the glass, they wouldn't change. These did. And the pictures really were holograms, not lasered dots that made up a face. Which meant this hologram was somehow projected into the glass by an unknown source. How else could she explain it?

Lexi huffed and took a single step back to view the entire wall. Maybe she could see something by looking at the big picture, like her father used to do. There was always a reason for everything, and this wall worked somehow, and she was going to figure it out. She was an engineer. This was her job, kind of. She took some structural engineering classes in college. But this wall was an engineering enigma. How in the hell did this thing work? What did they use to project the hologram onto the glass?

She took in another deep breath while staring up at the wall. "I have no idea how you're doing this," she said to the wall, as though it were a person: a stubborn, obstinate person who won't reveal their secrets, even up close.

Then Lexi was forced to face the truth. If she truly believed that these sentient beings were indeed another life form, then it was time she accepted the possibility that this wall, and how they used it, may be beyond her technological know-how. And these beings were capable of creating a glass wall outside of human comprehension. Like Arthur C. Clarke said in *Profiles of the Future*, "Any sufficiently advanced technology is indistinguishable from magic." And this was magic. Well, until humans figured out how the magician pulled off his trick. This was the first time there had been a real-life application for any of her science fiction reading. She wondered if Clarke ever realized how prescient he was and if he ever saw something like this wall. Or any disclosure.

It would be like handing Benjamin Franklin a computer tablet. He would have had the intellectual capacity to comprehend what it did, but not how it worked. Colonial American society wasn't technologically sophisticated enough, and neither were they, right now, able to comprehend how the wall worked. It was like Saif said in the basement. "It is obvious they are beyond human beings because we aren't on other worlds, killing other sentient life forms." How right he was.

She looked at the wall, shaking her head. *No, they were not!* She couldn't imagine a conscious life form, like herself, going to another world and kill a different species of beings. It wasn't in her nature. Some human beings probably could, but not her. Maybe it was for the best that astronauts take physiological tests before going into outer space. She would bet a million dollars this being's space program had no such test, or he would have failed, but then again, their space program specifically chose them for that quality, to be assassins. It made her wonder about their culture and value system. If these three were an example of the whole group, the human race was in big trouble.

Suddenly, while she was staring at the second pane of glass, another face popped up. Lexi froze for a moment. She had never been so close when a face appeared. It looked absolutely enormous in the glass, dominating nearly all of the glass square. Her eyes were as wide as they could get, filled with the holographic image on the wall. She was unable to move or even breathe for about fifteen seconds. When she did start breathing, it was in huge gasps. She turned around and, at a full sprint, ran for the main exit of the station, making a frenzied, serpentine configuration around people, benches, and bags. She barely reached the hallway to the exit when she stopped and vomited with almost projectile force.

A few seconds later, running from somewhere inside the station, came John. "Birdy, what happened? Did someone go up on the wall? I didn't see anything." He quickly glanced up at the empty wall. She couldn't answer him because of the ongoing retching. He didn't flinch or move because of the acrid smell of Lexi's stomach content; he had seen much, much worse.

A few moments later, Marise cautiously arrived at their side. Her hand began making slow comforting circles on Lexi's back. "Sorry I waited to come over here. I didn't want everyone running over here all at once. It would have drawn even more attention," she replied to John.

"Lexi, who is it? Who did you see on the wall? Is it one of us again?" Marise peered at John, then returned her attention to Lexi. "Do you know the person?" She knew whatever Lexi saw was upsetting enough to make her body react in such an extreme way. It was probably one of them again.

Lexi was still hunched over, violently heaving. Saliva and tears streamed from her face. Nothing remained in her stomach, and yet the dry heaves continued unabated.

John looked at Marise again. It had to be bad. And it must be one of them. They had to figure out how this bloody wall worked and find a way to stop it before Lexi ripped herself apart from the inside. He tenderly pulled her hair back from her face.

"Yes. Yes. I know the person," rasped Lexi, finally leaning up, barely able to speak to them. Both the vomit and the words tasted bitter in her mouth.

"Then who is it?" demanded John, anxiously waiting.

Lexi lifted her head. "IT'S ME!" she wailed.

John and Marise froze. There were no words. It took a moment for both of them to process what Lexi was saying and all the implications that went with it. It wasn't them. It was worse. Now the one person who could see the wall was on the wall. This changed everything.

"BUGGER it!" growled John, in as harsh a tone as he had ever spoken aloud.

"They even have my hotel and room number! How can they do that? How do they know that?" pleaded Lexi. Tears still ran down her face, while snot poured out of her nose. She didn't bother to wipe them away.

People in the station were beginning to notice her and the smell. The vomit couldn't help but draw attention to the group. John looked around and noticed the interest in Lexi. He was about to speak when he saw Saif running up from somewhere inside the main terminal. He appeared very upset, drawing in huge breaths while clutching his stomach. He spoke before he got to the group. "I know. I know," said Saif.

Lexi was shaking like a leaf from shock, and John was half holding her up. He had had enough of Saif and his panic attacks, which he obviously was having again. Lexi was in real trouble and trauma, and so were they. John took his frustration out on Saif. "How can you know? You only just came up. Did you know Lexi just saw herself on the wall? Unless you can now see who's on the wall as well?"

Saif clutched his stomach as another wave of pain hit. His face was bright red, tears were running down his face, and he barely got the words out. "No, I can't." He breathed out for a second, relieving the pain. "But I know what *I* can do."

"*Qu'est ce que c'est? Maintenant*? Right now, you figured it out?" questioned Marise anxiously, completely surprised.

"Well, what is it, then!" urged John, annoyed.

Saif started walking away from the group. "They're coming!" He headed down the hallway toward the exit.

John, Marise, and Lexi, almost in unison, turned around and gazed inside the main terminal. There were only a few people milling about this late at night, and the beings from the wall were nowhere to be found. They looked at one another in confusion. Maybe Saif got his adaptation wrong? It could just be another panic attack. He seemed to have a lot of them: first when they met him on the street, then at the interrogation, and now?

All three turned to find Saif had already reached the end of the hall. He stopped by the exit, frantically waving for them to follow.

On the other side of the terminal, the two sentient beings appeared out of nowhere. Lexi saw them first. Her breath was taken away. Saif was right. They should have trusted him.

The sentient beings were walking toward the wall. The third one, who they'd left in the basement, was not with them.

Perhaps he hadn't gotten loose from his chair yet. But bending his body in odd directions didn't seem to be a problem.

Lexi, John, and Marise watched the pair reach the bottom of the wall. One of them looked up, noticed Lexi's face on the glass, and hoisted himself up with ease to touch the second pane of glass with his index finger.

Lexi watched her face disappear. It was too late. They had her information. "That's it. It's over. I have to get out of here. Now!" she hissed.

They fled toward Saif, whose frantic beckoning became frenzied. They walked briskly toward the exit where he was waiting. When Saif saw them approaching, he slipped out the door.

John and Marise practically carried Lexi out of the train station and across the main plaza in front of Gare de Lyon. All three followed Saif like cubs behind the mother bear. Saif's brisk pace kept him far ahead of the others. When he reached the large boulevard at the end of the plaza, he made a sharp turn left and continued down the street, only occasionally looking back to make sure the group was still following.

As they made their way across the plaza, Marise and John continuously turned around, checking to ascertain if the beings were in pursuit. If so, they might have to make a run for it, dragging Lexi with them.

When Lexi made it to the boulevard, she finally mustered up the strength to take a quick glance at the station doors. She was distraught. "Are they coming out the door yet?"

Marise looked back at the station again. "No. The quickest way to your hotel is through the other side exit." She calculated, trying to think through the navigational options.

Saif, still far ahead of the group, crossed the boulevard to walk on the opposite side of the road, heading toward the river. He looked back at the others again. Supporting a weakened Lexi was slowing Marise and John, but Saif knew he was in no physical condition to help carry her. His stomach was still cramping from the waves of pain. He needed to keep moving, but he didn't want to walk too fast or far ahead because they needed to keep him in sight.

Saif felt a momentary sense of gratitude, knowing what his instincts could do, even though they manifested through pain. It didn't bother him that he was the only one left out while they revealed their adaptations. He'd never heard of people who had flashes or who could see ultraviolet light. But the Koran was full of people having prophetic dreams: Sura Yusef, Sura An-Antal, Sura Al-Fath, Sura As-Saaffat (May Allah be pleased with them). But there was never a woman who, as the Prophets Yusef, An-Antal, Al-Fath, and As-Saaffat (May Allah be pleased with them), dreamt about the future. He had to reflect on this new prophetic dream information about Marise.

Now, knowing his adaptation, he could put all the pieces together. The chronic waves of pain acted as a detection system to warn him of the presence of the Jinn. It was a gift from Allah Almighty. And this was too powerful a blessing to be taken lightly. Such a gift most men would abuse and use to gain power over others, and even over the Jinn. A Jinn captured was a deadly weapon. Perhaps the stabbing pain in his stomach was there to remind him there always was a price for such an advantage. The opportunity cost was to feel pain when it was being used; it would never allow him to abuse this gift. It reminded him that he was only a mortal human.

The mere thought of the Jinn put a quick stab back in Saif's stomach. He was happy to be human and to serve with this gift, as long as Allah Almighty saw him worthy. But what bothered him the most was the Jinn using Middle Eastern bodies as their "human" cover. They were not worthy of such human faces.

As the three followed behind Saif toward the river, Lexi was practically inconsolable. She was still unable to walk unassisted, and she began to sob. Seeing herself on the wall was the last thing she expected to happen. Her face was so enormous in the glass. She was thankful that only she and the other beings saw the image. If *EVERYONE* in the station had seen her face, she probably wouldn't be able to walk now. Marise and John would have, literally, had to carry her out of the station.

She glanced at Marise and John and was thankful for them as well. Thankful that she made the selfish decision to bring them along, and now here they were helping her. If she was alone, and her face went up on the wall, someone would have found her dead, not in her hotel room, but in the station as they walked out the exit. She felt a tremendous debt of gratitude for these two people, and Saif. Without him they may not have left the station right away. Just as she saved them, now they all saved her. Any fleeting feeling of superiority she felt over these people for helping them out was now gone. They were on equal footing: all victims of the assassins' wall.

Saif, ahead of the group, turned right at the river and continued walking, only rarely looking back. He didn't need to anymore. Unlike the first time the trio had followed him out of some morbid curiosity, now, they were linked to him and trusted him. And with each step away from the station, his stabbing pain diminished. By the time they reached where he wanted to go, his stomach would be back to normal.

As the group turned the same right corner, John looked up ahead at the lone figure of Saif. He wasn't clutching his side anymore, which meant the panic attack was coming to an end. "Why is it I always feel as though we're following Saif everywhere we go?" he joked, trying to lighten Lexi's mood.

"And I'm the Parisian," offered Marise.

"We should be following you, then," said John, the teasing provided a welcome distraction.

"I don't care where Saif wants to go. I'll go. I trust him," stated Lexi. She looked at Marise, then John. "I'm sorry, you guys, if this is how you felt after I came to get you. I really didn't empathize enough with how this felt." She wiped tears that were gently running down her face. "I thought I was stronger than this."

Marise lightly kissed her cheek and rubbed her arm gently. Marise knew Lexi was stronger than Lexi gave herself credit for. Strong in her heart, which was the best type of strength, especially for such an unexpected emotional shock. That made her situation different. Marise's dreams had emotionally prepared for the wall and the events that followed. Lexi hadn't seen this coming. Oh, the humor of life. The woman who could see into the ultraviolet spectrum couldn't see this coming.

As they followed Saif along the riverbank, Marise knew the fresh air was good for Lexi. It was important to take a moment and breathe. Take the time to let Lexi regain her thoughts, emotions, and composure. A shock was a shock. No human was unsusceptible to it. It was in our nature. Part of our survival instinct. Probably something those aliens had no idea about. Yes, Marise realized it, that word in her mind. *Alien.* She was ready to accept the fact that they weren't human. Her "heart feeling" suddenly got lighter at the thought. She was on the right track.

Maybe human instinct had its purpose after all. Here was an aspect of humanity she never took seriously and thought useless in the modern age. But the adrenaline rushing through Lexi's body made her sick and she fled the station, which saved her life. If Lexi hadn't vomited, the aliens would have seen her. And killed her.

Marise gave Lexi another small hug of comfort. She should have guessed. It was only a matter of time before Lexi was going to be up on the wall. Who saw ultraviolet light? No one, but for Lexi and the aliens. Sounded like an adaptation that would eventually bring humanity evolutionarily forward into The Great Connection. It seemed so obvious now. She was so ignorant, for only now catching the obvious. This must have been how Lexi felt after realizing that the people on the wall were being killed. At least now they knew everyone's adaptation: John's flashes, Saif's stomach, her dreams, and Lexi's eyesight.

Marise looked out at the river. What was 'The Great Connection?' She had to figure this out. She vowed that neither she, nor anyone else in the group, would be caught off guard again by not thinking ahead.

John picked up the slack as they continued by the river. He was practically carrying Lexi. She seemed to have lost the will to move and flee after seeing herself up on the wall. His heart went out to her. At least he had some type of warning with the flashes. She didn't. And this was what happens when coping with the unexpected. He quickly glanced at Lexi, suspecting that she remained silent until she calmed down and remembered that she was not alone. They all were in the same boat. And he was not going to leave her side.

Then he was momentarily angry with himself and the flashes again. He received no flash of warning that Lexi was going up on the wall. His flashes had officially transitioned. It was a change that was hard to appreciate given all the other needs at hand. He pulled Lexi up by the arm.

Lexi still had tears running down her face as she walked, or rather, as John and Marise dragged her. It took all her energy to keep putting one foot in front of the other. To say she had hit rock bottom was an understatement. Her heart had sunk so low it was now presiding in the area of her feet, which may be why it was so hard to pick each one up. What was she going to do now that she was up on the wall? Of course, she figured out her reason for being on the wall only *after* she was up on the wall. Life was always easier in hindsight. She should have picked up on it earlier, but she was more focused on the other people, not herself. Who cared if she could see into the ultraviolet spectrum? Right now, she would have given anything to take that away. But she couldn't. Her eyes had been an issue since she was a little kid. And that's how she viewed this: an issue. What good did it do to see into the ultraviolet spectrum? Who cared? Those beings did, that was who, and they were willing to kill her for it. What was funny, ha ha, to her right now was she could have sworn, on a stack of Bibles, that her eyes were nothing special. Aside from one giant glass wall, in one station, her ability served no purpose whatsoever and was not worth losing her life over. She didn't want to end up like Monsieur Lapeyre. Maybe it was cowardly of her, but she didn't want to die. She was not ready. Then again, neither was Monsieur Lapeyre, Louis Calendrier, Georges Martin, or even her father.

She looked up as they crossed a street; walking down the side road was a group of American Marines. Her father was a Marine. And she wished he were here now. She needed his advice about what to do next. That was what she missed the most, the advice. Not that her mother wasn't an exceedingly bright woman, but her father had a viewpoint that always brought everything into focus. He could see the big picture. She watched the Marines longingly. *"I miss you, Dad. And I wish you were here,"* she whispered.

Assassins' Wall: Gare de Lyon

CHAPTER 37

More Arches

ARC DE TRIOMPHE DU CARROUSEL, PARIS. NIGHT.

After more than an hour of walking parallel to the river, Saif had given up his pace ahead of the group and allowed the others to catch up. He was only a few feet ahead of them now and his stomach had stopped the waves of pain, making it easier to walk.

Lexi felt, and looked, a little better. She was more composed and walking on her own. For the last hour her emotions had been all over the map. Now she was angry: angry at herself for not seeing this coming, angry at whoever built the wall, angry at those beings for killing everyone, and angry because it was going to be that much harder to save the next person on the wall. She would never accept the fate of death from the wall, not without a fight.

John was still walking beside Lexi, who in spite of looking a little better, wasn't fully herself yet. "I'm sorry to bring this up, Birdy."

She turned to him. The tears had dried up, but her eyes were still puffy.

"But we will eventually need to find someone to retrieve our luggage."

"I've been thinking about that," answered Marise, who was still on the other side of Lexi. "I'm going to ask my sister to go to your hotel room and pick up all the luggage."

"No, Marise! I don't think it will be safe. I would never want you to risk hurting any family member for me."

"Don't worry, Alexandra. I believe they only kill the people who are up on the wall. My sister wasn't up on the wall, and she doesn't have any adaptation that will move humanity forward. Trust me." Marise laughed. "She is the only person in my family who doesn't have dreams."

"But ..." Lexi interrupted her.

"Also, I'm going to tell her to watch out for the men, tell her what they look like and what they are wearing. I'll tell her to leave and text me if she sees them. She can bring your luggage over to my offices at the Université Paris Diderot." As soon as she said the words her heavy "heart feeling" was gone. She had completed what needed to be done, at least from the dream's standpoint. She knew somehow her sisters were involved in all of this. When she told Lexi and the others about her dream, she didn't have the heart to tell them everything, just the parts pertaining to Lexi and the wall.

In her dream, her sister Claudine appeared behind Lexi as they were trying to get around the cement wall blocking their path. Claudine stepped in to help. When she did, the wall crumbled down. Now it all made sense. Claudine would come in and get the bags. And this will be over. Lexi could go home. Claudine would demand, in return for this favor, to hear every detail of what happened and which dream prompted it all. She, like everyone else in the family, loved to hear about prophetic dreams, especially ones that had already come true. And with that thought, Marise's "heavy heart" feeling lifted off her chest. The dream had come to fulfillment until the next dream. But a quiet question still remained unfulfilled in her heart and mind. In the dream, when the wall came down, why was her deceased older sister Maxine standing on the other side of it? She didn't know.

John saw the perfect opportunity to speak with Saif. Lexi didn't need to lean on him anymore. He took a few giant steps forward to catch up with Saif, who suddenly turned right, away from the river. He walked underneath an archway opening and John followed. With a few more quick steps, John finally fell in step with Saif. Saif turned to John and gave him a quiet smile. It seemed only Saif's brain knew what their destination was — which was acceptable as long as it wasn't Department 93 again.

John perused the area. At first it was a bit difficult to gets his bearings in the dark, but he had a faint idea of where they were. Up ahead on the other side of the road was another large plaza, making up the entrance of the Louvre.

"Saif, how did you figure that out?" asked John, in step with Saif.

Saif never altered his gait. "My adaptation?"

John nodded his head yes.

"I was across the main floor, hiding next to one of the other exits, when I saw Lexi suddenly turn from the wall and run across the floor. I went inside the terminal and saw her reach the hallway, then get sick to her stomach. And I got upset too when I saw her, a little stab in my stomach. I knew she was throwing up because of what she saw on the wall — over what the Jinn had put up there. Then my little stab turned into a wave of nausea. The feeling started to get worse and worse and worse; it builds, you see. It begins with a sharp knife stabbing, then come waves of pain. Pain so debilitating I have to hunch over. Sometimes I also vomit from the pain. I knew I was on the verge of having one of these panic attacks and about to throw up myself. Then it clicked in my mind: Lexi's vomiting, and my vomiting. The Jinn affected her, and they affected me. My stomach pain was because of the Jinn."

Saif looked at John. "I knew they were coming."

By the time Saif was done with his explanation, the tired quartet had reached his desired destination. The ladies were right behind the gentlemen. They caught up to them during Saif's explanation. They all hovered around the beginning of the Triumphal Way and the Arc de Triomphe du Carrousel.

John glanced up at the arch. It was a smaller version of the Arc de Triomphe, only this one had three arches: one large and two smaller ones on each side. Looking through the main arch, he could see the actual Arc de Triomphe farther down the Triumphal Way. "Why come here, Saif?"

"I've told you; public places are better; people moving around. You can see who is coming and going. It makes great cover, like a train station. And there are always people walking around here. It's safer out in the open. One of the Jinn wasn't going to kill us in front of hundreds of people."

"Well, not without you knowing they are coming first," retorted John.

"Yes, it would seem," agreed Saif. "Also, I need to walk for at least half an hour for my stomach to feel better after one of my attacks."

Lexi sat down on the ground. It had been a very long day for her. She started first thing with retrieving Marise and ended with seeing herself on the wall. What a day. If anyone had told her this was how the day was going to go, she would not have believed it. And honestly, she probably would have never started it all. 'But isn't that always the case when events snowball out of control? You never realize how big disasters are going to get until it's too late.' She was tired and after all they had been through, she thought it was acceptable to take a short rest.

"Have those panic attacks ever happened to you before?" questioned John.

"Yes, many times, not including today."

"And what do you do when you get these?" John felt like Lexi in the hotel room, asking him these exact questions, only this time it was him interrogating Saif. It was important to know how all this works. Saif had his own personal alarm system and that could be useful.

"Usually if I can, or I'm allowed, I go for a walk. It always calms me down," replied Saif.

"*Oui*, because you were walking away from those men," said Marise.

Saif nodded.

Lexi watched Marise, John, and Saif in deep discussion.

"Then how were you able to function when we kidnapped the other one?" asked John.

"During it all, I thought I was really nervous. I'm usually the one being kidnapped, not the one doing the kidnapping."

John looked at Marise. It all made sense. That was why he tried to hand Lexi and then him the knife. Saif couldn't do what had been done to him. He had courage, not vengeance.

"And the other few times you had these panic attacks, when did you have them?" interrogated John.

"I haven't had one for a long time, until today. Right before I met you all on the street. I was in the apartment when an attack came on. I decided to go for a walk and get some fresh air to help calm me down."

"We should have asked you in Lexi's hotel room why you were out walking," said Marise, knowing Saif had some sense, like her and John, before all of this happened. She didn't want to force a confidence from him. She thought he wasn't ready yet to admit it to strangers. In retrospect, that wasn't the best decision. Knowing what he could do might have saved them time.

"And the other incidents?" asked John.

"I'm not ready to speak about those yet. To anyone," answered Saif, not in a harsh manner, to John. The images still haunted him.

"It may help us figure out when and how this works," said John, trying not to be too pushy.

"I understand, my friend. But my heart is not ready to speak of those horrific events yet. Please give me time to adjust to all of this. We did only just learn the Jinn existed. I need time to think and pray."

John nodded his head. He wouldn't force Saif to relive a trauma from his past. He respected the time needed to reflect on all that had happened. He felt the same way. He needed an hour or two to get a handle on this whole situation, figure out how that man did that with his finger. And he had to admit that he was not sure that it was a human finger.

Lexi looked up at the Arc de Triomphe du Carrousel, then peered through the main large arch all the way down to the Arc de Triomphe de l'Etoile in the distance. It was a never-ending stream of arches. "How many of these things are there in Paris, Marise?" she asked, pointing up to the monument.

"Six, I believe. If you include La Grande Arche, but I don't consider it an arch. The name is incorrect. La Grande Arche is a hypercube."

"What's a hypercube?" wondered Lexi.

"A three-dimensional visualization of a fourth-dimensional cube."

"Oh. That's interesting. I did think it looked like a cube when I first saw it. But have you noticed how all the other arches look just like the wall?" Lexi looked up to the Arc de Triomphe du Carrousel again. It was as though all the arches, perhaps even the hypercube, were tormenting her. All over Paris were these huge arches. Whether they were made from glass or stone, it didn't matter. They all reminded her of the arched glass wall and all the innocent people who had an undeserved sentence of death on their heads.

"I wonder why that is?" she asked, not to the group, but to herself and the arch. Were these stone arches just another version of the glass arch in Gare de Lyon? Did they serve the same purpose? Have the same malicious intent? There were too many to ignore. She had personally seen five. So why did Paris have so many arches? It was a key question that kept reverberating through her mind. At this point, after seeing her own face on the glass wall, she refused to take anything for granted. She thought it was a piece of art, and she was very, very wrong about that. After everything, she couldn't allow herself to take all these other arches for granted. There may be some ulterior motive people were not aware of yet. Why else would the builders of the glass wall chose the same arch shape? She glared up at the whole Arc de Triomphe du Carrousel again. She couldn't figure it out. Yet, there was one fact she knew for certain.

"You know," said Lexi calmly, "we can't save everyone."

Saif and John turned around and stared at her. Marise, who was standing by her side, looked down.

"I *CANNOT* spend the rest of my life sitting in a Paris train station, reading names, trying to save all those people. I am not a superhero." Lexi was dead serious.

Marise leaned down to touch her arm. "You couldn't anyway now that your face and name are up on the wall. Eventually they will recognize you."

"I know," Lexi said in a resigned tone. "So, I can't go back to Gare de Lyon and wait by the wall anymore. And I can't let the people who will eventually be up on the wall die. I *CAN'T*! I have seen too much death, Marise." It wasn't just Messieurs Lapeyre and Calendrier she was referring to, but also her dad. Her heart sunk for a moment, reminding her of the pain of grief.

Lexi stood up, wiped her hands of the dirt from the ground, and joined the group, forming a small circle. She started with John and slowly looked each person in the eye as she spoke. "I couldn't let you all die. You have too much life still to live and too much to offer the world. Like my dad did." The mere thought of him brought tears to her eyes, only this time not out of anger, but out of the heart-wrenching, hollowing feeling of remorse.

"When did your father pass away, Lexi?" asked John. He knew it. There had to be a reason she was doing all of this, but grief wasn't the motivational factor he was expecting.

"About two years ago. He was still young and had so much life to live. I'm the one who found him on the kitchen floor, dead. I'm glad it was me, really, who found him. My mother couldn't have handled it." Lexi wiped a few tears from her eyes. "Once I figured out what was going on with the wall and that people were being killed ... did I tell you ..." She turned to John. "I found Monsieur Lapeyre dead on his couch: eyes wide open, saliva dripping from his mouth, cold as stone. It broke my heart. My dad's eyes were open when I found him. And I couldn't let that happen to the three of you. I couldn't find you all dead, like Monsieur Lapeyre and my father, and pretend not to know what was going on when I watched the news."

Saif, at that moment, realized he was wrong. He took Lexi for a Westerner who had never suffered, had been given every indulgence in a pampered middle-class life, and didn't understand sacrifice. Death in any form was an equalizer. Whether you were wealthy and privileged, or poor and downtrodden, death was so horrific; it brought human emotions to the same level. It never allowed a person to view the world the same way again. Lexi now had this view of the world.

"And it seems I was right to go get you all." Lexi smiled and wiped away the final tear. "According to that guy … being … thingy, you all have adaptations *vital* to humanity."

"*We* all." John reminded Lexi. She was one of them now, part of the Club. Maybe he should make membership cards. He could even put a little hologram on them. She would get a kick out of that; it would put a little smile on her face.

"What about the others on the wall after us?" asked Lexi. "What will they bring to humanity's evolution? I can't even imagine. Hell, I would never have guessed that flashes or dreams or panic attacks or even seeing into the ultraviolet spectrum would be the key to humanity's evolution, but it seems they are. And these weirdo adaptations are so valuable they are worth killing for." She guessed what they had to do. "There is only one way to stop it. We have to take it down."

"And how do we do that?" quizzed Saif.

"Blow it up," replied Lexi, looking up at the Arc de Triomphe du Carrousel, not feeling the slightest bit of remorse.

"Blow up *the whole train station*?" challenged Marise in a combination of worry and shock.

"No, just the wall. We have to take it down before another person pops up on the glass."

"Birdy, we don't even know how it works," pleaded John, who was always on the side of gathering scientific information before resorting to destruction.

"True. And honestly, we may never understand how it works, but we know what it does. That's how they're getting their information, and if it's gone then they won't get it," she concluded. It felt good to be able to channel her anger to the situation and the wall.

Saif put his head down with the words "blow it up." "You realize doing this will make us terrorists." He looked at the faces of each person in the group. "From this point on, once you cross this line, you can never go back. Ever." He was speaking from a place he knew all too well. Once violence was the option and something was destroyed, it could never be put back together again. Or put the Jinn back in the bottle.

"Can anyone else think of another option to stop all of this?" questioned Lexi, who deliberately made eye contact with each person. No one uttered a word. "I can't."

"What if someone is hurt in the explosion?" asked Marise, looking even more worried.

"We only need to take down the wall. Small explosions at the four corners of the wall should bend the steel and break the glass wall," said Lexi.

"It has to be timed right," said Saif, realizing their minds had been made up. "No trains coming into the platform, unloading a bunch of people. Nighttime would be best. Or early morning."

"Agreed. I don't want anyone other than maybe these sentient beings hurt," remarked Lexi. "But they can't be around anyway, otherwise we'd never get close enough to the wall to leave the explosives."

Marise realized the long-term ramifications of a bomb going off in her city would be terrible. It would hurt the economy, tourists would be deterred from visiting Paris, and it would promote the continued perception that the French government had no control over extremist violence and the minority population. "I don't know, Alexandra."

"Marise, if we don't do this and take the chance, how many more people will be killed by these guys — a hundred, a thousand? I can't sit around waiting for the rest of my life. And that's not an option since I was on the wall. Think about it. How long had the wall already been up in Gare de Lyon? A week? A month? A year? How many other people have already been killed? We don't know. Were their sacrifices for nothing? For the past and future people, we have to do something. Don't you agree?"

Marise took a long moment. "*Oui*," she admitted. Right now, until they understood what the wall was and how it worked, there was no other option.

"Not to put a damper on all your plans, Birdy, but how do we get the explosives needed to bring down a wall in a foreign country?" asked John.

"I don't know where to get explosives," declared Marise, half-expecting everyone to look to her for a solution since she wasn't in a foreign country.

Saif looked down at the ground, disappointed. This was what he hated being brought to — A foolish stereotype brought on by a few radicals years ago. A stereotype that would probably never go away — at least until this generation was dead and gone. Of course, if another bunch of militant extremists decided to pull a last-ditch effort to drum up support and bomb something in the name of Islam, the stereotype would be fueled all over again. But that was not him. Saif wanted to be the antithesis of those men. He knew exactly what would come into a Western mind when he mentioned explosives. The correlation would be made without a thought. They would have to understand that, sometimes in life, circumstances were a bit more complicated than that. In fact, a lot more complicated. Stereotypes were easy. The truth was complex and hard. And things were about to get a lot harder.

"I do," said Saif softly.

Everyone turned and stared at Saif.

It was the judgmental looks he was afraid of. Thinking that he too was a terrorist and used his religion as justification for death. Why else would he have had explosive material readily available? If only it was that simple. But if they wanted to bring down the wall, he was their only option right now. "Come on. We'll have to go get it."

Saif, a bit downhearted by their reaction, began to walk ahead, as always. And with Saif leading the way to retrieve explosive materials, it meant only one destination: Department 93.

Assassins' Wall: Gare de Lyon

CHAPTER 38

M.E.D.

APARTMENT, DEPARTMENT 93, SEINE-SAINT-DENIS. MIDNIGHT.

Sunday

Saif was standing with his friend Mas'ud from the other apartment. They were in a small room surrounded by large computer server racks. Lights were blinking on and off from every shelf, and there were at least ten of them. The two friends stood close together, whispering in Farsi. "After you left, those two men just opened the door. I don't know how, Saif Ullah, it was locked — they walked right in and looked straight at me," said Mas'ud.

"Did they say anything?" questioned Saif.

"They said your name and then looked around the apartment for you."

"And they didn't touch you or harm you in any way?" asked Saif, worried.

"No. They walked right past me into the bathroom and then into the closet to look for you. After they checked the entire apartment, they left. They never said a word but for your name."

307

"Praise Allah Almighty. I'm so pleased, my friend, that you are unharmed." Saif put his hand on Mas'ud's arm.

"Do you know who they are working for? Are they from Iran?" inquired Mas'ud.

"No, Mas'ud, my friend, they are from no country we have ever encountered."

"After they left, I quickly packed up your laptop and then mine and abandoned that apartment."

"You were right to come here. We will need to go to the other apartment outside Paris immediately. We shouldn't stay here for too long, especially after we all do this," said Saif, pulling out a few backpacks from a box.

"I agree." Mas'ud picked up three bags from a shelf and walked into the next room.

On one side of a disorganized-looking room, was Lexi, John, and Marise, sitting silently. Computer parts, server racks, spare monitors, and other random pieces of furniture intermixed with piled-up boxes filled the other side of the main room of the apartment. It was almost an exact replica of the basement they were in earlier.

Mas'ud carried in the three bags, and then Saif with two other backpacks entered the room, closing the door behind him.

Mas'ud turned to Saif, still speaking only in Farsi. "Saif Ullah, are you sure you want to do this? This type of violence is the antithesis of everything we have fought for. Who you are. Are you doing this for them?" Mas'ud pointed at the motley, pathetic-looking group assembled across the room. Saif turned and looked at them as well.

"You have worked too long to let this bring you down and be labeled a terrorist." Mas'ud looked disdainfully at the group. "You are not. And do not think they will defend you if you are caught. They will use you as a scapegoat and make you out to be a terrorist since you are Persian. These Westerners do not appreciate or understand what you have sacrificed to get to this position."

Saif spoke kindly to Mas'ud. "It wasn't just me who is sacrificing. All of their lives will be permanently changed after this." He looked sympathetically at Lexi, John, and Marise, who were watching them interact. "They just don't realize *how* much yet." But how could they? Their societies had never truly prepared them for it. Those nations had enjoyed a child-like safety bubble. In truth, their lives started changing the minute they chose to follow Saif back to Department 93.

Mas'ud shook his head. He threw all the bags down on a small coffee table in front of the group, then finally addressed them in English. "Do not touch these with your bare hands." Mas'ud showed them his plastic gloves. "Put gloves on before you touch your disposable clothes. And here is your discard bag." Mas'ud held up a giant black bag.

Mas'ud turned to Saif, speaking in Farsi, "I pray to Allah Almighty that you know what you are doing, Saif Ullah Mohammad. And these Westerners do not lead you astray."

"Allah Almighty had led me this far, and to these people, Mas'ud. Who am I to question His will? And walk away from these people? With what I have seen today, Allah Almighty's glory is far greater than I ever thought possible." He understood where Mas'ud was coming from, but Mas'ud hadn't seen the Jinn's finger and been through all the panic attacks, only to realize his gift was from Allah Almighty.

Mas'ud looked disgusted and left the room.

Saif walked over to a box across the room and pulled out some plastic gloves.

"What was your friend saying to you, Saif?" asked Lexi, knowing full well the tone of voice and the pointing at them were not a good sign.

"He thinks this is a bad idea," explained Saif.

This brought a moment of relief for Marise. She wasn't the only one who thought this was a very bad idea. What surprised her was that her only ally was Saif's friend.

Saif handed each person plastic gloves to put on. He already had plastic gloves on as well. "Here, please put these on first." He then walked over to another box and pulled out oversized hoodie sweatshirts. "Then put these on over your current clothes. It may get a bit hot. And I'm afraid the baseball cap needs to be taken off, John. It's too recognizable."

"In my pocket, then," responded John, tightly rolling up the cap. He was not about to take his lucky cap off his body. They had been through too much, and John was too superstitious to change their luck. 'Go, Mets!'

From another battered box, Saif dug out a few oversized sweatpants. "These as well," he instructed, handing the clothes to the women. "We need to try to hide your shape from the cameras. These may at least conceal that you are women."

Everyone slowly took their time putting the clothes on over their original clothing. It was a bit difficult and cumbersome.

From a different box, Saif pulled out for himself a white Thawb — a long white traditional Middle Eastern men's robe — as well as a Bisht — a dark black cloak worn over the robe. "Also, it is important for you all to know, Mas'ud told me when the Jinn entered our apartment, they only looked for me and never harmed him."

"*C'est bien ce que je pensais*," whispered Marise to herself while putting on the too-large sweatpants.

John slipped on his discard sweatpants, which were a bit tight and small for his over six-foot frame. "How do you know your friend, Saif?"

Saif was putting on the Thawb over his clothes. "He is a colleague of mine. And a friend."

Marise finished putting on the gray hoodie and waited patiently. "What is your profession, Saif?"

He stopped putting on his discard clothes, looked around the apartment, and smiled. "I'm a computer programmer ... from Iran."

That stopped the whole group from dressing.

Saif walked over and touched the computer sitting on a table. "This," he said, tapping the laptop lovingly, "is my weapon."

"And how do you use that weapon?" Marise asked carefully.

A defensive rush rose up inside Saif. He was sick of the ignorant conclusions these Westerners always jumped to just because of his ethnicity. If they were going to blow up this wall together, then it was time to tell them the truth.

"I'm not a terrorist, if that's what you're all thinking!" he answered harshly. "I write computer programs and host forums so people in Iran and other Arab countries, who do not have access to the full World Wide Web, can view bits and pieces of the free internet, free news, and free videos. Not this censored internet they try and convince their people is the real World Wide Web. These leaders keep their people in cages, hoping it will allow them to stay in power. I believe that only by seeing their cage will the people inside them realize they have never been free. On my forum they can see what stories have been censored because of the content, what videos are forbidden, and get a glimpse of what is going on in the rest of the world. And if *they* choose, *they* can do something about it."

"You do all this on the internet?" questioned John.

"Not as you think of it. We use relay nodes in many different countries to cover the origin of the information and users' identities. We are constantly changing them to evade officials.

"Oh, my God," said Lexi surprised by the complexity.

"Mas'ud and I are the administrators who build and fund the relay nodes. We also are the moderators, oversee content, write the encryptions and the software."

"Can anyone find this forum using an internet browser?" asked John.

"No. You must know how to get to a bridge relay by downloading special software and knowing a like-minded person who can lead you to a relay and knows the encryptions. I repost Western articles, news, videos, and social media for people to see. Then hopefully they can share this information with others. It may not sound like a free internet to you all, but it is the closest thing people in censored countries have to freedom of speech."

The word "free" kept ringing in Lexi's ears. She felt horrible. Here this whole time she feared that Saif was a terrorist, or someone who was practically a terrorist. Not only was he not a terrorist, but he was a fighter for the freedoms she took for granted back home. And given the recent censorship in the states by search engines and social media giants, she got a taste of what a controlled internet felt like. "I apologize, Saif. I misjudged you."

"And I you, so we are equal. My friend," added Saif. Yes, many judgments were being made all over the world that were wrong, especially about the intentions of the Middle Eastern people. He didn't know any more if he and his opinions were the silent minority in Iran, or if they were now the silent majority; he did have almost five million people visiting his forums every day. And those people had to be silent. They didn't have the ability to tell the rest of the whole world they were there. They felt the truth in their hearts, as Saif knew in his — these anons were not alone. It was what kept him going.

"Is that why you said Arab men have been after you before?" pressed John.

"Yes. I have been arrested, even tortured, in other countries before. That is why we moved our operation to France. Do you all know that the French have the best resources to break into computers on the planet? I didn't know that until I got here. They almost shut down our relay nodes a few times. Their procedures and practices are inspirational. And with my newest idea I got this morning, even more censored countries will be after me when I am done."

"What's your idea?" asked John.

"Write a new program that can let anyone turn their computer into a relay." Saif smiled at the thought. All he needed was the time to write the code and set up another forum — not in France.

Lexi put on her black hoodie. She looked down, knowing Saif was right. It was hard to discern that she was a woman.

Everyone took a moment and a breath to look at one another in their discard clothes.

Saif pulled out two final pieces that finished his full Middle Eastern garb, a black Agal cord and a white Keffiyeh for his head.

"Why did you choose to wear this?" wondered Marise, pointing to his traditional outfit.

"I figured the Jinn seem Arab in appearance. When we are caught on the train station's security cameras leaving bags that take down the wall, the suspect profile of an Arab man in traditional attire will make it harder for the Jinn to continue using Arab faces as disguises. In the future, these three Jinn won't be able to just loiter around train stations, not without raising suspicion."

"That's a really smart move, Saif," said Lexi with quiet admiration in her voice.

"Yes. But it also puts me at higher risk as well. And feeds the stereotype that all Middle Eastern men are terrorists, but that can't be helped now. We will use perceptions to our advantage and then deal with it later. By that I mean *my* culture."

"Many older British men and woman are still prejudiced against the Germans for World Wars I and II," retorted John. "It takes time, Saif."

"Yes, but for now we can use prejudices to our, to humanity's advantage," said Saif. He picked up one of the backpacks. "Please keep the gloves on until the wall is down."

John took the backpack from Saif. "We must be careful with the explosives," warned Saif.

Saif walked into the next room and came back with a very small device. It was a single small plastic explosive, a little more than a cubic inch in size, strapped to a large chip and another plastic outer square with an opening for a single small battery. Small wires inside the cube and the device connected all the pieces. He carefully put it in John's bag.

"Saif, what are these?" asked Marise.

He walked back into the other room and picked up another one. "A device that performs a micro-explosion on our computers."

"Micro-explosion? I've never heard of that before," said Lexi.

"Mas'ud and I originated the idea ourselves. In the past we've needed to destroy our forums before they got into the wrong hands. We used to smash the hard drives by hand, piece by piece, which took too much time. On a few occasions we were almost caught.

"One day we were watching the news about the I.E.D.'s being used in Iraq and Afghanistan We figured a miniature version of that could be used to destroy a computer hard drive remotely. Now if we have to quickly change locations and our equipment has to be demolished, these Micro-Explosive Devices, or M.E.D.'s, destroy the drives."

Saif held up the cubed device that filled the palm of his hand. "The explosion itself is small." He examined the tiny square. "And we place these devices on the drives. No one gets hurt, besides the computer, that is." He took the second Micro-Explosive Device and put it strategically in John's bag.

"Forgive me," interjected John, watching Saif carefully handle the M.E.D. "I don't mean to state the obvious, but why don't you use laptops?"

Saif smiled. "They do not have the processing power and memory storage we need to run this relay node, or the physical locations needed for the forum members to have access to it." Saif nodded toward the door. "In the next room are the server racks that make up this core forum node. It has to exist somewhere."

"The M.E.D. is a very inventive way of solving your problem, Saif," said John. "Have you ever been caught since using them?"

"No. We almost did in Syria, but that's a long story," recounted Saif, placing another Micro-Explosive Device, this time in Marise's bag.

Marise stood up and walked to the room filled with the rows of large computer servers and a high-power air-conditioning system. "Is this your only core forum, Saif?"

"Oh no, the only one in Paris. We have them all over. That's the beauty. The relay nodes are always changing. One goes down, another comes up. It's almost impossible to follow. Not unless you know where to go."

Lexi got up and joined Marise at the door, looking at the light show of the servers hard at work. "Wow, Saif, I'm impressed. I had no idea any of this existed."

"Neither does the average Westerner." Saif joined them at the door and took out more M.E.D.'s. "This is all we have in Paris. I hope it's enough to bring down the wall."

"It will be if they are placed at structurally weak points," replied Lexi, watching Saif place an M.E.D. in her bag. "I know this may sound weird, Saif, but it makes me feel better knowing we are only using small, controlled explosions at key points to bring down the wall. It's kind of like a building demolition. Not an explosion that will hurt people."

"I agree. That is why we made them so small, that and a little thermite." Saif gingerly placed Lexi's bag down, then picked up an old-school burner cell phone. "We set it off remotely using mobile phones."

Lexi raised her eyebrows.

"Don't worry, this phone wasn't on any known French telecom network. I wouldn't be foolish enough to do that." He put the small mobile phone in his pocket.

"I'm praying Mas'ud won't have to abandon this site soon."

"And if he does?" challenged Marise, walking over to Saif.

"He will have to remotely overwrite the hard drives, which can take hours."

"How long have you been in France, Saif?" asked Marise.

"A year or so. He should be safe here. But we will have to move after the wall comes down. The French government will step up their 'anti-terrorist' searches."

As Saif double checked his preparations, the level of complexity and thought he put into his actions astounded Lexi. She never would have thought of a lot of this. As she gazed down at all the random discard clothes, then to the small backpacks and bags, the implications of what she was about to do hit her for the first time. A hollow pit suddenly plummeted into her stomach and a piercing sensation hit like she had never felt before. She started shaking a little. "I'm afraid."

"Of what, Birdy?" questioned John.

"Of all of it! I'm afraid to go back into Gare de Lyon after being up on the wall. I don't know how all of you had the courage to do it. The last place on earth I want to go right now is that train station. I'm afraid something will go wrong with the M.E.D.'s and a human might get hurt. I'm afraid of getting caught after bringing down the wall. But mostly I'm afraid of *them*.

"It means humanity is truly not alone anymore and that scares the *SHIT* out of me! I really thought with all the science fiction I've read and watched over the years that I would be OK with this, but after being on the wall I realized I'm not."

No one spoke or moved.

"And I'm afraid because they are so much more technologically advanced than we are. I've looked at the wall. There is no known mechanical reason why it works. It's beyond us. They are beyond us. And they are killing people. And we don't even know how yet! It's funny, I thought my worst fear was being up on the wall. But I was wrong. It's sentient beings from another planet that are more advanced than us and *malevolent*."

No one moved an inch.

"I'm afraid and I don't want to do this." Lexi was now visibly shaking even more.

John walked over to her and lightly wrapped his arms around her. He looked around the room at the other concerned faces staring at Lexi. The answer was obvious. Each person in the room was on edge, just holding their breath waiting. "We're all afraid, Lexi. You're not alone."

Everyone had their own specific fears: Lexi of the beings' technological superiority, Marise of the bombing of her beautiful Paris, John of the lack of control and scientific understanding of the situation, and Saif of hurting innocent people with his explosives. There was enough fear to go around and then some.

"Do you still want to go through with this, Lexi?" Saif stepped closer to her and John, who was still holding on tight.

"We have no choice. The wall has to come down. It's the only way to stop the killings," she said mournfully. "As long as we are together in this."

John let go of Lexi and quietly nodded yes. One by one, Saif and Marise nodded yes, as well.

"OK," agreed Lexi. The group consensus didn't diminish her shaking or her primal desire not to be any part of this but doing what needed to be done to save human lives won her over. Monsieur Lapeyre. This was for him.

Saif got one more M.E.D. from the next room.

"Where did you learn how to do all of this, Saif, since you're a computer programmer?" asked Lexi.

Saif didn't look up as he returned. He couldn't bear to see their reactions when he said this. "In an old al-Qaeda Jihadist core forum. Nothing is ever truly erased on the internet." He waited, putting the M.E.D. in the backpack. Without looking up to witness the grim look on all their faces, he added, "It was the only place to find the manufacturing manual for an I.E.D.," he finished, figuring that would shut them up for a while. And it did.

CHAPTER 39

Realization

STREETS, PARIS. EARLY MORNING.

All four walked along in silence, heading toward their final destination, Gare de Lyon. Each person was covered from head to toe, hoodies up, sweating in the discard clothes, and carrying bags filled with volatile explosives.

The weight of what Lexi was about to do got heavier with each step closer to the station. She silently prayed that she didn't have her own version of Saif's panic attack when she placed her backpack filled with M.E.D.'s by the wall.

Saif and Marise were walking side by side ahead of Lexi and John. The streets at this time of early morning were empty and silent. Not a lot happens in Paris pre-5 a.m. on a Sunday.

"I've been thinking," disclosed Marise. The streets were so quiet that it wasn't a problem for John and Lexi to hear her clearly. "I'm almost one hundred percent sure they aren't human, but I have been thinking about what he said about the EVO squad."

"Yes," said Saif, turning to her. It was the first time he chose to position himself within the whole group, rather than walking ahead.

"And about what he said about human evolution," said Marise.

John spoke up from behind. "Yes," he said, taking a step in closer to get right behind Marise.

"And about our adaptations." Marise looked lost in thought for a moment. "He said they are killing off everyone from the wall who had some kind of evolutionary adaptation that will move the human race forward."

"Yes, the sentient being did. I'm not calling him an alien, by the way, it sounds a little hokey after everything we've been through," pronounced Lexi, stepping in close behind her.

"What does *hokey* mean?" asked Marise.

"Oh, cliché, corny, antiquated. These guys are all too real for that old-school name."

John realized even he was having a hard time coming up with another answer to explain the finger. He had watched Lexi cut it off, and to admit that the finger was a fake would mean, by proxy, that Lexi would have been in on any deception. He quickly turned and glanced at her. He could see that she was still shaking a little, apprehensive about what they were about to do. If she were part of the EVO squad operation, then why be nervous? And for that matter, why did she warn him then? The only conclusion was that Lexi was not a liar, and the finger wasn't a fake. The digit she had excised was indeed real. The next cognitive leap was to believe either (A) there was a sub-species of humanoid beings originating on Earth whom humans had never found before to study their physiology, or (B) the beings weren't from Earth at all. Either choice was a huge scientific leap for him.

"I have a theory," declared Marise. "What the sentient beings ..."

"Thank you," Lexi interrupted gratefully from behind.

"... are doing will not kill off all the adaptations that will move human evolution forward, but rather more adaptations like ours will survive."

"How?" asked Saif.

"We obviously have abilities or adaptations that allow us to survive this hostile environment — there must be a reason."

"Which is ...," said John.

"They have them wrong," answered Marise.

"What wrong?" asked Lexi.

"Our adaptations."

Everyone walked in silence for a moment.

"Because *our* adaptations are how we have survived: by your stomach, Saif, my dreams, John's flashes, and Lexi's eyes. All of these prevented us from being put in harm's way. Those beings couldn't kill us off *because* of our adaptations. Whoever put our names on the wall, if they had the correct adaptations, they would realize what we could do. They would know that our adaptations would prevent us from being killed. They must be wrong."

"Which meant there will be more people with our kind of adaptations surviving," said Lexi.

"*Oui*, I believe so," affirmed Marise.

"If that is true ..." pondered John, thinking deeply.

"It would explain the four us," replied Marise.

"And more to come, which is why we have to take down that wall, *NOW!* More and more humans are evolving toward *The Great Connection*." Lexi paused for a moment. "Does anyone else think that's kind of a weird thing to say? I would have guessed "The Great Connection" would be the knowledge that human beings are not alone in the universe: a Great Connection with other sentient beings from all over the universe. Instead, he said that in the Great Connection humans would have 'adaptations that would surpass them all,'" she said, mimicking the being's voice and cadence. "Let me ask you, how is that a Connection?"

"Yes, it's an odd turn of phrase, Lexi," acknowledged John. "Perhaps the word connotation has a different meaning for him. My guess is English wasn't his first language." John smiled at her.

"Or his second," mused Saif, reminded that he'd seen the Jinn understand Arabic, French, and English during their interactions. Maybe the Jinn had a way to understand all human languages. It was time to start thinking of any possibility, even if it sounded outrageous, to explain the Jinn. It might be the only way to be prepared for whatever lay ahead.

"Then what are we up on the wall *for*?" wondered John, in frustration. No one answered. No one knew. But if Marise was correct, there had to be a specific reason why, maybe even a reason potentially beyond his flashes or the others' abilities. He needed to find the connective tissue between all four of them. It was the key to their survival. He had no idea what it was yet, but he felt it was hovering just out of reach.

Assassins' Wall: Gare de Lyon

S   J

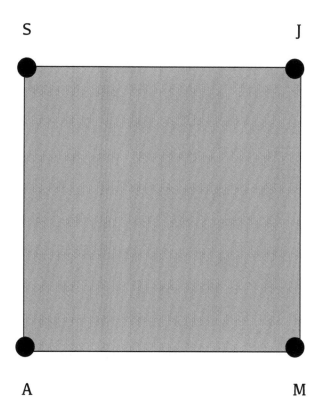

A   M

{A, M, J, S}

A *square* has four equal sides and four
right angles working together to create a
shape on a 2-dimensional plane.

(n = 2)

Assassins' Wall: Gare de Lyon

CHAPTER 40

The End and the Beginning

GARE DE LYON. PARIS. EARLY MORNING.

It would be a very long time before any of them ever walked into Gare de Lyon again — if they ever walked in again. They agreed beforehand, so not to raise any suspicion, that each person would walk in alone, place their bag down in their chosen corner of the wall, and then leave. And when the next person saw the previous person finish, they would start heading into the main terminal. That way none of them were seen together.

Lexi volunteered to walk into Gare de Lyon first. She asked to go first. Everyone assumed it was because she was the first to realize what was going on with the wall. But that wasn't the reason. She had a plan. She secretly worried that, despite the early hour, a new face would already be up on the wall. And by being first, she had time. It put a pit the size of a grapefruit in her stomach to think that *she* was the last person on the wall. She couldn't remove herself from it anymore. She was in its blood. She was part of the wall. But perhaps she could remove the next victim.

Walking into the station, Lexi purposely chose the same entrance she used four days ago. She couldn't believe it had only been four days. It felt like a lifetime ago, when she was the unexceptional tourist admiring the innovative holographic face 'Art' on the sculpture glass wall. This entrance was the beginning and the end of Gare de Lyon for her.

It was very early in the morning. The first trains were set to roll in any minute, and Lexi wasn't exactly sure when. It never occurred to her to look at the train schedule since she wasn't taking a train out of Paris. She hoped Saif or Marise knew exactly when the trains came in and that was why they picked this time. But it was probably an assumption they made, as well.

NOTE TO SELF: Stop making assumptions.

From the hallway entrance, she looked around the main floor of the station, and as luck would have it, it was completely deserted. Despite her fears, whomever unlocked the doors pre-5 a.m. was already gone. The universe had someone open up the station at the right time and by grace there was no one around, which meant they could leave the bags, bring down the wall, and no one would get hurt.

Gare de Lyon laid bare and empty seemed like a very lonely place. It was kind of like a stadium sitting empty before a game. It was a place that was designed to hold people, to serve a purpose, and without those people it seemed to have no soul. No real reason for existing. It always made her sad to see a huge, hundred-thousand-seat stadium sitting empty. Just as Gare de Lyon made her sad right now. She kind of felt sorry for the station. It was just an innocent bystander in all of this. It didn't put up the wall. It was doing its job without complaining or objecting for more than a hundred years. Poor old Gare de Lyon. It really was a beautiful train station.

Lexi looked to her left, over to the other entrance on this side of the station. Saif was sneaking up to the main floor. If he felt anything in his stomach, he would immediately make a "no" signal and end this whole mission. Saif nodded his head yes, meaning all is clear and it was OK for her to go into the station to drop off the first bag.

She looked across the station over to the wall. Her heart froze in anticipation as she turned her head. The wall was empty. She briefly sighed in relief. She half expected to see herself up there again, even though none of the others' images had been reposted. Better to be prepared. She wasn't last time, and the shock had almost broken her.

Lexi turned back to Saif and shook her head no, the signal that no one was on the wall. It was time. She was still shaking a little as she made her way across the floor of the main terminal. She looked at the empty benches, the Express café, and the little pastry kiosk that made its happy home under the destination board, which was lifeless at this time of morning. But lifeless was good. It meant no one would be killed.

As she approached the glass wall, Lexi looked up at the second pane of glass: the source of all their troubles. She marched

333

over to the farthest right side of the wall, the side closest to the destination board. At the bottom where the steel support beams met, she put down her bag on the ground, hands shaking. She silently prayed and took in a deep breath, hoping that this did indeed work and the wall would be destroyed in a few minutes.

After she put the bag down, Lexi took a few large steps back to look at the wall again. It was her moment to say good-bye to it. She really did think it was beautiful the first time she saw it. But now all she saw was death.

"This wall was death," she said both to herself and to the wall, so it could hear her. She wanted *IT* to know, she knew what was is, and she was calling it out for the world to hear. Its secret had been discovered.

Lexi glanced down at her bag again, to double check that it was in the proper position before leaving the train station. It looked ready to go; all it needed were the three others to join in for the wall to come down. She planned on going home to New York and not entering another train station in the foreseeable future, even the subway. She intended on taking cabs or Ubers around the city. Well, as long as she could afford it. She was realistic. Cabs were expensive. The train was cheap in comparison. *BUT NO TRAIN STATIONS!*

She thought of maybe taking a quick picture of the wall. But that seemed a bit morbid. It reminded her of the late-nineteenth-century Victorian practice of taking pictures of your deceased loved ones, especially children, to remember what they looked like. Taking a picture of the wall felt like doing the same thing, but this wasn't her baby. It would soon be down and dead. Instead, she opted for one last look at the top to try and burn its image into her memory. It would be hard to forget.

Taking another small step back, she slowly observed the glass wall. Her eyes made it up a few feet. "Oh, shit!" she howled, so loudly that her words reverberated throughout the empty station.

Marise, toting the second backpack, had barely entered the main terminal when she heard Lexi's distress call. Abandoning any attempt at casual stealth, Marise ran to the wall.

"What? Another name?" Marise called from behind, quickly making her way over.

Lexi was transfixed and horrified. "NO!" she wailed again even louder.

Marise rushed to Lexi, "*Qu'est ce que c'est?*"

On the wall in the second pane of glass was a holographic picture of a man. Lexi was staring up at him; her eyes were filled with his picture. Then she lifted her head up even farther, to the square above. "There are TWO!"

"Non!" Marise screeched at the wall, as though it could hear or care about what she was saying.

"It's in the square above the other one!" shouted Lexi, pointing to the third square from the bottom. There it was — a beautiful holographic 3-D face of a blonde woman. The two faces were too much for her to process. Lexi froze. She stared up at the wall with her mouth agape. "Oh, my God!" she said slowly. The two faces — a man, and a woman — stared blankly out into Gare de Lyon.

"I don't understand. The wall has only ever shown one person before!" squealed Lexi in confusion. If ever there was a doubt in her mind about taking down the wall before, now she felt truly justified in blowing it up. Two new targets. It probably had to do with all the people the aliens had failed to murder. The four of them! Now they — whomever controlled the wall — were putting two faces up at a time to make up for it, so they could catch up. Or maybe there were an increasing number of adaptations that need to be killed off?

Still staring up at the faces high on the wall, Lexi reached into her pocket and pulled out the plastic baggie with the cut-off finger. She retrieved the gooey finger out of the plastic bag. "I have to take them down."

The finger felt rubbery and cold to the touch, and it was still dripping with what looked like a yellow mucus. "Aww, yuck," Lexi said, watching as the finger continually dripped out fluid.

Lexi stepped directly below the wall. She looked up at the steel frame high above her head. She strategically placed the cut-off finger in her left hand, between her thumb and index finger. She jumped up, grabbing the steel frame, trying to do a pull-up like she used to do in high school. Lexi struggled to even pull her head up to the second pane of glass. With the cut-off finger in her hand, only her right hand was able to hold the full pressure since the left couldn't grab the frame firmly. The slimy finger was ruining her grip. She barely had the leverage to pull her head up past the steel frame. Her left hand slipped, and she dropped back to where she started on the ground.

For the first time, Lexi was in awe of the sentient beings. They were not just technologically superior to human beings, but also physically superior. The amount of effortlessness they displayed while getting up to the second pane of glass was remarkable.

While Lexi tried to figure out a way to pull back up, Marise realized there was no time to waste. She quickly walked over and placed her backpack down in the right interior frame of the wall, where the center opening met the ground. Two bags down, two more to go.

It was time for another plan of attack. Lexi needed both hands to pull up, leaving only one option. She quickly put the cut-off finger in her mouth, like a flamenco dancer holding a rose. It tasted like a dirt pie with a hint of roses. She jumped up again, grabbing the steel frame, pulling up with even more of a struggle. She managed, with a tremendous effort, to get her head up and over the steel frame. Once she caught her breath, she quickly maneuvered her elbows in place, bracing them on the steel frame. Her face was staring directly at the second pane of glass.

That's when she realized her next big problem. The finger was pointed in the wrong direction. It was parallel to the glass. She had to turn it around so the fingertip could press against it. She couldn't grab the finger with her hands because it was taking all her arm strength just to keep herself up. If she let go with one hand, she would fall, and she probably wouldn't have the arm strength to get back up here again. She could try and turn the finger in her mouth with her tongue, but there was so much yellow goo coming out the end of it. For the fingertip to touch the glass, she would get the yellow mucus inside her mouth, and she didn't want to swallow any of that muck. Lord only knows what that junk was. It could be poisonous to humans. The only other option was for her to turn her whole head and move it forward.

Lexi maneuvered her head left; the fingertip was now facing the glass. She slowly leaned forward. Her shoulders and arms were shaking from the strain. The steel frame was at least five inches deep. She made it forward only a few inches.

"LEXI! Saif's right! Get down from the wall!" roared John from below, breaking the eerie silence. Lexi turned her head to look down, finger still in mouth. Standing directly underneath her was John, who looked very upset. Goo from the finger splattered all over his discard sweatshirt.

Marise surveyed the station. Saif was barely halfway to the wall, still in the middle of the station. He hadn't been within earshot, not without yelling, loudly.

Having heard John's howl, Saif approached from across the station when he heard his name. "What is it?" Their quiet plan was slowly crumbling.

"You just told Lexi to get down." John replied, watching Saif rush up to the group.

"No, my friend, I never said anything." Saif took John's bag from him and walked toward his designated third corner, the left center opening, to put it down.

By this time Lexi was hanging on by a pinkie. Her head, shoulders, and arms were barely clinging to the steel frame. She was shaking from the strain of keeping herself up, and her chin was dripping with a combination of the yellow mucus and her saliva.

John angrily yelled at Saif while Saif placed John's bag down in the third corner. "Yes, you did! I just heard you! You told Lexi to get down off the wall."

"No, my friend," answered Saif calmly, "I did not."

John looked to Marise for support, but she shook her head. "No. He never said a word, John."

Saif looked up at Lexi, who was losing her grip on the wall. She had slipped down a few more inches, and her face was barely above the steel frame. "But John's right, Lexi. The wall will be down before they can read the names. Please come down now."

Her left arm finally gave out and she fell, not to the ground, but to her first position before the pull-up. She hung like a ragdoll from the steel frame. Using her now free hand, she took the finger out her mouth, still managing to hold onto the frame with just one hand. "Eww. This thing tastes *nasty*. We should write down their names, just in case."

Saif walked over to put his backpack down on the fourth and last corner, at the far left of the wall. "No. You're wasting time. Get down, please. Before they come back."

"Fine," she retorted, knowing it was time to give up. "I really didn't have enough strength to pull up again anyway."

She finally let go, and John caught her by the waist. "Thanks," she said in a tone of disappointment, not at him, but at the knowledge that she didn't complete her mission. She pulled out the clear baggie and placed the finger back inside. It still had a never-ending flow of yellow mucus coming out of it. It should have drained itself out by now. A human finger would have. How much fluid can one finger hold?

Saif looked over from the fourth corner to the group standing together. "You all go. I'll meet you outside in a few minutes. I need to double check the placement of the components and put in the batteries."

Lexi, Marise, and John started toward the exit.

John watched Lexi as they walked. He had to admit the sight of her up on the wall had disturbed him beyond belief. She could have hurt herself or fallen down. When he heard Saif yell, it echoed his own feelings. She needed to get down. He couldn't believe Saif said nothing. He heard him clear as a bell. A man's voice was right next to his ear, but Saif was yards away. Maybe there was an echo in the station that carried his voice?

After finishing with his backpack, Saif moved over to John's bag, opened it, and checked the positions of the M.E.D.'s and the electrical wires. He put a small battery in the device. He needed to make sure all the components hadn't shifted or disconnect while they were walking to the station, and that no critical parts had fallen off. It was a very delicate explosive that had only been used on stationary hard drives, never jostled inside a bag before. Who knew the damage that could have happened in motion? They would need all four bags to detonate in order to bring the wall down.

Saif wanted to slowly take out the M.E.D.'s from one large bag and put them in each individual backpack in the station, but that would have been too obvious for the cameras and too time-consuming. Which was probably for the best. Lexi's stunt cost them valuable time. They didn't know when the Jinn would be back. The thought of the Jinn put a little stab deep in his stomach.

Lexi, John, and Marise were more than halfway across the station. Lexi turned around to stare at the wall and the two faces. John watched her longingly look back. "You wouldn't have been able to reach the second picture, Birdy. It's too high up."

"I know. I should've had you climb up." She looked at John, who was over six feet tall. He could have easily just jumped up with the finger and taken the second picture off the wall. "I wasn't thinking."

"I wouldn't have been able to reach the second one, either." five yards was a bit of a stretch, even for him. He probably could have made it if he really, really, really tried, using the frame as a pivot, but he didn't want to upset her with that fact right now.

As they approached the main exit, Lexi took in her last view of Gare de Lyon: the architecture, the stairs up to Le Train Bleu, and its green color. She remembered initially thinking the color was warm and inviting. She never got the chance to look up what the color green meant in Goethe's *Theory of Colours*. But could she say the color was warm and inviting now? No. But green was the color of life. Photosynthesis. Light into energy. It is the color that made life possible on this planet. And they were fighting for that now. Life. Human life on Earth ... Paris was green.

As she panned the station, she saw them. Coming in from the other entrance on the opposite side of the station were the two sentient beings. All she could do was quickly breathe in air, making a loud "Huh." John and Marise quickly turned at the sound and saw them walking across the main floor. Lexi glanced over to the wall and to Saif who was already looking up, watching the Jinn walk across the station toward him. He had made it all the way to Marise's backpack, checking its position and was putting in the batteries for the explosives when the feeling started, a sharp stab in his stomach. He knew what it meant. The Jinn were approaching.

Saif quickly put the batteries in the M.E.D. He still had to finish working on Marise's backpack then move on to Lexi's bag. He had to have all four bags working. If he called out to the others to warn them, they may have rushed to the wall. And he didn't want that. If all else failed and he was here finishing with the bags when the Jinn arrived ... Saif stopped for a moment, taking in a deep breath to quell both the stabbing pain and his realization.

He was prepared to go down with the wall. A tear rolled down his bright red face. It surprised him how quickly he made the decision. But he understood in his heart, he must stop the killing of human beings and the only way to stop it was for the wall to come down and the Jinn to lose their target list.

Saif finished putting the last battery in Marise's backpack. He quickly peeked up. The Jinn still hadn't seen him hunched down, next to the wall. He swiftly ran, half hunched over from pain, along the backside of the wall to Lexi's bag and squatted down. He glanced up toward the Jinn again. They still hadn't seen him. He pulled out the mobile phone from his pocket, holding it in one hand, ready to press the code. With the other hand he unzipped Lexi's bag.

"No ..." said Lexi breathlessly, as she and the rest of the group watched Saif install the batteries in her bag. She looked at the beings; they were only now passing the destination board. They would see him any second.

John knew why Saif was holding his mobile phone at the ready. It took him only a few seconds to figure out what Saif was prepared to do. And he couldn't allow that. Not without at least trying to help him. He watched Saif quickly peek again. He realized he had to give Saif a little more time to finish — just enough to put the battery in the other M.E.D.

John lightly pushed both Marise and Lexi toward the exit, then stepped further inside the station toward Saif. He turned around to the women. "Get outside," he said so low it was barely audible. He took another few steps forward, as the two beings passed the destination board. He was not going to let Saif go through this alone.

"SAIF!" yelled John from across the station. He was prepared to go get him. He was a decent-sized, tall, sturdily built man, and the two beings looked smaller than him, so if worse came to worst he could fight the two of them off, until Saif got away. Fight then flight. It wouldn't be the first time.

The two beings observed John and quickly started running toward him at a fast pace.

John stepped another foot closer, waiting for their impact.

The women didn't fully retreat down the small hallway. They stood back, monitoring the spectacle breathlessly, waiting to see if they were needed. They were all in this together. If Saif was unable to input the code to blow up the wall, then Lexi or Marise would do it. Saif showed all of them what sequence of numbers to press. Just in case. It was generous of John to be chivalrous, but the women knew they were the back-up of the back-up plan. The wall had to come down. No matter what.

Saif peeked again, not wanting to make too much movement. The Jinn were less than ten meters away. He quickly placed the battery in the last M.E.D. and zipped up Lexi's bag, still holding onto his cell phone. He immediately began sprinting toward the opposite doorway, away from John and the Jinn.

Only with that flash of movement did the beings notice Saif leave the bottom of the wall. The two beings immediately turned their attention away from John to Saif, who was running across the main floor, past the escalators.

"GO!" screamed Saif to the others.

At the sight of Saif running across the station, Lexi and Marise turned and ran down the hallway toward the exit. Their movement caught the attention of their pursuers.

John waited at the beginning of the hallway to see if he needed to help Saif again.

The two beings pursued Saif across the main floor, ran past the benches and then the escalators. Within a few feet of Saif, one of the two swiftly turned around to stare at the wall. He saw the bags placed at each corner. *Those strange bags didn't belong there, which meant only one thing.* He grabbed the other one by the arm to stop him from running after Saif. They twisted around toward the wall and began racing toward it. They must leave their prey. *That is Saif Ullah Muhammad from the wall... And the man who called out from across the station is John Michael Edward Stanton Barry. And the two women who were in the hallway are Marise Louise André and Alexandra Julian Peters. All four joined together. They know. And are working together. How?* But their prey was far less important than the portal.

When John saw the beings give up on Saif and turn back toward the wall, he started sprinting to the exit.

Lexi and Marise made it outside the main door of Gare de Lyon and ran into the large plaza in front. They stopped and waited.

Saif barely made it to the hallway of the main terminal. He clutched his side from his panic attack — no, his adaptation.

His face was flushed, and tears of pain ran down his cheeks. He rotated around and saw the Jinn running toward their bags. As they reached down to grab one, each in a separate corner, he pressed the code #517517 into the mobile phone.

The beings and the bags ignited. The bottom half of the glass wall blew up. The light from the four synchronized explosions momentarily blinded Saif. The wall cracked slowly at the bottom from the explosion down below, then it crashed down in deafening shards.

The explosion was much larger than Saif had planned to detonate. He realized that he put too many M.E.D.'s in each bag. He quickly scanned around the rest of the station. Not a single human being was in sight. He silently said a prayer of thanks as he started running down the hallway.

John was finally outside when the vibration from the explosions momentarily stumbled his gait. It felt like a mini earthquake.

Lexi and Marise, waiting in the plaza, jumped from the rumble of the explosion. John made it up to them and they all waited anxiously, looking at the exits for what felt like an eternity, until Saif ran through the door.

When he reached the three standing together, he yelled, "Keep moving!" He ran ahead of them, having the momentum from his sprint. They quickly followed behind.

At the end of the plaza Saif, trailed by the others, made a left-hand turn on the boulevard, quickly crossing the street, on the same path toward the river they traversed earlier that night. All four ran down the street, away from Gare de Lyon, away from the wall, and away from the malevolent beings. Forever.

After making it a block down the street, Saif stopped. He ducked in an alley behind a café, no external cameras were in sight, and he quickly took off his clothes since he was wearing the most recognizable outfit. The ladies stepped in front of him, blocking the view from the street, and John blocked the view from the alley. Once Saif was finished, which took barely a few seconds, he rolled the clothes up in a ball and everyone continued running together down the street toward the river.

"Did it get them?" asked Lexi, keeping pace next to Saif.

"Yes," answered Saif. He could have taken down the wall without killing the Jinn, but they knew his face, knew his friends' faces, even Mas'ud. The Jinn had to go down with the wall or they never would have stopped pursuing them.

"Are you *sure* those beings were killed?" repeated John, running at a decent jog but nowhere near the speed at which he left his hotel the day before.

"Yes. Very sure," confirmed Saif. "No living creature, wherever they were from, could have survived that explosion. It was big."

"Was anyone else in there?" questioned Marise, a strain in her voice. She lagged a bit behind, continually looking back down the street at Gare de Lyon in the distance, waiting for the police to arrive, but the street remained empty and quiet.

"No. No humans were in the main terminal," insisted Saif.

"Oh, thank God," said Lexi. A huge wave of relief washed over her. The thought of accidentally hurting a living human being ... She had decided deep down in her heart that if anyone besides those sentient beings were hurt in any way from the explosions, she would turn herself in immediately. It was the right thing to do. She would take full responsibility for her actions and the bringing down of the wall.

"Yes, Allah Almighty has been gracious tonight."

The streets were still empty at this time of morning, another fortuitous circumstance that allowed them to run without questioning eyes observing their escape. Marise was a little bit worried when it came to security cameras all over Paris. Other cities, including London, had hundreds of thousands of them constantly being monitored by police on every street corner. The French, as usual, took an old-fashioned viewpoint of life and technology. They were hesitant to embrace that level of full surveillance, not wanting to infringe on a person's "*liberté.*" And that hopefully allowed them to take down the wall. France, in part, was responsible for saving all the people who would have been up on the wall. If she had a glass of wine in her hand she would declare a toast, "*Vive la France!*" It was impossible for her to love her country more, and she needed a glass of red wine, from the Bordeaux region, immediately.

"And the wall?" questioned Marise, making sure.

"Gone," replied Saif, making a sharp right turn at the end of the boulevard onto the street that parallels the river.

Lexi smiled to herself. It was over. The wall was down. The sentient beings were gone. No one was going to be up on the wall ever again. It was all worth it. Monsieur Lapeyre's death was not in vain. All of the proverbial leaps she made, they all made, were worthwhile. Tears filled up her eyes. The whole experience was beyond belief. And it was all over. She was ready to go home. She pulled out her phone and immediately texted her mother, typing, "I'm leaving Paris soon."

"Make a left turn on the bridge. The Université is not far down the river. My sister is meeting us there," revealed Marise.

The group turned left and crossed the bridge. As soon as they were over, they made another hard left turn and continued walking down the sidewalk, the river still on their left.

Marise opened up the discard bag. Saif immediately put his large pile of clothes in the bag, then took it from her. They slowly began to take off their discard clothes, hoodies, gloves, and sweatpants.

"You knew this area the whole time since we are so close to your work?" asked Lexi, taking off her hoodie and putting it into the large discard bag.

"*Oui*. This is my arrondissement," answered Marise, who already had her discard sweatshirt off.

"No wonder you looked so at ease," said John, having a bit of trouble walking and taking off his sweatpants. He stopped at a tree along the walkway, leaning on it for stability.

"Except in *Departement 93: une zone de sécurité prioritaire*," said Marise, who was also having trouble walking and taking off her sweatpants. It seemed human beings did not have the art of taking off pants while walking down to a science.

John understood how Marise felt about that neighborhood. It was the only time this whole trip that he was uncomfortable as well, besides when he was running out of the hotel. He could hardly wait to return home to London. Take a moment to sit and relax without the fevered rush of where to go next and whom to save. Most importantly, there would be no more flashes. He had had enough flashes in the last week to last him a lifetime.

This trip to Paris was not what John intended to have. He truly believed he would go visit all the tourist sights, starting with the Arc de Triomphe since that was the first flash. And he never even made it to the arch itself, only seeing it from a distance. But now it was time to go back home, play with his dog and not think about any train stations, glass walls, or yellow-mucus-dripping fingers, ever again.

Actually, who he really wanted to see was his mother. He had so many questions to ask her about his flashes. His memory was a bit hazy, especially from when he was really young. He needed to ask her if she ever noticed a pattern to the flashes. Did she or anyone else in the family have them? He couldn't remember ever talking about it with her; he just remembered her reacting to the flashes as if they were a normal occurrence.

Right now, he was so desperate to sit down, have a cup of tea, eat his favorite chocolate digestive biscuits, and tell his mum everything that happened in Paris. She always loved a good tale and this one was worth at least three cups of tea, two sandwiches, and a whole box of biscuits. And he longed to be home and hear his real name, the name all his loved ones and closest friends used. John was his formal name. The name work colleagues and strangers used when they first met him. Now, his heart yearns to be called Michael.

Walking very fast down the street, John saw it.

Flash: A glass wall.

He stopped a moment after taking off his discard sweatshirt. He looked at Saif, who was next to Lexi.

"Saif, are you *sure* the wall went down?" He checked, unsure of himself and what he just saw. Maybe it was just his imagination replaying events. It had all been a bit traumatic. His blood pressure was still high, and his face felt flush from all the running and the adrenaline of the wall coming down. He pulled out the Mets baseball cap from his back pocket and put it on, found his pack of cigarettes and lit one up.

"Yes, my friend, I saw it come down with my own eyes," answered Saif, still carrying the discard bag since he was the only person in everyday clothes.

Everyone was breathing heavily, and they all finally put the last bits of clothing into the bag. For the first time they were following Marise down the sidewalk.

Lexi was finally back in her own clothes and ready to return to the States, eat junk food, drive down to D.C., visit her mom, and see her Dad's grave. She couldn't take the train right now even if she wanted to. And maybe she would go to a Mets game. She looked over at John. He was wearing the baseball cap and staring down at the ground. Perhaps John wanted to come to New York to see a Mets baseball game? Honestly, she had to admit, it felt good just to be thinking about normal things, anything other than the wall.

Lexi did a double take when she saw John put the cigarette to his mouth. "What's wrong, John? Is everything OK?"

John snapped out of his little trance, looking up from the ground. "Why? What made you say that?"

"You're smoking. You said you smoke when you're upset. Are you worried about the bombing?"

"No," replied John.

Flash: A glass wall sat in the middle of a busy train station. People are walking below it and around it. It stood gleaming.

John blinked his eyes and continued walking down the street in silence, taking another very long drag from his cigarette. This time there was no mistaking it. This wasn't his mind replaying events. It was worse. A pit, much like what he imagined Saif must feel, settled into his stomach.

The whole group continued walking quickly in silence. The distant sound of police sirens could be heard over the river. Not a word was said among them. Lexi kept looking over at John, waiting for an answer.

John finally turned to his friends walking beside him, trying to build up the courage to speak. They would not want to hear what he was about to say. He spoke hesitantly. "I have something to tell you all."

Everyone slowed the fast-walking pace to focus on John.

"I just had another flash."

The group slowed their walk down to a crawl.

"What was it, my friend?" asked Saif.

"A glass wall."

"Gare de Lyon's wall?" pressed Lexi, who couldn't believe what she was hearing, not after what they just went through. She silently prayed it was a flash from the past, not the future. But did John have flashes about the past? He never specified.

"At first, I thought it could be. But I've noticed something about my flashes recently. They are telling me what direction I needed to go in." John paused for a moment to think and take another puff from his cigarette. "I've been thinking about something we haven't considered or even dared to contemplate. What if that wasn't the only wall?"

This was a visible blow to everyone in the group except John. No one spoke for a while. The implications of this suggestion were beyond words. And the truth was no one was in any place to hear it.

"*Mon Dieu*!" Marise finally uttered to herself.

"I never thought that was a possibility. I was so focused on this one, it never occurred to me there might be another one," said Lexi.

"John, do you know where it is? The new wall you're seeing?" questioned Saif.

"Yes, I think I do." He took another long drag from the cigarette. "It's in Victoria Station." He paused. The words were impossible to say. "In London." The idea of another wall, this one in his hometown, had officially put a permanent pit in his stomach. There was no running home for safety. It was home.

"How can, you be sure?" challenged Marise.

"I travel through Victoria Station, and I know it very well. In my flash I saw another wall there and people walking by it."

Everyone continued silently down the street.

Saif, who was always ready for the unexpected, took the news better than anyone else. Maybe it was the years of going from traumatic experience to traumatic experience, like this one. He had learned to survive by picking up his head and moving forward. The wall was down in France, so there was no reason to stay. It might be a good idea to move Mas'ud out of the country as well. Shut down the forum and start a new one somewhere else. Perhaps England?

"I think it would be a good idea to leave France," announced Saif. "England might be a good place to go until the news and the investigation of the bombing quiet down."

Marise couldn't believe there was another wall, but it had been almost thirty-six hours since she last slept. She needed to rest her mind, think clearly, and hopefully dream. Saif was ready to go to England, that was obvious; John was going home there anyway, so she was the tide turner for the group and especially for Lexi.

She had long suspected the only reason Lexi came this far was because the first person she saved was a woman. It was hard for a man to truly understand this dynamic. A woman trusted another woman. There was an automatic bond there. A woman felt safer with another woman, especially among strangers. If

Marise had been a man, Lexi would have given him the warning about being up on the wall, then probably left him alone; men were loners by nature. But since she was a woman, there was compassion. There was a bond, with trust, and a feeling of safety, as well the immediate sense of community. Having a woman as a companion when all this started allowed Lexi to feel secure enough to approach the other strangers, who were men.

If Marise went to London, she assumed Lexi would go as well. She wouldn't leave her alone. "*Oui*, I will go. We all should go," she declared, turning to Lexi.

And there it was — all on Lexi's shoulders. She had to make the final call. For a moment she said nothing and continued walking toward the University. The thought of another wall ... more people being killed. Could she do this again? The answer was *NO*! No, she couldn't. She didn't have the strength. She never wanted to sit in another train station again for as long as she lived. She wasn't sure if she would ever get over this trauma and what just happened.

If they thought it was difficult finding a way to bring down the wall in France, she couldn't imagine how hard it would be in England. Their citizens weren't even allowed to carry firearms, or weapons of any kind. How were they going to find a way to bring down another glass wall? What were she, Marise, Saif, and John going to do? Push the wall over?

She just wanted to go home to the States. Pretend all of this never happened and go back to living life in her bubble of ignorance. Thinking, like every other human being on the planet, that humans were the only ones in the known universe. But then again, denial was never her forte. What did she say a few days ago while sitting in Gare de Lyon? She would rather have the knowledge and be able to do something about it than live in blissful ignorance. Her father always used to say, "Be careful what you wish for, Lexiz Boo-Bear, you may get it." *Well, thanks Dad!*

She had the knowledge. She knew about the wall. She knew what it could do. And she was the only one who could read it. Her head was telling her to go home, put all this behind her and get back to living. But her heart was whispering the truth. Why did her heart keep getting her in trouble? If it wasn't for her heart, she never would have picked up the French newspaper, and all of this would never have happened. Her heart kept nagging her. Saying that John, Marise, and Saif going to Victoria Station without her was pointless.

Lexi stared over at John, who was chain-smoking another cigarette. What if John went up on the wall again, and she was not there to see it? London was his home. What if another sentient being saw him on the wall and went after him? Could she live with herself knowing she could have helped him? What if John *died* because she couldn't be bothered to go to England and went home instead? And most importantly: what about all the other Johns, Marises, and Saifs she had yet to help, all those people who would be up on the wall in Victoria Station. Could she allow them to die? Because they unknowingly had some adaptation?

Her heart reminded her, feeling momentarily heavy, that there really was no choice. She had to go, even though traveling to England to find another glass wall was the last thing on Earth she wanted to do. If the options were hell or England, hell would be the preferred option. Then again, she never liked hot climates, and her eyes didn't react well to hellishly bright light.

She paused a moment: trying to remember all the mental notes she made to herself during this visit to Paris. All of the wisdom she had imparted to her brain, to be brought up at a later date to be used when she truly needed it, like now. Find a rational thought or concept that might help her cope with the current situation. But her mind went blank.

NOTE TO SELF: Stop making notes. You always forget them, anyway.

END NOTES!

Her heart won.

Lexi halted and after a few steps, the group stopped. They spun around to face her. "OK," she said, slowly looking at each person: Marise and then Saif and finally John.

"Next stop, Victoria Station."

Assassins' Wall: Gare de Lyon

EPILOGUE

Head Worm

EUROSTAR TRAIN, CHUNNEL. MORNING.

Sunday

Something had been eating away at Alexandra Peters' mind for a while. She couldn't remember if it had been there for days, hours, or the last week. It all seemed such a blur. In fact, the last five days had been a whirlwind: Traveling to Paris, finding a giant glass wall in the Gare de Lyon train station spewing out names of people about to be killed, running all over Paris in an attempt to save those people from almost certain death, and all the while trying to outwit and survive the assassins at the same time. Unfortunately, Lexi was unable to save poor Monsieur Lapayre, George Martin, and the other gentleman she saw the first day she arrived.

Lexi sighed audibly and glanced at her beaten-up reflection in the train window. There were black shadows under her brown eyes. Her hair was pulled back and messy from non-stop running. Not to mention the worry furrowed in her face — a deep concern that only she could see in her reflection. The lines in her face seemed slightly deeper and her cheeks hollow. This was what naturally happened when you didn't get enough sleep, but there was something more. Her reflection intimated what had been slowly growing in her mind. A thought borrowed deep inside her head like a small worm eating at dirt to make its way — not an ear worm — like a song playing over and over in your head. No, this was a head worm. A *thought* that just wouldn't go away and repeated over and over, getting louder and louder with each pass through her mind. The noise built a home in the back of her brain and slowly took root, like weeds that grow in the most unlikely of places and prove nearly impossible to pull or kill. The first whisper of this thought went unnoticed amid the clamor and rush of the past few days, but in the quiet reminiscence on the Chunnel train ride to England, she could almost hear the head worm eating away at her brain. Chomp, chomp, chomp.

Perhaps what she felt was all part of the psychological process of the brain absorbing and taking in the extraordinary information. Maybe for most people this head worm was as ordinary as peach pie during times of shock or strain to the mental system. Maybe too much dopamine or adrenaline created this worm.

Lexi knew she should be thinking and mourning the explosive mess they left behind in Paris. Poor Paris. It was such a beautiful, green city. The ramifications of the bombing in Gare de Lyon were going to be far reaching for a very long time. The citizens of Paris would take a long time to recover and trust each other again. A feeling she, as a New York City resident, knew all too well. Even more than two decades after 9/11, if a plane flew too low along the Manhattan skyline, most people were paralyzed in fear, and held their breath waiting for impact. And now France would be left to grapple with the same fate. Not as though Paris hadn't seen enough pain and suffering in the last decade of the Charlie Hebdo killings, the 2015 suicide bombings, and the endless protests. And almost a full century after the Nazi occupation, which must have left emotional, if not physical, scars on the older generation of Parisians. Now all of Paris had to endure the same fear cycle again for a current generation, brought to them by Lexi and her cohorts. Will it ever end? But if the French were able to move on from the Nazi occupation, they would most certainly be able to move on from this bombing — in time. They had resilience.

Lexi also felt a pang of guilt because Saif was dressed in full Middle Eastern attire while lying the M.E.D.s down under the glass wall, thereby increasing the scrutiny over one-third of France's population. It wasn't fair play, especially given the tensions between the native Parisians and the newest neighbors. But hopefully, as Saif had gambled, his traditional attire would stop any other assassins loitering around other train stations and from using Arab faces as disguises.

And now the thought of a potential new Assassins' wall in England, and the other victims that could potentially be targeted wouldn't' stop eating away at her mind. She had to stop thinking in order for her stomach to handle it all. At least the wall behind her in Paris was gone from the world, forever. No more killings, no more deaths.

Given everything that had happened, her mind should be filled with thoughts of Paris, Saif's Arab garb, the group's responsibility for the bombing, and new wall at Victoria Station, but it wasn't. The head worm ate further into her brain. It was gaining ground and growing stronger by the minute. And it kept mumbling to itself while eating. Its chomping muted all her other thoughts: *Humanity was no longer alone, and humanity was in trouble.*

The mundane seriousness of everyday reality paled in comparison to the big-picture ethics quandary that was presently eating away at her brain.

Lexi turned away from her tense reflection to see John taking a brief nap on the Eurostar train in the seat diagonal to hers.

It was dark outside the train windows in the Chunnel, somewhere under the water between France and England. The lights inside the cabin were dimly lit.

Lexi turned back to her reflection, and focused past her image to the outside for a view that wasn't there — only the darkness of the head worm. On a scale of what she thought would be important, maybe the thought should have ranked lower than a Paris bombing, or their flight from responsibility, or even another wall operating in Victoria Station. For a reason only her mind and the damn worm seemed to comprehend, her real number 1 ranking, as of this moment, was the fact that humanity was no longer alone in the universe, or on this planet, and they were in big trouble. Why was this thought echoing in her mind?

Overwhelmed by shock and danger in France, Lexi's brain took in this information, acknowledged it, and filed it away under the "I always thought so pile." And now that she had a bit of time to herself, some quiet time to actually think and reflect on all that happened in the last week one simple thought kept coming forward — UGH, damn head worm. Burrowing away and eating at her brain: Human beings were no longer alone. *HUMAN BEINGS WERE NO LONGER ALONE*. Humanbeingswerenolongeralone ~ enolaregnolonerewsgniebnamuh. Human beings were no longer alone, like, for sure, 100% definitive, no doubt about it, not alone.

And what "should" have been an exciting fact to her, being a science fiction aficionado, had now become a burden — to know that and the human race as a whole, and its future, was being threatened by murderous aliens who would stop at nothing to halt our evolution. It was isolating to realize that except for John, Marise, and Saif, no person alive would believe her.

It's not as though the aliens — *stop using that word* — the Beings landed their spacecraft on the White House lawn, announced their arrival, welcoming the human race to the wider universe. Oh no! That's not what happened at all. We got the crazies landing here. Of course we did. Why wouldn't humanity get the interstellar asylum rejects? The lunatic ones hell bent on killing us for what we *might* do, evolutionarily speaking. What a joke. "Star Trek" lied to us; the nice ones didn't arrive first.

Lexi turned back to John, his blond hair glimmering in the light from above his seat. The motion of the car probably put him to sleep. It had been a rough 48 hours for him. Well, for all of them. She would have been sleeping too, if it weren't for this damn head worm eating away at her brain.

She turned her attention back to the dark window, and the worm inside her head. It shockingly answered back, "We are no longer alone."

She shook her head in response to the head worm. And what did humanity do now? She didn't have the answer yet. The worm clearly had to dig deeper and tunnel further into her brain to find the answer. There clearly was some medulla left for it to chomp on.

Lexi took in the atmosphere of the train on this quiet Sunday morning. The moving cars rocked the few passengers back and forth. The rhythmic pattern was relaxing. She observed the different passengers, some asleep, others silently on their smartphones and tablets. She wasn't ready to reconnect to the world yet. She was still processing and dealing with her shaken inner world. It was the calm after the storm, or was it before the storm? Or was it both?

"Are you alright, Alexandra?" Marise leaned over from the seat across from her, having noted the heaviness of Lexi's absentminded staring.

"Yeah," sighed Lexi in a super-hushed tone. "I'm fine. Just thinking. It's so quiet in here ... and my mind is *very* loud in the deafening silence."

Marise stared at Lexi for a moment. "You did the right thing, you know."

"What? By coming to England?"

"... all of it, Alexandra." Marise put her hand out for Lexi to hold for a moment.

Lexi huffed loudly, accepting the kind gesture, then quickly shrugged her shoulders in partial non-agreement. She wished she could agree with Marise. The weight of the bombing lay oppressively on her heart and her head, and the head worm couldn't shut up.

John opened his eyes. He was obviously just cat napping. "Don't worry Birdy, We're all going to get through this. We're not alone."

"I KNOW! That's what worries me!" announced Lexi, a little too loudly in the quiet car. Damn, head worm! It must be in John's head too. She wondered if ALL of them had a new visitor in their brain.

Saif, who sat across from John by the window, opened his eyes and smiled tiredly.

All four — Lexi, Marise, John, and Saif stared at each other for a moment, like a platoon of soldiers might take a moment after a long firefight or a respite before the next battle. They made quite a troupe. Formed and attached via trauma bond. They indeed had the look of a squadron after a battle and their faces were weary and worn.

A voice came over the loudspeaker, "We are about to enter St. Pancras Station. Please gather your belongings."

No one had any inkling about what these four had been though.

Lexi stared out the window for signs of the station as the train slowed down. The head worm grew louder: What did that alien thing say? Kill all human beings that move humanity evolutionarily forward.

What did that mean? Technologically? Spaceships? Leaving our planetary system? How were we a threat to them to begin with? Evolutionarily? Were we evolving to be too tall or hairless for them? Using our opposable thumbs to our advantage.

Damn, Lexi knew what Le Pouce thumb sculpture in La Défense finally meant. Our thumbs were our advantage. It's how we beat the evolutionary scale of these beings. Maybe she should have cut off its thumb, not its index finger. It all felt like a joke. A giant cosmological karmatic joke. '*I wish this head worm would go away.*'

Lexi shook the head worm into silence as she grabbed her bag from the storage overhead.

"How far to Victoria Station?" asked Lexi, as she placed her bag on her seat.

John helped Marise get her very large bag, then grabbed his own. "Actually, I was thinking we should drop off our bags at my place first, then head over there, straight away."

"That is a smart idea, John," said Saif. "Why wait, since we don't know what we will find there?"

"Or who," quickly interjected Marise.

"I'm praying for nothing. No wall, No guys, NOTHING!" asserted Lexi with an inch of denial in her voice.

"Ok, Birdy." John kindly gestured to Lexi. He knew that was what Lexi had to tell herself to get her inside Victoria Station, so be it. People always tell themselves little lies in order to move forward and do something they don't want to do. He could hardly blame her for it. He practically did that same thing the whole way to Paris, telling himself that the trip was a quick weekend jaunt to see the Arc de Triomphe. He lied to himself to get him there. The truth of what had occurred would have been almost too much for him to handle beforehand. What mattered the most, despite her fears, was that Lexi was still with them. Denial was definitely a coping mechanism that worked. But John knew what he saw in his last flash: A gleaming glass wall standing in the middle of Victoria Station, London, England. There was no doubt about that. His flashes were as sure as Christmas day, but without the presents.

"We are not alone. And are you ready for what comes next?" echoed the head worm in Lexi's head.

Despite the chomping away, none of the group — not Lexi, nor John, Marise, or Saif — had the slightest idea that their journey was about to become weirder and wilder than any of them could ever imagine.

PART 4

Human Beings have the most incredible weapon in the
known universe entirely at their disposal:

Imagination.

If only they knew how to use it properly.

Assassins' Wall: Gare de Lyon

CHAPTER 1

Victoria Station

VICTORIA STATION, LONDON. NOON.

Sunday

What should have been a day of rest became, in fact, a day of running. Amid a long day of fight, flight, destruction and evasion, Alexandra Peters, Marise Andre, John Barry, and Saif Muhammad cautiously entered their second train station for the day. Actually, it was their fourth, but who's counting. It might be weird to count train stations, yet that is exactly what Lexi did. But this station was her new number 1 worry. It was with dread, anxiety, and fear that she along with her weary cohorts entered what they hoped would be their last train station for a long, long while.

"I don't have it in me to look first." Lexi walked through the entrance and kept her eyes on the ground. "John, you're going to have to tell me if it's here or not."

"I will, Birdy," replied John who knew this very busy train station all too well.

Only a few feet into the station, Lexi stopped dead. She took in a few deep breaths. What they were looking for was another glass wall just like the one that is in Gare de Lyon station ... or was, until early this morning. It was down now thanks to the four of them.

Lexi was having a moment of P.T.S.D. symptoms. Or perhaps it was a panic attack. "Is this what you feel like, Saif? When you saw those beings approach you?"

Saif, the fourth and final man who joined their motley crew, observed Lexi struggling for breath, sweating, and momentarily frozen in place.

"Yes, my friend. But this is a natural physical reaction to past trauma. It's the body reliving what it went through, only in the mind."

"This is so much worse than I imagined. I should have had more empathy for what you were going through."

"It's hard to truly understand, unless you go through it yourself." Saif added with a half-smile at her. "Give yourself a little time. You only went through all this, this morning."

Marise was at Lexi's side. "Let's stay here till you get your bearings, Alexandra."

The three waited a few minutes until John circled back and waved them in.

"Oh God," murmured Lexi when she saw him wave. "There must be one here."

"Do you need another minute?" asked Marise.

"No. I'm not sure this feeling is going away any time soon, so I might as well get it over with. It's now or never, Marise."

All three slowly walked into Victoria Station.

It was another beautiful sunny station, built in the 1800s with high walls and glass ceilings. Lexi looked up and down the walls, noticing the cherry red color festooned throughout the station. It could have been because of all the Union Jack flags hanging down from the rafters, but London was giving her red vibes.

They all turned a corner and found themselves in the main terminal concourse. And there it was. Just like in Gare de Lyon, standing loud and proud in the middle of the floor, was a giant glass sculpture shaped like the Arc de Triomphe. It was a carbon copy of the one in Paris.

Lexi had a brief moment of paranoia. "Saif, it went down, correct? The one in Paris?"

"Yes, Lexi. It is down. I checked the news on my laptop during the Chunnel train ride. I saw videos from inside the station. It broke into a thousand pieces."

"OK. Thank you." Lexi exhaled another breath and took a step closer to this new Assassins' Wall.

John walked up to the group. "What's wrong?"

"Alexandra is having a little moment here," answered Marise, nodding toward Lexi.

"Birdy, what's going on? How can I help?" John turned to Lexi. He was feeling very confident on his home turf of London.

"Just give me a second. I have to remind my brain this isn't the wall from Paris. This one could be inert."

"I think it is," responded John. "I'll make another lap around the station. There's no one loitering around the bottom. Our friends aren't here."

Saif immediately walked away, then paused and called back to the group. "I'll be back."

John took off in the opposite direction as they both paced circles around the perimeter of the main floor and subtly scouted the glass wall in the center of it.

Marise and Lexi slowly made their way to a nearby set of benches.

Saif was the first to return. "No, nothing. I feel nothing and see nothing."

"Good." Lexi breathed a sigh of relief.

John finished his perimeter recon and wandered it back to the bench. "Nope, they aren't here."

"Well, I guess it's time for me to do my job." Lexi stood up and straightened her clothes. "I'll go have a look. See if there are any holograms or names in the glass."

"Want us to go with you?" offered Marise.

"No, thank you. I think the boys did proper recon. I'll be fine." She smiled at John and Saif and stepped forward to the wall. "Off I go ..."

The Assassins' Wall loomed large in the center of the station. It was glass and tall, it's structure like that of Gare de Lyon. If she didn't cognizantly know that wall in France was down, Lexi would have sworn this was it. As she approached the giant glass wall, she felt her chest tighten. She needed to be within twenty feet or so to see the 3-D hologram picture in the glass.

Victoria station was teaming with people walking to and fro. If Gare de Lyon was a swarming beehive of activity, then Victoria Station was a large ant farm of dignified marchers on a mission. The amount of people walking around made it hard to see the bottom of the wall.

Lexi weaved in and out, meandering ever closer with each step. She never took her eyes off the glass panel where the target faces appeared on the Paris wall. But as she got closer, there was nothing to see but the enigmatic glass itself.

She stopped about twenty feet away and stared up at every translucent inch of the towering arch. "Maybe," she mused to herself, "this one wasn't going to have the names or pictures in the exact same spot. Maybe it is on a higher or lower pane of glass."

Lexi crept closer and checked out every last inch of the wall. There was nothing. No pictures. No names. No lighting. nothing. She began to cry a little, her emotional release was immediate.

She turned slightly toward the group staring at her from the benches, and slowly shook her head no.

"Oh, thank God," she said out loud.

Lexi slowly made her way in a figure eight around and through the arch of the glass wall. And still there was nothing.

John left the group and headed to Lexi's side. "Nothing?" he asked as he approached.

"No. Nothing."

John sighed. "Good."

"John, I'm sorry I didn't ask you this before. When you had your flash, was it just the wall only? Did you see anything on it?"

"No. The wall wasn't the main focus. It was actually kind of fuzzy. I knew it was a glass wall like Gare de Lyon, but the main highlight was this station."

"Probably should have asked you that before. I was so preoccupied."

"It never occurred to me either."

"Maybe they haven't activated this wall yet." she countered.

"Then why did I have the flash of this one?"

"Just so we know?" answered Lexi, trying to find a reasonable response for an unreasonable situation.

"That's not how my flashes work," said John, perturbed, as he turned and walked back to Saif and Marise.

"I guess we came all this was for nothing," announced Lexi to Marise as she approached behind John. She was ready to leave Victoria Station and never return. She had been there long enough. Good-bye England, Good-bye Europe.

"I think we need to wait for a bit. Make sure this is inactive." John turned to Lexi. "Didn't you say you had to wait almost two hours for Marise to pop up?"

"Yeah, but there are no beings loitering around the bottom of this wall."

"True. Can we please give it a little time, just in case?" He looked anxiously at the group.

"*Oui*," answered Marise. "We came all this way."

Saif nodded in agreement.

Everyone stared at Lexi, who was the linchpin. Without her eyes to actually watch the wall, there really was no point. The others couldn't observe the faces.

Lexi didn't want to answer. The further she was from this wall, the better.

"Birdy?"

"Sure." She answered hesitantly.

"Let's give it a few hours."

"I think we should split up. Watch for our friends or anyone loitering around the bottom of the wall," Saif proposed to the group.

"Saif, you keep talking about the beings coming here. Do you think they survived?" asked Marise.

"The news didn't mention any dead bodies. Or people who died in the blast. Nothing but the wall "falling" down because of structural problems."

"Really? Officials are covering up the bombing. Probably not to cause public panic." speculated Marise.

"I wonder how they got the beings out," pondered John.

"At least we aren't murderers," interjected Lexi. "And the trauma for Parisians will be nowhere near what I was imagining."

"Those Jinn were next to the bags when I set them off," stated Saif, as sure as the sunrise in the East.

"We must concede, Saif, that maybe they had a way to get out, and survived," countered John. "Technologically speaking."

"Probably don't die like us," mused Lexi. "That finger is still endlessly leaching that yellow mucus substance the last time I checked at John's place. It's gross."

"There are too many permutations of possibility. But I feel like my flashes don't just happen. There is a reason. I saw this station. I feel like we should stay," John insisted.

"We will, my friend," promised Saif.

"In good news, the police won't be looking for the vandals who brought down the wall. So, it may be easier for us here." Lexi had an inch of encouragement in her voice. Maybe this wasn't the jailed terrorist situation she thought this would be.

"But someone knows the truth and then covered it up," warned Marise. She was even more suspicious and worried now. This suggested some type of coordinated government involvement. This logic wasn't the good news Alexandra thought it was. In fact, it was perhaps the opposite. This situation ran deeper than they suspected — it wasn't about secret murderous aliens killing humans to delay some evolutionary adaptation. This was the tip of an iceberg. And they were blindly flying blind, naively trying to rescue the helpless targets from the wall and from the assassins.

A few hours later, John, Marise, and Lexi were perched on the benches, eating sandwiches. Saif, meanwhile, was mysteriously exploring on his own. Every once in a while, he would walk over and subtly check in — making quick eye contact with one of the three — but other than that, they didn't see him.

"I think they figured out about us, and that something went wrong with the last wall," said Marise, finishing the last bite of her sandwich.

"They are changing tactics," speculated Lexi. "Why do you think that Marise?"

"It's what I would do."

Lexi stared over at the lifeless wall. "I hope you're right." She took another moment and looked around the busy Victoria station. It seemed as though the traffic never stopped. There was always someone going somewhere.

"Where do you think they come from, Marise? Planet-wise."

"Qu'est que c'est? There is a whole universe of possibilities."

Saif finally rejoined the group. John handed him an extra sandwich.

"Nothing?" queried Saif.

"No. You?" returned John.

"No. Not that this bothers me. Perhaps the ones here don't alert my stomach."

John raised his eyebrows. "It is a possibility. Best we do not assume anything, my friend."

Another hour passed sluggishly.

Lexi kept checking the wall but had nothing to report. She switched spots with Marise and John occasionally to mix it up. "It's weird having you all with me. I'm so used to watching the wall alone."

"But that's good, isn't it, Birdy?"

"Yeah, I think I've spent enough 'Alone Time' with the wall." She laughed at her irony.

After another quiet hour, Lexi was beginning to feel hopeful and even a little lighthearted. Maybe everything was going to be OK. Maybe she could actually go home. Go snuggle with her cat. Go to dinner with her best friend. And may blow off some much-needed steam. Maybe she would be allowed to go back to "normal."

"It's been over four hours, guys. I think this one is deactivated. Marise was probably right. They changed their tactics," announced Lexi jubilantly.

"Oui! We've been here all afternoon."

"I promise the flashes are never wrong," pleaded John. "Please just a little more time?"

"Fine, but I'm going to walk around and stretch my legs a little." Lexi stood up and John got up to accompany her around.

"No, thank you. I will be fine. Don't worry. I will keep you all in sight. HA! Get it? Sight! Since I'm the only one who can see the wall. Aren't I funny?"

"Ironically, yes," answered John dryly. "Will you see yourself out?"

Marise and John watched Lexi wander around the station.

"I wish she weren't the only one who could see the wall holograms," huffed John.

"Why? Do you want to see it?" wondered Marise, curious.

"I mean it, so Lexi doesn't have to always be here watching the wall. That way we could take turns."

"I *don't* want to see the wall." finished Marise, "I'm afraid all those faces would haunt me forever." Marise was already haunted by dead faces in her dreams. It would be too much to see them while awake as well.

Saif bolted up to the two of them. "Where's Lexi?"

"Stretching her weary legs." John pointed to Lexi, but in a less than obvious manner. "How's the tummy?"

"I think this station is abandoned as an assassin center headquarters. Maybe they stopped using it since the last wall went down?"

"I was just saying that, too," replied Marise, glad to see that Saif now agreed with her, like Mas'ud.

"The best analogy I can think of is this: if it were me, and I knew a computer was hacked, I'd never use it again. Perhaps they will never use the wall again?"

"I believe they know about us. I would change it up, if I were them," agreed Marise, nodding at Saif.

"Yes, maybe you all are right. But my flashes have never been wrong before."

"We aren't saying your flashes are wrong, John. Maybe they were using this wall around the time the Gare de Lyon wall came down. So, you flashed it as it was being used."

"Yes, could be." John sounded more and more convinced. "I'm not fully aware of the nature of flashes. Perhaps it is a "present" thing."

"Your flashes were correct, John. You did see a wall in Victoria Station." Saif pointed to the glass wall hovering over the station like a mass of locusts waiting to eat the field.

"And the wall was just standing there, in your flash. Plain glass without any faces on it. Correct?" quizzed Marise.

"Come to think of it, yes. It was ONLY the wall itself. I took it for granted that Lexi would find the 3-D holograms here. I assumed that since I can't see the holographic faces in real life, I wouldn't see the images in my flashes either."

"Then you are right," remarked Saif. "Your flashes may have been a warning that a potential wall was here, only. Not that it was currently being used by the beings."

"I apologize, I never had the need to be so particular with my flashes, or to analyze them in such depth. I usually see them and go."

"Understandable, my friend. No one would expect otherwise." Saif smiled and touched his friend's shoulder.

"Maybe we should try again tomorrow for a little bit. Come and see. It has been a very, very long day. We haven't slept properly in 36 hours. I don't think Alexandra has slept in a few days either. We all could use the rest," urged Marise.

John nodded, and glanced over at Lexi, who had almost finished her loop around Victoria Station.

"What's up?" asked Lexi, as she sauntered over to the group.

"We are ready to call it a day," said John, standing and stretching. "I'd like to take you all out to dinner at my favorite place in London."

Lexi smiled, glad she wasn't the only one imagining normal life and ways to celebrate their near escape. "Great! There is nothing on the wall, so I'm ready to call it."

The troop of four began to walk out of Victoria Station and away from the glass wall. This one was just a glass wall. The assassins were long gone.

"John, I have to be honest. I couldn't be more relieved that this one is abandoned, or not operational." Lexi had a bounce to her step. "And I'm ready for a good real dinner."

John nodded his head, but his heart felt a strange unease.

"This is the best outcome of all. One that my heart was afraid to let myself imagine. A blank wall," said Lexi jubilantly.

John nodded his head again, lost in thought. He was having a hard time coming to terms with the flash being wrong. He couldn't remember a single instance in his life when his flashes hadn't warned him of something important. But maybe he should just take the win. John reached into his back pocket and pulled out his Mets cap.

Lexi smiled when he put on the baseball cap. "You officially earned that cap, John. It's yours for life."

John smiled, but it was hollow. He was trying to recall a time when he was ten ... if a flash had been right about a dog which was chasing him down a street. But he remembered it did actually happen. Preoccupied, he kept digging deep to find a flash that had been inaccurate.

"Don't worry," murmured Lexi, who took his focus as concern for them. "You won't be stuck with us for much longer."

John nodded his head, but his heart skipped a beat.

"We will come back tomorrow one last time to check on this abandoned wall," interjected Marise, also noting his concern.

"No!" a voice shouted in John's ears. He turned to Lexi.

"No what?"

"No, what, what?" wondered Lexi.

"You just said, *NO*. No, to coming back tomorrow? Or no, turn back?"

Lexi eyed Marise, and then turned back to John. "I didn't say no, John."

"My friend, none of us spoke. Did you hear someone in the crowd?" asked Saif, concerned. For the first time, he was worried about John hearing voices. It was never a good sign. The trauma was getting to him.

"Marise was the last to speak," said Lexi, who put her hand on John's arm.

"Someone just said NO!" John stopped dead, halfway out of Victoria Station. "In my ears."

"John ..."

Flash: A 3-D holographic face of a man in a glass pane of the wall.

"No!" grumbled John sharply. "God, no."

"That's too many no's, John. Which no do you mean?" asked Lexi.

"No, Go back. There is a MAN!"

Saif frantically looked around the station. "Where?"

"On the *WALL*! I had a flash."

John turned around and ran back to the main floor of Victoria station. The rest of the group chased right behind him. He stopped dead at the entrance to the main terminal.

"There!" John pointed up to the wall.

"I can't tell ... this is too far away," said Lexi, surveying the wall and its surrounding details. "I have to walk up to it."

She began moving towards the wall when John started walking with her. "Let me go alone, please. I'm OK." Lexi reassured John.

"Fine, we will follow a little behind. Saif?"

"Feeling alright, John." He looked just as confused as the rest of the group.

"Are you sure?" Lexi questioned John.

"Yes! A man, late 50's with blue eyes, graying hair, pointy nose. But he was in pastel color."

"Yeah. That's what I see. Don't think I ever mentioned the pastel colors before to you." Lexi was convinced. "Saif, do you have the knife?"

Saif nodded and thought to himself, '*That and other things.*'

Lexi trying to control the urge to hurry, moved as close as she dared to the imposing arch without drawing attention. As soon as she hit a good angle, she saw it. On the second pane of glass was the 3-D hologram. It was just as John described. Older gentleman, late 50's, graying hair. But that wasn't all. Above the hologram of the man, in the third pane of glass, was another hologram. A woman. Early 30s' by the look of her. Blonde hair, brown eyes.

Lexi glanced at the now assembled group a few feet away. She held up her fingers, signing the number two. She swiftly looked around. There weren't any of the sentient beings hanging around this wall. No one was climbing up to take the holograms down, and no one was staring up at the hologram.

Lexi doubled back to John, Marise, and Saif. "There's two. Like the last time in Gare de Lyon. The guy with the gray hair and another target hologram above him. A woman."

Lexi reached into her bag and began pulling out the ziplock bag with the sentient being's finger, which was still oozing.

"What are you doing?" queried Saif, concerned.

"I'm using the finger to take the pictures down."

"I'm not sure you should do that, Alexandra." warned Marise.

"Why?" Lexi asked, confused.

"That finger could have been programmed for the French wall only. If you use it, the beings may know we are here. And alert them to our helping out other people. I don't think we should show our hand, or that finger, here, just yet."

"And Lexi," contemplated Saif. "What if it calls that Jinn to its finger. He will know where it is — and where we are."

"And I'd have to pick you up to get to the third pane of glass, Birdy," remarked John. "I'm not sure how wise that would be in a station full of people. It would draw everyone's attention."

"Especially if you are touching an empty pane of glass with a constantly oozing amputated finger." Saif looked calmly at her. "To do such measures would take time and planning. We can't get sloppy, or we may be discovered."

"FINE! But I have to write the names down, now." Lexi grabbed her glasses and notepad from her bag and headed back to the wall.

"Don't be too obvious, Birdy. In case someone is watching." John whispered as he took a step with her toward the wall.

Lexi nodded.

Saif looked around the station from the different strategic positions he'd cased out earlier in the day. "In case something goes wrong, let's fan out."

The huddle broke, and each walked in a different direction.

As Lexi approached the wall, she pretended to be writing a rote mundane everyday list. She wrote the whole way there. She hoped that whomever may be watching wouldn't realize *what* she was writing.

As she walked, she wrote: A ... B ... C ... D ... E ... F ... just a little closer. H ... I ... It was easy enough to remember the alphabet and not be overly distracted by what she was writing.

As she got closer P ... Q ... R ... Tom Stevens ... T ... U ... V ... Knightsbridge ... X ...Y ... Z ... Tilda Perry. Now I know my A, B, C's ... Chelsea.

As she quickly wrote the names, she kept an eye out for their former friends. Not a single bi-ped altered her senses. And she knew Saif would have walked up and warned her.

She hastily went around the wall and met the group back at the starting point.

"OK. I think we should split up," announced Lexi. "Two people should take one name."

"Fine. Saif, I'm with Birdy."

"But ..." countered Lexi.

"That's fine," answered Saif.

"What? You don't want to go with me?" teased John.

"No. It's just ... Saif has the knife."

"Ever the American, wanting to be armed," laughed John.

"Or Marise and I could go get the girl, and you and Saif would get the man."

"Please, *TIME*!" hurried Marise.

"OK. Sorry." Lexi tore the paper with the two names on it. "Saif, you and Marise go get Tilda Perry in Chelsea. And we go get ..."

John looked at the piece of paper. "Thomas Stevens, God bless his soul. He's in Knightsbridge, that's close."

"Good! And I think our friends aren't here" remarked Lexi. "No one was under the wall trying to take down the names. I think they aren't here yet. Maybe the sentient beings from Gare de Lyon were supposed to come here after it was destroyed."

"They are gone," remarked Saif.

"Then it should be no problem getting these people."

"I agree. I do not think they are here," answered Saif.

"But we must be cautious, just in case," finished John.

"They are here!" Marise's voice emanated stone-cold certainty. "We just don't know *WHO* it is yet. Otherwise, there would be no names on the wall." Marise had her suspicions. Why wait hours and hours to put a name on the wall. Whoever uploaded those holograms had waited for someone to arrive first. But who was it?

"Good point." Lexi said grimly, trying to brace herself to do another battle. She didn't know how soldiers had the fortitude to pick up and go at a moment's notice. At least they were trained. She was not. Last week, she was sitting in her small office calculating micro-meteoroids impact on aluminum. Now she was in London preventing assassins from killing unknowing targets. Did she have the energy to do this again? That question really didn't matter, did it? There was a name — no, two names — on this new assassins' wall, and someone had to stop the victims from being killed.

"In any case, we have to get them, assassins be damned ... Let's go."

TO BE CONTINUED IN ASSASSINS' WALL: VICTORIA STATION

Assassins' Wall: Gare de Lyon

<u>ACKNOWLEDGMENTS</u>

There are too many thank you's, but if you indulge me, I will try. First, to my original editor Amber Esplin, who is an accomplished writer in her own right, words couldn't even begin to thank you. Next, to my other editors Sharon Rasmussen and Amy Noel, thank you both for helping shape the story as you see it today. You both are *super* women. To the late Jean-Francois Chaufour and his lovely daughter Anne-Claire Chaufour-Fregnan at Le Refuge restaurant in Old Town Alexandria, thank you for your precise translation of all the French. To Jüergen Kummer and the late Sarah Oster, thank you both for taking the time out of your trip to Paris to take pictures and videos inside Gare de Lyon. And finally, to the generous few who preferred not to be named, thank you for your insight and feedback, it was invaluable.

Assassins' Wall: Gare de Lyon

ABOUT THE AUTHOR

Amanda Dubin is an author and independent filmmaker. Her novels include *Last Stop, Earth*, a science fiction novella for children and *Universe Olympics: Heat 1*, a space adventure for young adults.

She currently resides in Alexandria, Virginia. She attended film school at Boston University, and then went on to win a grant for a short film from Miami Light Project.

Follow her social media:
Instagram: DubinAmanda
Twitter: @DubinAmanda
Facebook: AmandaSue.Dubin
Youtube: Amanda Dubin

Made in the USA
Middletown, DE
14 February 2024

49811622R00225